Chapter 1

Cult Island

Deep inside the ship carrying the members of Alpha Z, within its engine room, dark and barely lit, the plasma engine hummed steadily, pulsating energy to the rest of the ship. Next to it stood Stephan, the head engineering officer, who was busy working on the ship's systems.

In the heart of the ship, Stephan accessed its mainframe through a terminal connected directly to it. The screen he stared at had an unusual appearance, being an ancient program, created hundreds of years before Stephan's birth. It was only ancient, though, in its display. In terms of performance, it ran as well or better than the newer editions, Stephan would argue, but with white characters lost in a dark, black abyss, it gave other users a different impression.

Stephan knew the use of the antiquated program was unorthodox and that others would most likely never understand why it was his system of choice, but he liked the program anyway. Something about it just seemed right, when so many other things did not. It was not necessarily the blocky shape of the white characters or the bright and harsh light they emitted. Neither was it the jerking movement of the blocks of text that occurred when the system was processing. It was some quality within the program as a whole, more than the sum of its parts, which struck a chord inside him in a way he could not quite explain.

A quiet, yet distinct, noise interrupted his thoughts—the meek but sharp noise of the edges of several sheets of paper striking a hard surface. Stephan walked over to the tray and picked up the printout of what he already knew was their next assignment. After ordering the pages and binding them for the delivery of his report to the captain, he read the assignment.

Usually, Stephan merely skimmed the text, acquiring the necessary information—only what his captain would find important for the report. When Stephan finished, he could do nothing but stand there, gazing at the pages in his hand. He couldn't believe it. With quick movements, he flipped back to the beginning and reread, taking in every detail.

Cult Island. The familiar words he had thought and read a thousand times now seemed almost foreign to him. The phrase commonly used to describe the island would be the destination of their next mission. His stomach dropped when he read it. He typed the island's coordinates into the mainframe, pausing as thoughts of the inhabitants of Cult Island came to his mind. They were a reclusive people, so much so that hardly anybody believed they existed. The mere mention of them in conversation almost always resulted in a major faux pas, the effect of which would most likely be many lost invites to future dinner parties.

Stephan, though, did believe in their existence. Being a strong, but secret interest of his, the topic had consumed much of his off-duty time in fruitless pursuit of some evidence regarding the mysterious hermits. On one occasion, he found images of them. In every single one, the island's inhabitants, always two in each photo, wore cloaks with hoods that cast shadows across their faces. They would usually be standing next to a major political leader or another prominent figure of immense power and position. Stephan never spoke of what he found. Such photos were often explained away as being mere facsimiles, made by people with too much time on their hands. Being so isolated on such a small piece of land, Stephan often wondered how the inhabitants of Cult Island lived.

What brought Stephan even more confusion than his team's new and inexplicable destination was the lack of an objective. After reading the assignment yet again, he still did not know why they were going to the island or what they would do when they would arrive.

His gaze shifted toward a faint red light that was part of the mainframe's structure. It triggered a new string of thoughts about a recent operation involving Alpha Z, the military special operations unit Stephan belonged to. He and his comrades had fought a terrorist cell just inland from the coast of Ghana. They were now heading back from the mission. They'd been tasked with defeating the terrorist cell. Part of that objective had been the necessity of capturing or killing the leader. Analysis had proven that the defeat of a cell without the capture or death of its leader would merely delay the cell's objectives until that leader could replenish its numbers. Alpha Z had not, as it so happened, captured or killed the terrorist leader. The small battle had gone well until it took a turn for the worse, and through a series of unfortunate events, the terrorist leader had slipped away.

The mishaps accrued quickly as many of the fifty Alpha Z combat specialists waned in their performances. No evident cause had yet to be determined for this or the series of small, yet critical, system failures which also plagued their efforts. Stephan's own laser sniper rifle had malfunctioned unexpectedly.

This kind of failure of Alpha Z was unheard of, but what made this particular event further stand out in Stephan's mind was something he could not explain. Just before the leader of the terrorist cell slipped away, Stephan, who was the farthest away from the fighting, made eye contact with the leader through his rifle's scope. In his gaze, he thought he saw a slight, almost imperceptible red hue in the leader's eyes, which held an intensity and fury he had never seen in any enemy or ally. However, when he checked the video footage of the skirmish, he found no red color in the man's eyes and no indication that any of the other combat specialists had seen it. He wanted to dismiss it seeing as there was no known psychological disorder or illness described in the ship's extensive medical library would create a manifestation of this sort, but he knew the memory would fester in his mind.

Stephan felt the report in his hands—the tactile feeling of the paper against his fingers. It made him feel less alone in his own preference for an outdated means of communication. He was ready to give his report to his captain.

Chapter 2

The Report to the Captain

Alexander Bennet, captain of Alpha Z, sat across the room from General Weathers, with two rows of lesser officers, one row on each side of the general. Their meeting, having been tense up to this point, had consisted of a robust and heated discussion of Alpha Z's failed mission in Ghana, specifically the failure in apprehending or terminating the terrorist leader.

This shouldn't have happened, not to Alpha Z. We are above this! Alexander thought. This hostility toward Alpha Z was not, however, an isolated situation. Alexander knew of the rumors regarding the illegal, genetic enhancement of several key members, himself included, had been circulating among the top brass. These rumors were false, but they had caused a certain amount of animosity against them. Alpha Z's renowned status bordered on celebrity, and it was clear the fame garnered jealousy and insecurity among those who sought it for themselves. *Such is the game of the pursuit for power,* Alexander thought, quoting the ancient war maxim in his mind.

The meeting dragged on while the lesser officers hurled accusations of blame at each other for the failed tactics implemented during the Ghana mission. The general, who had been patiently observing the contentions until it became clear they would not be resolved on their own, pounded the table with his clenched fist. The loud thud silenced the lesser officers and order was then resumed.

"Squabbling on this matter is pointless," General Weathers barked, his tone deep with a commanding quality. He then addressed Alexander. "Captain Bennet, has the cause leading to the terrorist leader's escape been determined?"

Alexander swallowed and cleared his throat. "Not as of yet, sir. We have conducted a thorough investigation of all possible factors that could have contributed to the mission's failure. So far, all results show nothing, either with the personnel or with our weapon systems, to indicate any malfunction. Another diagnostic is well under way, and I should be receiving its report shortly."

This did not seem to satisfy the lesser officers, but General Weathers gave a generously warm look and nodded softly. In that moment, Alexander was grateful for the general. He was one of the only truly honest officers of the upper echelons of the United World Initiative (UWI) and fought for an impartial treatment of Alpha Z as well as all the other specialist groups of higher reputation. Alexander thought for a second about the origins of the word *specialist* and how it used to refer to one whose abilities were uncommon and unique. But this word did not fit with the functions of most of UWI's personnel as almost all of them were part of some "specialist" group. Alexander pushed the thought away as soon as it came into his mind to concentrate on the meeting before him.

"We look forward to receiving this report," the general said, interrupting Alexander's thoughts. "I'm sure we will find the source of these problems eventually. We will reconvene upon the completion of Alpha Z's next mission. Weathers out." With that, the holographic image of General Weathers grew weaker until disappearing altogether. The lesser officers gave their own sign offs, their images also fading away.

Alexander now sat alone in his office.

He stood and walked over to the transparent steel window, watching the English coastline pass by off the starboard bow. *How am I going to fix this?*

Alexander gazed at the passing landscape for some time. He ruminated on the meeting with the general and lesser officers. His thoughts dwelled on his status, both in a professional and informal sense, as he had always had a great deal of influence on those he came into contact with, especially those with little to no status of their own. It was something of value in his life but presented its own ills.

If he wanted to ascend to a higher echelon within the UWI hierarchy, he would have to give up the possibility of being in a position where he could directly command in battle, since paperwork and administrative duties dominated their work. This never gave him much cause for worry. The prestige of his current rank would be enough to secure a greater position if he did eventually decide to move up the ranks. No, he would stay where he was, even with the mounting tension against him and his officers.

A soft chime sounded from the other side of the room. He knew it was Stephan with the report. Alexander returned to his desk, which faced the general direction of the door, and sat down behind it. "Enter," he said with an authoritative tone. Stephan walked in, stood in front of the desk, and saluted.

"At ease, Lieutenant," Alexander said with a reproach which was playful for him but less so for his subordinate officer, "and deliver your report."

"Sir, the second diagnostic has been completed and the ship's systems each check out as optimal. No current or recent defect could be detected. I took the liberty, sir, of making a thorough scan of the ship's subsystems. They produced no results. Anything detected was not unexpected nor a possible contributing factor, to any great or small degree, to the recent system failing during the mission in Ghana. I have included the details of the diagnostic and deep system analysis in this report." Stephan placed the folder containing the archaic printed version of the report on the captain's desk. "In addition to the analysis, the folder also contains the details pertaining to our next mission."

Alexander looked a little surprised as they were still heading north along the English coastline, and not in the direction he would expect, as the objectives assigned to Alpha Z would usually take them away from their home county. The captain picked up the folder. "So, where will our next assignment be taking us?" Alexander flipped through the report, skipping the technical details and turning to the documentation on their next assignment.

Stephan hesitated. "Island X-1138."

Alexander stopped flipping the pages of the report for a second and then resumed with greater speed until he got to the text and photos detailing the destination. There was much less there than had been when he had received the details on the Ghana mission.

When he reached a certain page in the assignment, the captain stopped and slowly placed the folder on the desk. He looked up at Stephan and, after a long pause, asked, "Cult Island?"

"It appears so, sir, and it was made clear that there is to be complete discretion on this assignment. Also, we will rendezvous with Sergeant Yenien."

Alexander's body became tense when he heard the name. After a moment of contemplation, the tension eased.

"Well," Alexander said in a tone that reflected moving on from an unpleasant subject, "I suppose there is nothing more to do than make preparations for our next mission."

"I am in agreement, sir; however, will there be a need for another diagnostic?"

"Oh, no," the captain said with a false confidence. "If we have not recovered any information in two diagnostics, a third is unlikely to be fruitful."

Stephan nodded. "Very well, sir." He saluted in the traditional manner and exited the captain's office.

Alexander sat back in his maroon, leather chair. A feeling of deep dread came over him, ousting his previously held peace of mind. He knew of no rational reason for the malaise. Sergeant Yenien was difficult to work with, being a hardened officer of the Marine corps, whose temperament often bordered on the sadistic. But Alexander had worked with the sergeant on a few previous occasions, without this kind of awful anticipation preceding any of those instances.

There must be something about the island and its inhabitants, he thought, turning to the pages of the report.

Alexander closed the folder and steeled himself for whatever may be waiting for them.

Chapter 3

Cult Island

The pilot of Alpha Z's ship landed on Cult Island. After a quick roll call and weapons inspection, the unit marched toward Sergeant Yenien and his company of privates. Stephan was on the captain's right while Lieutenant Jessica Meadows, Alpha Z's chief medical officer, was on his left. The remaining crew members followed behind them in single file.

Strangely, the landing site detailed in the report had been much farther from their destination than what was necessary or required during most missions. Alexander suspected Yenien's influence because he was known to enjoy causing the inconvenience of others, particularly officers who outranked him. Most knew the cause of this sadism instantly once they saw his diminished stature. Yenien completely personified the "Napoleon complex."

As the members of Alpha Z headed toward their destination, the village where the inhabitants of the island resided came into view. The houses there were archaic, stone, thatched-roof huts. To Stephan, it appeared to be a place devoid of any semblance of modern technology. Eventually, a company of UWI privates could be seen in the outskirts of the village performing various duties. Amid the active privates, many robed figures stood still, standing in ordered lines, the hoods of their robes drawn, hiding their heads and most of their faces except for their mouths. Stephan recognized instantly the general attire of the village's citizens from his old photographs of random sightings. A chill ran through his body, the kind he had only felt a few times in his life when he would see something with his own eyes he thought unreal.

When they arrived, Captain Bennet, as well as the other senior officers, saluted Sergeant Yenien, who did not seem to notice them as he did not immediately return the salute but instead stood gazing at the activity of these men. Stephan could read instantly the smug satisfaction Sergeant Yenien openly displayed on his face, a satisfaction derived not only from making senior officers wait, but also from being in command of so many large and well-built men.

The senior officers waited uncomfortably for some kind of recognition. Stephan took in all of his surroundings. Something seemed off to him. He felt…unsettled. When the sergeant did eventually turn to address the other officers, he did not do so immediately but gave them a vacuous and empty stare.

Stephan noticed something strange about the sergeant's eyes. He thought he could see that slight, almost imperceptible red hue in them, just like in the gaze of the terrorist leader during the Ghana mission.

"Captain Bennet," Sergeant Yenien finally uttered while looking down at his clipboard, "you and your men are late."

"Sir," Alexander said heavily, "my apologies, but the landing site was unexpectedly far, being on the other side—"

Sergeant Yenien interrupted Alexander as he turned and barked another order to one of his privates to alter the length of the line the villagers were being placed in.

What are they up to? Stephan thought.

"Our orders were vague, sir," Alexander said, pressing on. "Perhaps if we knew of our function here, my unit could be of service."

"Your function will be given momentarily," the sergeant said curtly. His view was still directed toward the activity of his men.

Unable to make any headway with Yenien, the officers turned and watched the activities of the privates. The soldiers were forming lines with the robed and hooded cultists while the other company members could be seen going from door to door, gathering more of the hooded figures and bringing them to the lines. One of Yenien's men closest to Stephan looked at him, making eye contact and holding it. Once again, Stephan saw the faintly red hue in the man's eyes. His skin began to crawl. *Something is not right*, he thought.

"Captain, there's—" Before he could say anything, though, the private suddenly turned, produced a handgun from his belt, and pointed it at one of the hooded figures. Without hesitation, the soldier fired. The figure collapsed to the ground, motionless.

Stephan stared, wide-eyed in horror, at the fallen figure. The hood had fallen. Stephan saw that the cultist's ears were deformed, each pointed at the top. He also saw the unusually light skin of the figure, too pale considering how recent the shot had been.

"Sergeant, what is going on here?" Alexander demanded. "These are civilians! Stop this immediately!"

Yenien did not respond to Alexander's words but stood still, facing the private who had fired on the cultist. The private was staring at the dead body. He then looked to the sergeant, who nodded, and the private turned back to the line and lifted his weapon, pointing it at another cultist.

"No!" Alexander shouted. "Private, drop your weapon now!"

Stephan wanted to act, but he was paralyzed by the bizarre nature of what was happening, and he also did not want to break with protocol. He suspected similar reactions among the other members of Alpha Z.

The private did not respond to Alexander's command and was about to fire when the captain quickly drew and raised his own weapon. He aimed it at the private's hand, which held the gun, and fired. The soldier's hand twisted and contracted violently. The weapon fell to the ground. Although the hand had reacted, the private himself displayed no other signs of being in pain as blood dripped from his fingers. Stone-faced, he slowly bent over to retrieve the gun with his unwounded hand. The other members of the company went about their business as if nothing unusual had occurred. Sergeant Yenien stood calmly.

Stephan's eyes darted wildly from the cultists to Yenien and then to his men. He was rarely confused and did not enjoy feeling that way. He looked to Alexander, who was glaring at the sergeant with bated breath, and to Jessica, who held her hand over her mouth, horrified.

The captain's hand then made a motion. It was the sign to prepare to perform Defensive Maneuver A-128—an order to scatter in a predesignated pattern and await further orders. The maneuver would take Stephan west to the hills. He glanced in that direction. There was a hill with many trees dotting it. He understood the wisdom of the order since the trees would provide cover.

The private who had shot the cultist now had his weapon in his uninjured hand, pointing it at another cultist. Alexander's own weapon was still pointing on this private. "Stop this, private!" He fired again. The gun fell from the soldier's grip. The private again showed no pain or slowness of action.

Alexander made the motion to execute the defensive maneuver. The members of Alpha Z, in unison, scattered, running west, north, and south in a predetermined pattern, toward the cover of the trees or whatever cover the villager's houses would provide. While doing so, each armed himself in order to be ready to return fire. Sooner than what could be expected, Sergeant Yenien's soldiers produced their weapons, turning away from the cultists toward the fleeing members of Alpha Z. As they were about to take cover, the Sergeant Yenien gave the order to fire. The sounds of shots rang. Bullets pierced a few of Alpha Z's enlisted crew and they fell lifeless to the ground. Most of the others took cover behind a number of the villagers' homes.

Stephan and his guards reached the part of the west hill where they would have the greatest cover. Once there, they were sure to have enough coverage of the village. They were outnumbered four to one. They would have to take any advantage they might find.

Stephan set up his sniper rifle and looked through the rifle's scope. As he did, he was reminded of the reality of being the sole member of Alpha Z with any long-range weapons training. With effort, he shifted his thoughts back to the current situation. Through the scope, Stephan could see the bulk of the fighting currently taking place in the village below. He found a few exposed targets and locked the rifle's system onto them. He hesitated in pulling the trigger. It was not a hesitation for the sanctity of life; his training had successfully conditioned him to dislocate the instinct against killing another human being. Rather, it was a hesitation born from the knowledge that pulling the trigger would direct the attention of Yenien's men to his location and the advantage of his position would likely be lost.

The privates were now in the scope's site. He swallowed hard and fired off three rounds in rapid succession. The projectiles struck two of the privates clean through their arms and one through his leg. Stephan remembered the early private's non-responsiveness to gunshot wounds and observed them. Just as he had anticipated, the soldiers either stopped for only a brief moment or fell and then got up again, without so much as a single cry of pain.

"Stephan!" It was the captain coming in through his earpiece. "Come in, Lieutenant!"

"I hear you, Captain."

"Something's wrong with Yenien's men. I am authorizing lethal force."

For a moment, Stephan was caught off guard. It was standard protocol to use non-lethal force on any UWI personnel. Typically, tear gas, high velocity beanbags, or even stun rays were used, if the targets were of high status. It was unheard of to use lethal methods on UWI personnel.

Stephan's hesitation was only momentary as he had seen, through his scope, the unnaturally persistent nature of Yenien's men.

"Copy that." After placing a vulnerable private's head in the scope's sight, he fired. The soldier's head tilted suddenly to one side and his body went limp, collapsing to the ground. Upon seeing the lethality of the attack, Stephan let off a barrage of high-powered shots, striking the targets with his usual rating of high accuracy. With his rifle, it was not as difficult as it would be for many; it had an inertia-dampening technology that absorbed the force of each shot. Only a minor amount of kickback resulted from the round, allowing for a relatively rapid rate of fire.

Stephan continued to take down targets, relieved to find himself not garnering any attention. In the course of searching out new, vulnerable privates, he came upon a shed, behind which Alexander had alone taken refuge. Saul, one of Yenien's men, was on the shed's roof, carefully creeping toward the back where the captain stood. Stephan was about to target him when he saw another of Yenien's company rounding the corner, opposite the captain. Before Stephan could target either one of them, Saul leapt from the shed's roof and Stephan was powerless to intervene.

Alexander leaned against the shed's back wall. Around him, chaos ensued. Since he had given his last order, the fighting had escalated to unexpected and even unnatural levels. When he glanced behind him, he saw nothing but the bodies of his two rear guards. Since their deaths, he'd had to work frantically to cover all angles.

Alexander looked around the shed's corner. He found an exposed target and was about to fire upon the private when he sensed something closing in on him fast. As he turned, he saw the approaching private, wide- and wild-eyed, armed only with a knife. Almost simultaneously, he saw a figure descend from the shed's roof onto the attacker. Alexander recognized him. It was Saul, a former senior officer of Alpha Z. He knocked the private to the ground and struck his neck. The private collapsed limply to the ground.

Saul stood up and looked at his former commanding officer. For a few moments, Alexander could do nothing but stare back at the former Alpha Z officer. Alexander's rage mounted for a second until he exploded into action, grabbing Saul by his private's uniform and shoving him against the shed's rear wall. The resulting thud would have been loud if it were not drowned out by the surrounding carnage.

The captain put his face close to Saul's and shouted, "That private might have had information! You should have incapacitated him!"

After getting a closer and longer look at Saul, Alexander could see that his face was neither twisted in rage nor lifeless like those of the other privates. He seemed to have genuine humanity left in him. Alexander released Saul with another shove, his eyes narrowing a little. "You aren't like the others. What's happening here?" Saul only shook his head slightly. The captain resumed his position at the shed's corner. Saul, being unarmed, picked up the knife recently wielded by the man he had just killed and guarded the shed's opposite corner.

The battle, as it progressed, did not let up, continuing to grow in intensity, casualties mounting on each side until both groups were low in numbers. The smaller the company became, the more fiercely Yenien's men fought.

As the battle waned, Saul and Alexander abandoned the cover of the shed to join Stephan on the western hill. They found Stephan still using his rifle, but it was unmounted and he held it in his arms since his original position had been compromised. The only other member of Alpha Z acting as his rear guard was the medical officer Jessica Meadows, who had been alternating between the tasks of covering Stephan's flank and tending to the wounded.

A group of Alpha Z specialists had been pushed northward on the hill and were separated from Alexander and the others. They made a valiant stand before falling to the flood of privates. Before succumbing to them, however, they succeeded in dividing Yenien's men and causing great attrition among the larger of the division. The smaller division was defeated by the three remaining Alpha Z officers and the private, Saul. When the remainder of the larger mass of privates was engaged, they were easily defeated by the current and former Alpha Z officers due to the diminished numbers of Yenien's forces. At last, after many hours of continuous combat, there was silence on Cult Island.

Chapter 4

The Ambassador

The silence of the island was interrupted by the sounds of Lieutenant Jessica Meadows performing a scan on one of the fallen private's bodies. The scan was performed by puncturing the skulls with a medical device designed to read the cranium's immediate contents as well as neural imprints, revealing its activity up to the time of death.

Alexander watched as the medical officer worked, his face contorting in a look of disgust with each thrust of the device's sharpened, tipped rod and the sickening crushing noise that would accompany it. Saul and Stephan were each searching the bodies strewn about the island for Sergeant Yenien's, which would not be found. Stephan had the additional, wrenching burden of accounting for the loss of each slain Alpha Z specialist.

While conducting his search, Stephan thought it was strange that out of all the possible scenarios of who would and would not survive, those who did were the officers and Saul. What was further puzzling to him was Saul's lack of succumbing to whatever had caused the privates' sudden hostility. *None of this makes sense,* Stephan thought. *If it were a virus, how could it spread in such an erratic manner?*

In time, Stephan and Saul returned to Alexander and Jessica. Alexander was pacing back and forth nervously as Jessica was finishing her analysis. A sound emanated from the device in her hand and Jessica monitored the results. Her expression became one of puzzlement.

"Well?" Alexander asked with an impatient eagerness.

Jessica still monitored the results as she responded. "Nothing," she said flatly. "Absolutely no trace of any disease or psychological break of any kind." She looked up to Alexander, now appearing somber and concerned. "Nothing to explain their sudden hostility."

As the others looked to Alexander, the captain's gaze was locked on the body before them as if in deep thought, his expression heavy and grave. After several moments of tense silence, Alexander turned to Stephan, "Lieutenant, what happened to Captain Johnson and his crew after the Greece incident?"

Stephan knew of the incident Alexander was referring to, but he did not know how much of the incident the captain knew himself. He also did not know how much he was required to divulge.

"The former captain," Stephan began, "his officers and his crew were reassigned to—"

"What *happened* to them?" Alexander repeated the question with a stronger, more demanding tone.

Stephan took a deep breath, steeling himself before divulging highly classified information very few people knew, of which he himself was not supposed to know. "It is true that Captain Johnson was reassigned and relocated to an obscure outpost in the Southeast Pacific region, but what is not generally known by most is that he and his crew were executed shortly after starting their new assignments."

As Stephan spoke, his field of vision remained fixed on the ground, but in its corners, he noticed the reactions, and the body language, of the others to this revelation. He continued.

"The reassignment was done publicly, but the execution was done privately for an intended purpose. They seem to want a specific narrative unfolding in what seems like a natural way; the rise of a new batch of officers and crew, a glorious string of episodic and flashy missions with the eventual and inevitable fall from grace, with the UWI handling it delicately. This broadcasted sequence of events generally makes for captivating television and propaganda; however, it mainly functions as a psi-op, continually and subconsciously crushing any trust the audience may have in "heroes" or any strong individual figure. In this narrative, the UWI organization as a whole appears to be the savior. They want to quell any populist uprising before it even starts, before the thought of it would even occur."

The others were silent, quietly contemplating what Stephan had just revealed and its grave ramifications. Then Alexander broke the silence. "It's worse than I expected!" The captain grew solemn. "There will be a court martial. All of us will be implicated, and with no evidence to testify of our innocence, we will suffer the fate of Captain Johnson and his crew."

A strange, piercing voice, from outside the field of vision of any present, interrupted Alexander. "Not necessarily."

All turned to find a hooded and robed figure, standing higher on the hill, facing them. It was clearly a man's voice, but most of the face could not be seen because the hood cast a shadow, obscuring it.

"You're one of the…villagers," Alexander said. Stephan was relieved that his superior caught himself before calling this mysterious figure a cultist.

The figure pulled back his hood. He had many of the features Stephan had seen in the fallen villager earlier: the pale skin, the pointed ears, and the face's small, sharp features.

"I am Luxeniah, high ambassador of the kingdom of Geradia." As the ambassador spoke, Stephan noticed a depth in his voice. Stephan had never heard any other voice like it before in his many years serving in the proximity of highly accomplished leaders.

"We are pleased to meet your acquaintance," Alexander said, his tone taking on his carefully cultivated, stately manner.

"We have little time, so I will make this quick. I offer you and your officers sanctuary in the glorious kingdom from which I hail, if you come with me to pass through the Earthen Archway and serve me as my guard."

Alexander looked at Jessica and then Stephan, who seemed surprised but with an air of acceptance of what was their only way of escape.

"We could go with you, at least for a while, until all of this is sorted out, but let us return to our ship for supplies and weapons."

Luxeniah shook his head. "I would advise against such an action. Your ship has been loaded with explosives set on a timer. They will most likely explode before you could arrive."

How could he know so much? Stephan thought.

Luxeniah seemed to read their hesitation. "Why do you suppose you were ordered to land and leave your ship so far away from your destination?"

Alexander gazed at distant ocean, lit by a fading light. He turned and looked at Stephan for a moment and then at Jessica. When they both gave consenting nods, he turned to the robed cultist.

"Very well. My officers and I, "Alexander said, while gesturing to Stephan and Jessica, "will accompany you to the Kingdom of Geradia and, along the way, act as your guard."

Luxeniah gestured downward to Saul, who was sitting. "And what of him?"

"He is not my officer. He was one of Yenien's men," Alexander said. His expression took on a serious quality, and when he spoke, his mouth formed a line, almost a smirk.

Observing his response, Stephan did not understand why the cultist's eyes widened and his mouth opened a little when he heard this. It was as if he were disappointed. The ambassador then turned and offered his hand to Saul. "Then I shall commission him as well, and he, too, will be my guard."

Saul looked at the pale hand of the cultist, took it, and was lifted up to his feet.

The ambassador turned and walked briskly past the others, towards the northern part of the island. The others followed him. The island had grown dark after the sun disappeared behind the ocean's horizon. When the ambassador and his guard had traveled beyond the woods outside the village, a distant explosion could be heard in the distance, in the direction of the landing site of the vessel that had carried Alpha Z to Cult Island.

They all—all those who had been enlisted to be the ambassador's guard—looked at their new superior with a renewed trust and knowledge that they were in good hands.

General Weathers stepped off his personal transport's platform and onto the soil of Cult Island. He had landed close to the village where scores of UWI specialists were cleaning up after the recent incident. The surviving villagers were safe in their homes. A general classified priority of the highest order had been issued by Weathers to all personnel currently on the island to refrain from any contact with the island's inhabitants. It appeared as though the specialists were abiding by the order.

As the general walked toward the site of the incident, Sergeant Yenien approached him with an intensity beyond what the sergeant was infamous for.

"General Weathers!" The sergeant stopped and saluted impatiently.

The general returned the salute. "At ease, Sergeant, and deliver your report."

"Sir, we completed an inventory of all casualties and are still in the process of body disposal." Weathers noticed the exaggerated movements of the sergeant's mouth as he spoke. He spoke as one who was posturing, attempting to convey more power than what he had or was capable of. "As it has turned out, the captain and two lieutenants of Alpha Z, in addition to one of my own men, have not been accounted for. My own experience stands as a testament to their guilt. After the fighting was ending, I saw them run!"

Although the general agreed that the absence of Alpha Z's officers was suspicious, Sergeant Yenien's manner of speech dripped with bias and a premature trust in a hastily made assumption.

"That may very well be the case, but I have ordered a full investigation. This is outside the behavior of any of the Alpha Z crew—to attack a whole company of privates without cause."

"Sir, I understand your deep affection for the crew of Alpha Z, but I was there." The "deep affection" Yenien spoke of was a reference to the general's past training of many who held top positions in the Alpha Z specialist group. Weathers found the sudden shift in Yenien's manner of speech from his usual clumsy brashness to a strangely empathetic manner jarring. Yenien continued, "I saw them crack myself, most likely from the genetic manipulation. It seems as though the rumors are true."

The general listened while gazing at the specialists, who were placing bodies into containment pods, and without looking at Yenien, said, "Those have always been mere rumors, Sergeant; I don't believe they could have done this. I *know* them."

"*Knew* them, sir," Yenien said, correcting the general. He was going to say something else when a sharp chorus of barking noises erupted close by, interrupting Yenien. A few specialists were handling a pack of UWI canine units, barely restraining them by their leashes as the dogs growled and nipped the air as well as each other.

When the canine units were far enough away so that their noises didn't drown everything out, Yenien said to the general, "We'll know the truth soon enough, sir." He then saluted. The general met the salute and the sergeant followed the canine units up the hill toward the grove of trees he had earlier seen Alexander and the others flee toward. The general heard the barking of the canine units and the barking of Yenien shouting orders fade into the distance.

General Weathers continued to watch the UWI specialists handle the bodies of Yenien's former privates. Each specialist was dressed in black; Weathers found it a fitting color considering the typical nature of their duties. He winced slightly when his mind gave him an image of what the scenario might have looked like if Sergeant Yenien was right. He was not quite sure which of the many possible events in his mind was most likely, and he felt, for the first time, that the rumors of widespread use of genetic manipulation among the members of Alpha Z could have some merit.

The general continued toward the village. As he walked past the row of corpse pods, he thought to himself, *What happened here?*

Chapter 5

The Earthen Archway

Ambassador Luxeniah, Alexander, Jessica, Stephan, and Saul were walking in one of the many groves on Cult Island in almost complete darkness. Faint rays of moonlight streamed through the trees, lending them some vision of the terrain so they could make their way through the untraversed brush. They could not use any of their standard issued flashlights out of concern for making their presence known.

After some time carefully making their way through the dark woods, they came to a clearing. On the other side of it there was an opening to a cave. They walked to the cave and entered it. As soon as they were inside, faint yet distinct sounds could be heard behind them in the distance. They were growing louder.

"They have found us," the ambassador whispered quickly. Luxeniah produced something wrapped in large leaves. He pulled the leaves off of the concealed item to reveal a dead rabbit, which he flung into the darkness of the cave. "Follow me. Make haste!"

When he spoke, Luxeniah was almost against the cave's wall and, in almost complete darkness, seemed to disappear into it. Stephan then saw it—a fold in the cave's wall. When Stephan walked over to it, he could tell it was an opening to a crevasse. Inside it, Luxeniah was tearing the leaves into small bits and scattering them on the ground. A pungent, but naturally masking, odor permeated the opening in the rock.

Stephan and the others, by Luxeniah's direction, entered the opening and descended into a chamber within the rock, where Luxeniah, lifting his hand in the usual UWI manner, signaled to stop and remain motionless. Stephan was surprise and impressed by the ambassador's use of their military hand signals.

The distinct sounds from before hovered above them. The barking of the UWI canine units and the shouting of Sergeant Yenien's unmistakable caustic voice echoed down the crevasse and into the chamber. Stephan's heart raced for a brief moment until he realized the consistency of the shouting and barking of Yenien, his men, and the attack dogs. He relaxed since the reverb from the opening in the cave's wall could never be heard; it would be swallowed up in the symphony of collective sounds made by the group. After some time, as they moved deeper into the cave system, the noises faded away.

They sat silently for several moments. When he was sure the dogs were long gone, the ambassador revealed another chasm, which led downward and into another branch of the cave system that he knew was almost completely separate and unconnected from the one above. Through this branch of caves, they traveled throughout the night, stopping for only short rests along the way. The cave system went deep, so much so that it went under the channel separating Cult Island from the mainland of Wales. When they were under the channel, the caves grew cold. Thankfully, though, the channel was narrow, so the ambassador and his guard made great progress to what he had earlier referred to as the "Earthen Archway."

While traveling through the branch of caves, they each had to remain silent, in case the sound of their voices would be heard by Yenien and his men through one of the shafts that connected the caves below to those above. Alexander, Stephan, and Jessica refrained from using their transmitters to communicate since Yenien might have been recently outfitted with a similar device. Luckily, Luxeniah seemed to know the caves system well, so following him in complete darkness was surprisingly easy. They all had a strangely intuitive sense of where he was at all times. Alexander or Stephan would have inquired as to the reason for this, but each member of the guard was entering a mode of conduct they were each conditioned to follow called the Carn Doctrine, a set of UWI imperatives restricting any behavior that could be offensive to another culture or did not conform to the cultural standards of the land. Stephan recited in his mind a famous quotation of the military social scientist known as Carn: "In situations where cultural mores are unknown, the best course of conduct is silence and mimicry without the appearance of mockery." Stephan anticipated more silence than mimicry for a long while in whatever place they would be traveling to.

In spite the silence, at times, Stephan could have sworn he heard Luxeniah's voice. When he did, it was always faint and strangely without the echo the voice would surely have if spoken by one so deep within a cave.

Just before one particular bend, the ambassador motioned to the others to slow their walk. When they turned the bend, there was the dark, starry canvas of the night sky. Stephan felt the sudden mental adjustment from ambiguity as to what hour it was to certainty that it was night again. They had traveled throughout the branches of the underground caverns for a full day.

When they reached the cave's opening, a ledge jutting upward blocked their vision of the valley below. It continued to their left along the cliff face. Following Luxeniah's lead, they each crept to the edge and peered over it to find a narrow valley and a military encampment established in its center. Stephan recognized the manner of the camp's tents and equipment immediately as being of UWI's science division. Outside the tents, many modules of observational equipment could be seen strewn about the camp, as well as there being many science specialists who were positioning the equipment as if anticipating an event. The attention of most of those in the camp seemed to be directed toward something along the rock face farther to the left. The science specialists were positioning themselves around a large stone arch carved into the cliff's face. The arch was adorned with ornate symbols and artwork, which could not be clearly seen due to the distance, even though the whole camp was bathing in it. Stephan was not surprised because it was standard UWI procedure to overdo almost everything it could down to the smallest thing, such as the lighting of an encampment. While waste was the usual result of the practice, in this case, it served to conceal their presence quite well as the lamps' brightness would distract anybody looking in their general direction.

A movement in Stephan's peripheral vision caught his attention. He turned to see four more of the villagers behind their position walking past them. Stephan wondered where the villagers had come from. He assumed the caves, as there was no other way to get to the ledge they were currently on without passing through the encampment, but he found it incredible that the villagers had passed so close by them without making a sound.

The four robed figures, tall and clearly able-bodied, seemed poised and ready for something. Luxeniah's voice came into Stephan's mind, unmistakable this time: *Upon my mark, we will descend into the valley below and head for that arch to our left. Follow closely behind me!*

There was no mistaking their foreboding task, but Stephan did not know what the arch had to do with escape or how they would get past the myriad of UWI personnel. Not only were there the science specialists with combat specializations in addition to their scientific training, but more daunting was the presence of the mech-suit units—towering, bodily-shaped mammoths of a steel plastic composite, whose size and weight seemed to contradict the speed at which they were capable of moving and attacking. They were placed at strategic points throughout the camp, blocking the path between them and the arch.

There was a sudden increase in activity throughout the camp as the science specialists scrambled to man their equipment set up by the arch. A series of faint blue discharges manifested in the air within the arch. Stephan watched, unable to look away, even though the brightness of the discharges caused discomfort to his eyes. The series of bursts of blue light grew brighter and brighter until finally a flat plane of blue-white energy manifested itself, filling the space within the arch's sides. Along with the light, a torrent of wind swept through the encampment and along the ridge.

Near Stephan's line of sight, while witnessing the manifestation of energy, one of the four villagers produced a small, metal ball—what Stephan immediately recognized as being a small EMP bomb. The power of its discharge was typically too small to disable the measurement equipment or the mech-suits, but when the villager threw it to the valley's floor, it let out a high-pitched, piercing shriek that produced a bright flash followed by the extinguishing of most of the camp's lights. The camp was plunged into an almost complete darkness, lit only by the blue hue emanating from the arch.

The four villagers immediately leapt from the ledge to the valley's ground. They proceeded to attack the encampment. Without killing any of the science specialists, they rushed to incapacitate them and disable whatever equipment was not affected by the EMP blast. The camp was now a torrential, chaotic storm of panicked cries and orders from science officers attempting to restore order. Once a path had been carved out by the four villagers, Luxeniah signaled to the others and jumped down to the base of the cliff. Closely behind Ambassador Luxeniah, Alexander, Jessica, Stephan, and Saul each leapt from the ledge's edge and into the chaos below. The four members of Luxeniah's guard followed him throughout the fighting, each one weaving in and out of individual scenes of conflict, taking cover in pockets of darkness here and there until an opening would present itself, usually created by one of the villagers.

As a group, they were getting closer and closer to the arch's pulsating blue energy when a mech-unit dropped down in front of them, blocking the way. The suit's pilot could be vaguely seen from behind the transparent, metal faceplate. A mechanical, synthesized voice sounded from the suit. "Rogue members of Alpha Z identified...surviving member of company 198...." The voice cut out as many of the suit's indicatory lights died and the suit slumped over. One of the villagers stood up, standing on the suit's shoulders with a handful of wires in his fist.

Luxeniah and his guard hurried past the immobile mech suit. Alexander and the villager's gazes met and held as they ran past the villager. For a moment, Alexander felt as though he were in some way of great importance to the villager. Then the warrior broke the gaze, leaping from the mech-suit and into the fray.

When they reached the arch and its blue-white energy field, Luxeniah looked at each of the others. When Stephan met his gaze, he remembered what the ambassador had said about following him. Without speaking, the ambassador walked into the energy field, and when his body made contact, he turned into a white silhouette for a brief moment before disappearing in a flash of white light. Saul went next and then Jessica, their bodies disappearing in like fashion. Stephan was about to follow them when he noticed Alexander looking not at the blue-white field of energy but back at the chaotic scene they had been trying desperately to leave behind.

"Sir!" Stephan yelled in trepidation at his superior, not sure if his voice would be heard above the noise of the arch's wind and the sounds of the UWI personnel panicking and scrambling to restore order. "Sir! We need to go! There's nothing left for us here!"

Alexander looked at Stephan and, after a moment, nodded. Alexander motioned Stephan to step aside and he stepped into the bright, blue-white field and became a white silhouette before disappearing as the others had.

Stephan had his own moment of hesitation, but for a different reason. He imagined the science specialists, who had been studying this phenomenon for some time, trying to find out whether the disappearance of whatever touched the field of energy was a result of its transportation or destruction and wondered what would happen to him. Stephan decided to trust the ambassador, who had been right about the explosions on their ship, as well as everything else up to this point. He stepped into the field. For a period of time, Stephan felt as though he were in two places at once and that the places were incredibly far from one another. Stephan then found himself above a starry chasm. The Earthen archway behind him flew into the distance and he was left alone in a vast, starry void. Before he could feel any sense of impending doom, a sense he surely would have normally felt, the whole of his field of vision went dark.

Chapter 6

Awakening

Stephan awoke to the view of an unfamiliar sky whose constellations did not form any shape he was aware of, and he had an encyclopedic knowledge of all of them. Although the stars were visible, it was not night, but early morning, the time between night and the sun's appearance on the horizon.

Stephan slowly sat up. Rubbing his head, he viewed his surroundings, which were just as strange and unfamiliar to him as the sky's constellations. He was having difficulty placing where he was when the memories of the chaos in the encampment by the archway came flooding into his mind. He remembered the stark lighting of the science encampment, the mech-suit specialist who had blocked their path, and the blueish-white energy field of the Earthen archway. The events must have happened mere moments before, but they now seemed like a distant memory or a dream to him. Stephan stood up and further observed his surroundings. To his right was the archway, the energy field now gone. Next to it, Luxeniah was sitting, his back flush against the rock face. In between him and the archway lay Alexander, who seemed to be unconscious. Jessica was a few feet in front of him and was just then sitting up. When she got to her knees, she made her own search of the surroundings and saw

Alexander. She continued and made eye contact with Stephan, but said nothing, choosing instead to get up and help Alexander. When they made eye contact, Stephan could read a lack of interest in any aid he would have attempted to offer. He knew he did not have the training to be of much use anyway.

Stephan continued to look around and found they were all on a long cliff coming to a point, running away from the arch. On the point of the cliff stood Saul. Reading his relaxed demeanor, Stephan thought he must have been awake much longer than them all. From the corner of his eye, Stephan could see Jessica moving toward Ambassador Luxeniah, most likely to tend to him. He wondered whether or not the villager was unconscious, and then, without turning and as if to answer his question, Saul said, "There's no need to check on him. He was awake when I came to. He told me he just needed to rest." Jessica paused and then continued to the ambassador anyway.

Stephan walked to the side of Saul to see what his gaze was so fixated on. Saul seemed to be focusing on the mountain range, which was in the general direction that the point of the cliff was facing. Stephan did not see anything remarkable or noteworthy about it. They looked like ordinary mountains to him. He turned his attention to the waterfall to their right. It fell in a break in the cliff, which continued after it, all the way to the mountain range Saul was staring at. The distant mountains seemed to go on indefinitely to both the right and the left.

Stephan saw Saul once again, and the sight of Saul's pointless fixation brought to his mind a series of memories centering around Stephan's role as an intelligence specialist assigned with the task of monitoring the activities of several key individuals. It was the position he had held before joining Alpha Z as an engineering specialist. One person of interest he had been assigned to monitor was Saul. In either an ironic twist of fate or an orchestrated transfer made for some unknown purpose, he would later serve with Saul as a fellow officer in the Alpha Z ranks. As an intelligence specialist, Stephan observed every aspect of his daily life pertinent to the assignment's objective, which was to evaluate Saul's mental and emotional health, as well as his commitment to the UWI directive. It proved to be an impossible assignment since Saul's behavior was bizarre and inconclusive. Stephan would have classified him as mentally insane; he met all the criteria but one—he was technically capable of living a functional life, at least in performing his duties adequately. He would have classified him as dangerous, but although he came close, Saul never technically caused anybody any real harm. That is, until the time he attacked the captain, breaking his leg in an illegal move at the end of a martial arts match. It was a match the captain had won. The assault brought upon Saul a severe and dramatic demotion all the way down to the lowly rank of private. He would have classified Saul as one having nefarious intentions against the UWI, but any behavior that could have been labeled as such could be explained away in many other ways.

The difficulties related to Stephan's assignment were not limited to Saul's physical actions alone; both the manner of his speech and its content were almost always unorthodox. He once said, while in idle conversation, that life was too easy, being too comfortable and sterile. This infuriated Stephan, as well as those who heard about the controversial statement, as everybody well knew that life was perfect the way it was—the way UWI had dictated it to be. It further infuriated Stephan when, on another occasion, Saul had commented that he thought life to be hard, cold, and lifeless. *Couldn't he keep anything straight?* Stephan would think.

As time passed and Stephan continued to monitor him, Saul stopped saying anything unorthodox. He ceased saying much at all, other than what was required by the necessities of his duties. It was at this time that Stephan delivered his disaster of a report. All of his reports of previous monitoring assignments had been perfect. Stephan requested to be transferred to Alpha Z, to maintain rather than monitor and to serve as an engineering specialist with long-range combat capabilities.

Since his reassignment, Stephan often thought about that assignment, and although he had no objective evidence for it, he could never dispel the idea that Saul somehow knew he was being evaluated. This was absurd, and so Stephan never dared breathe a word of the idea to anybody, but the thought would have explained much of Saul's supposedly unexplainable behavior. It also gave a tenuous explanation for why his superiors were not disappointed by his announcement of his transferring to a new unit and specialty. He had originally assumed he had given such an unsatisfactory performance that the higher ups were glad to be rid of him. It was vaguely possible that he was guided in some way to that decision. Although absurd on the face of it, Stephan knew of several past examples of this kind of psychological manipulation.

Stephan broke from this string of thoughts. With no ship to maintain, or any kind of technology other than his laser rifle, he found himself out of his element and without purpose. He resolved, at that moment, to revert to the skills and mentality associated with his previous position as an intelligence officer. As there was nobody else, he would observe and record his observations and be grateful to have some duty to perform.

After taking in another view of the lands Saul was facing and still finding nothing noteworthy in the distant mountains, he looked down and found the base of the cliff they were standing on far below them. Stephan then proceeded to the other side of the cliff and viewed its continuation in the other direction as far as he could see. Along the cliff's edge was a large stone wall with towers regularly dotting it. He followed the wall from its most distant part to the cliff he stood on until he came across a stairway ascending all the way up to a higher elevation level with the wall and towers. The base of the stairway was to the right of the archway.

Stephan shifted his focus to the land at the base of the cliff where he saw the land strewn with charred trees and patches of grass. It was as if there had been a long series of small skirmishes, the results of which accumulated over time to form the damaged land. From the corner of his eye, Stephan noticed movement around Jessica. It was Alexander stirring, trying to stand. He walked over to his captain, eager but subduing any sign of it, and offered a hand to help. Alexander, who was now using one arm to bring himself slowly to a one-legged kneeling position, refused the offer, shaking his free and open hand. Appearing confused, he smirked and lightly shook his head.

Alexander stood, and while surveying his own surroundings, observed Luxeniah, still sitting next to the arch. "What's with him?" he asked Jessica, gesturing to the ambassador.

"I'm not sure," Jessica reported. "He's been in that state since Stephan and I recovered, but Saul said he sat down and just needed to rest. I checked him. He is conscious but unresponsive. His eyes flutter from time to time underneath his eyelids, but I don't think it's the result of an REM cycle. I think he just needs some time."

"That seems to be something we have in abundance." Alexander looked at Luxeniah. Up to this point, the ambassador had been so capable, but now he was passively sitting there.

Alexander continued surveying his surroundings and found that Stephan had slipped away. His lieutenant was crouching some distance away from them, intently studying something out of Alexander's sight. As Alexander approached Stephan, he found the object of scrutiny to be a patch of crystals. They were unlike any he had ever seen.

He drew nearer to Stephan and spoke quietly to him. "Lieutenant, use the laser option on your rifle to cut off a sample of that crystal."

Stephan gave him a puzzled look and appeared almost alarmed. "But, sir, the Carn—"

"Don't worry; the crystals are far from the ambassador. He won't notice a small piece missing. A sample might be something we could offer the UWI when we return. They're always on the lookout for new materials."

Stephan got up, stepped backwards, and aimed his laser rifle at one of the shards in the patch. Alexander took a step back. Stephan pulled the trigger and a high-pitched, screeching sound accompanied a bright, hot beam. Alexander glanced at the ambassador and saw that he was still motionless. When he returned his attention to the crystal patch, he saw that the laser had no effect.

"I don't understand!" Stephan was now feeling the point where the laser made contact with the crystal. "I've cut diamonds with this rifle!"

Alexander looked around and found that the crystals were common in this area. There were several patches on the cliff. Looking from patch to patch brought his sight to the point of the cliff, to where Saul was still standing and grimaced a little.

Strange footsteps broke Alexander's concentration. He looked in its direction to find a figure cloaked in the shadows created by the sun's lowly position. Stephan and Jessica also took notice, turned, and stood ready. Even Saul responded and turned from gazing at the distant mountain for the first time since any of them had awakened.

The dark silhouette moved forward. It emerged from the shadows to reveal a being like Ambassador Luxeniah in skin tone, height, and the shape of his ears, yet he was remarkably different in his dress and countenance. Like the ambassador, he wore a cloak, but it was made out of a different material, which appeared to be the thick fur of beasts. Silently, he moved toward Alexander, drawing his sword. Stephan became fixated on the figure's blade, noticing its unkempt, jagged edge. It warned him that it was a dangerous weapon. This impression went against what Stephan knew—that each one of them was much better armed than this assailant. In spite of this, Stephan gripped his laser rifle, ready to use it if necessary.

With his combat sense piqued, Alexander drew his own weapon, a standard-issued pistol kept at his side. He hesitated at first, remembering the Carn Doctrine, but when it seemed necessary, he pointed his weapon at the slowly approaching enemy and yelled, "Stop!" Stephan and Jessica now had their firearms drawn and fixed on the attacker.

The figure did not alter his course, so Alexander fired. A few sparks appeared in front of the approaching enemy, accompanied by the high-pitched, metallic sound of a glancing deflection.

Stephan could not fully understand what had happened when Alexander fired his pistol. He had an idea of what might have happened, but he did not see the movement of the assailant's arms, if he had indeed deflected the shot.

The enemy continued, so Alexander, his senses now fully active, quickly fired several more shots, each time a spark appearing in front of the unknown being with the same high-pitched sound of metallic impact. Jessica also fired, but the sparks again appeared, with the same sounds as before. In an instant, the attacker was in striking range of the captain. He lifted his sword and swung downward. Stephan was about to fire his laser rifle when the rough blade was stopped just before striking Alexander's face by another, smooth blade. Wide-eyed, Alexander let out a quiet and feeble wheeze.

The blocking, smooth blade was held by Ambassador Luxeniah. For a moment, the two swords shook before the eruption and a fury of swings, parries, and thrusts. Their actions increased in speed until the others could not see them, except for brief moments here and there when one would pivot or adjust his stance. The fury of activity only lasted an instant. When both became still again, the rough blade had fallen to the ground. The attacker was gripping the wrist of his injured hand as blood dripped from it onto the ground.

The attacker stepped backward. Luxeniah matched his step, stepping forward. The intruder was furious, his eyes locked with Luxeniah's stern gaze. Without speaking, the mysterious figure ran into the shadows from where he came. His blade lay on the ground in front of the High Ambassador, who stepped forward and retrieved it.

When he had regained his composure, Luxeniah turned toward the others. "I wish your introduction to the realm of Xaliud were more cordial, but that Coltrous infiltrator will not be bothering us again any time soon." Luxeniah motioned to the stairway. "We must be moving now; we are in common land." He walked to the base of the staircase, which led up the hill. The others followed. As they approached its base, Stephan stopped and looked up at the stairway, resembling more of a monument than a means of ascending the cliff. The marble stairs themselves were bordered by a wall on each side. They started up, Alexander and Luxeniah in front, followed by Stephan and Jessica with Saul behind.

"We should be safe from here on out. The common lands end at the top, and there are no places of opportunity for our enemies to hide and attack us."

As they made their way up the stairway, Alexander and Luxeniah conversed on the intricacies of leadership.

"A leader must lead his men as a rider trains and rides his horse, by breaking it through consistent application of discipline," said Alexander.

Luxeniah responded, "Ah, yes, an undisciplined army is a defeated army...."

As they continued in this manner, Stephan took an interest in the reliefs that populated the stairway's bordering walls. The first was on the left. It portrayed two divided groups with a few prominent and more detailed figures in the center. The figures depicted looked as though they were sculptures trying to escape the confines of the marble wall. These figures were showed engaging in a warm exchange, clasping right forearms in the traditional Roman way. The tone of the relief struck Stephan as being positive, with the figures joyfully embracing each other's company. As joyful as the figures' countenances were, there was a bitter sweetness to it. The piece as a whole seemed to depict a farewell of sorts.

Stephan then noticed on the leftmost portion of the relief an arch, which strongly resembled the one they had passed through shortly before. The relief's leftmost figures seemed to be parting ways with the other figures so they could pass through the arch. Stephan also noticed that those on the left were much taller than the beings of the rightmost group and were creatures very much like Luxeniah. He thought that they must be of the same or a similar race. *Xalians*, Stephan thought, creating a word to describe those who were from what Ambassador Luxeniah called "the realm of Xaliud." Stephan mused as to whether the Xalians and events depicted on the wall were historical or fictional in nature.

They progressed farther up the monument stairway and came across the next relief, the first on the right. This one showed a long line of creatures, as tall as the Xalians who were like the ambassador, yet were different in their manner of dress and countenance. They were dressed in the furs of beasts with thick leather belts securing them to their bodies. *The Coltrous,* Stephan thought. These Xalians seemed to be similar in dress and manner as the one who had earlier attacked Alexander. Some of these Coltrous seemed sad, but they all shared a sort of seething fury in their sadness. The line led from the cliff and the archway all the way down a trail that continued down the cliff. The proportions of the relief were artistically and skillfully exaggerated in some parts to show the extent of the line's length. Stephan could see that it extended all the way down the cliff's trail and well into the land below.

Stephan was confused by what he had seen so far; he did not understand the connection, if there was one, these two events shared. He sensed, however, that they were indeed related in some manner.

After passing the second relief and walking farther up the stairs, Stephan took in the third relief, the second on the left wall, with hope that this one would bring with it some clarification as to the connection between the pieces. The third relief was the largest so far. It showed an enormous battle. Those fighting in it were of all three of the previous groups; first, there was the Xalians, of the tall ilk of Ambassador Luxeniah, adorned with embroidered cloaks and fighting with decorated swords. Alongside them was the shorter race of man, dressed in a manner similar to their Xalian allies. Opposing them were the Coltrous. Although intertwined in the battlefield, it was easy to tell the two groups apart. The battle seemed ferocious, the sculpted bodies in the foreground twisting, gnarled, and wrapping themselves around each other in mortal combat.

The pattern continued, and the fourth relief, the second on the right, appeared to bring with it a different look. It did not have the exaggerated features of the second relief, nor was it relating events from a singular location. Stephan noticed that it was more like the first, but instead of there being two large groups divided by one small group, there were two lands separated by a great body of water. On the left land were many small gatherings of peoples, both man and Xalian, performing many kinds of works, works distinctly different from those on the right lands who were those from the second relief, the chained, brutish people clad in the skins of beasts. They appeared to be the Coltrous.

Stephan focused on the individual groups left of the many waters. One was in a library learning from books and instructed by bald, robed men. Another showed its figures learning from a blacksmith, fashioning swords, spears, and other weaponry. Yet another gathering involved both man and Xalian in a throne room, with what much have been a king or some manner of ruler in the center, with two groups, one on each side, engaged in congenial conversation and debate. There was also a group learning and teaching the art of construction in the course of constructing the tower of what would undoubtedly become a castle, as portions of a half-built wall were attached to the half-completed tower.

Stephan shifted his focus on the lands to the right of the dividing waters. The Coltrous there were engaged in many destructive tasks not at all similar in nature to those of the other groups. They were generally engaged in acts of thievery, debauchery, and all manner of darkness. These people, dirty and unkempt, were not happy like those on the left, but looked grave and vengeful. There was a group of men and Xalians in these lands conversing with a group of the Coltrous, handing them books and tools. However, those of the right lands would not accept the gifts, throwing them to the ground and shouting at those who were attempting to show them generosity. Further inland on the right lands was another group raiding a village. Another was learning from an old, cloaked woman with a face of many warts and a long, pointed nose. Stephan did not spend much time looking at this side of the mural because time was running out and the images brought sadness and darkness to Stephan's mind, so he turned to look at the next relief. As he did, he noticed Saul viewing the reliefs. He felt a pang of embarrassment and resentment at the common observations the two shared, but he quickly worked past it, knowing he had a duty to perform, the duty of learning as much about this world as was possible or at least whatever would be of importance later on.

The fifth relief, the third on the left, was much simpler than the others were. It only showed a small group of Xalians without the presence of man. The only trace of mankind was the structures in the distance. Also, in this piece, Luxeniah's people were dressed differently. They were more rugged and like the Coltrous, but without the hatred in their countenances. In the center of the mural, four prominently depicted figures, who were the only ones in the relief dressed in embroidered cloaks, were sharing books and tools with the others. Some were accepting the gifts gladly and gratefully while others were reacting like the savage Coltrous in the previous relief by throwing the gifts to the ground. One even held his arm out, palm flat, toward a pile of books and tools starting to catch fire; he seemed to be causing the pile to become engulfed in flame.

The sixth relief, the third on the right, was not as simple as the last relief, but it was still populated by few figures. It showed the Coltrous traveling across the many waters of the fourth relief to the right land mass. Most of the boats of the fleet were more than halfway, and a few were already on the beaches of the right lands. Strangely, a few boats of the Xalians were traveling to the lands of the right side as if to follow the Coltrous, but they were far behind, being closer to the lands on the left.

The seventh relief, the fourth on the left wall, followed this manner of simplification, showing, in one part of the relief, only the four Xalians from the fifth relief being nursed back to health by four bald, robed men. In another part of the relief, the four were being taught to read from large tomes and to write with ancient quilled pens. In yet another part, the four Xalians were learning to use tools, and in another, they were making weapons. One weapon in particular seemed to be the most prominently displayed and Stephan recognized it from previous reliefs. It was a broadsword—ornate, detailed, and held high by the tallest of the four Xalians. The other three, as well as any man in its presence, seemed to look upon it with great interest, almost with reverence. Other scenes showed the forging of the weapon by the tallest of the four Xalians, hammering the metal that would become the weapon's blade, the other three surrounding it with outstretched arms and flat palms pointing at the metal.

They continued up the staircase where the eighth relief appeared on the right, being the fourth on that wall. It showed the results of a small battle, with bodies of both the primordial Xalians and men strewn across the ground. The four Xalians from the previous relief were among the bodies of the fallen Xalians and were being dragged and lifted away by the familiar bald men with robes, who were becoming regularly recurring characters or figures in this story or account. In the distance, a castle could be seen, and closer to the foreground was a monastery, which seemed to be the destination of the robbed men and the wounded warriors. Stephan thought that both the castle and monastery appeared to have similar architecture when compared to the structures in some of the previous reliefs.

Ambassador Luxeniah and his guard were now approaching the top of the stairway monument, and the final relief came into Stephan's view. It was the ninth and fifth on the left. It depicted the archway with its energy field and hordes of the primordial Xalians pouring through it in what to Stephan seemed to be blind fury. There were minor differences in the landscape, but its location resembled strongly the archway's Earthly location. The Xalians looked different to Stephan from those in the other murals. They had a mindless appearance, their faces more like those of feral beasts than sentient beings. He wondered about the reason for this difference.

His thought process was interrupted, though, when the group ahead of his stopped.

Luxeniah turned to view the stairway and the cliff on which the archway rested in the distance. The others turned, following his lead. "As you can see," he said, "we are a people who remember their history and often dwell on the lessons it can bring."

Alexander pursed his lips and looked to Stephan as though he wanted to say something but hesitated. "My lord, as much as we appreciate the sanctuary you've given us, I can't help but wonder why you have taken such an interest in us. Why go out of your way and risk your life for those who are not of your kingdom or kin?"

The lord gave a slight smile and replied, "A danger has been building for some time. It threatens all of us, and I believe you four will be pivotal to the survival of both our realms."

Luxeniah appeared as though he were going to continue, but then he paused. His eyes narrowed slightly and his head turned as a smile crept across his face. "Is that not right, my dear Cambrian?"

Luxeniah turned around sharply. The rest also turned to see the question's recipients—two strapping, young Xalian men. Their manner of dress was fine, suggesting positions of prominence within the Geradian Kingdom's military. They had their weapons drawn; one wielded a one-handed sword and the other a spear. When the two Xalians saw who had just spoken, their combative postures eased.

The one Stephan assumed from his manner and dress was the more experienced of the two spoke first. "Lord Luxeniah!"

Lord? Stephan thought. He watched Alexander and Jessica's reactions, and although subdued, he could tell they were as surprised as he was.

"My lord, forgive us!" The more experienced of the Xalians knelt, and the other, seeing the gesture, followed the example.

Lord Luxeniah chuckled. "Arise, Cambrian! Why does my return bring with it such formality?"

"Your return, my lord, has quite the opposite effect. Your return is a joyful and glorious one! We were tracking a Coltrous infiltrator; tricky and slippery that one is. To my relief, he has not brought you or those of your party any harm."

"He did not bring us harm as we dispatched him mere moments ago."

The Geradian brightened, and after looking over the others with an impressed look of being impressed, clearly assuming they had played a significant role in the fight, he said, "Not only has your return brought joy but an easing of my duties, of which I am not worthy."

Lord Luxeniah chuckled again. "Now, my dear Cambrian, as head of the local militia of the royal guard, you are entitled to rest, are you not?"

"In the year you have been away, my grace, fortune has smiled upon me. I am now the second helmsman of the king's royal guard!"

"Ah, surprise does not take me as it was not only fortune's smile but my training that brought this gift."

"Yes, my lord. I wish to stay, but the duties you so prepared me for call me away. I humbly ask for your leave."

"And you have it. Farewell, second helmsman!"

With that, the two Xalian guards saluted and rushed off, jumping from ledge to ledge. Stephan and the others were taken aback by their speed and agility. Their skill and strength were similar to that of Lord Luxeniah when he had fought the Coltrous infiltrator earlier.

Being at the top of the stairway monument, they turned around once again to view the stairs, the reliefs, the cliff, and the surrounding lands. They, the lord's party, had learned of both the darkness and the light of the world of Xaliud, for some purpose they were unaware of. They were now on their way to find out why.

Chapter 7

The Kingdom of Geradia

The road to the Castle of Geradia ran alongside the Hadriatic cliff-fortress. Led by Lord Luxeniah, Stephan and the others strolled along the road, affording Stephan a chance to view his surroundings, which were both strange and strangely familiar at the same time. The landscape shared many of the same elements as the Welsh, English, and Scottish wildernesses. He could tell, from long afternoon walks throughout the Welsh countryside, that the trees, grass, and other plants were of the same kind as those back home. This was the familiar part; what was strange was not only the similarity itself in such a foreign place but also the sizes of each plant varied wildly from their Earthly twin. In every flower, in every tree, and in every vine, the size did not seem to match, and the resulting experience of noticing these differences was both a little jarring and delightful at the same time.

The strangeness of Stephan's environment did not end with the foliage, however; all the animals also appeared to be of the same kind as those he had seen and studied in his youth. What was doubly peculiar was the variation of the sizes of the beasts, even within the same breed. As with the foliage, when compared to Welsh and English wildlife, the animals here were either significantly larger or

smaller when compared to their Earthly twins. When he saw a fox
darting ahead of them and across the road, it was leaner with longer
legs. When he saw a white-tailed eagle, however, it was smaller than
those back home.

Ahead of Stephan, Luxeniah was still walking with Alexander,
but he was speaking to all of them now. He was orating on various
asinine topics such as the past ownerships of several farms they had
passed earlier; the history of the road they were then walking on; and
when and what was good to hunt around these lands. Stephan had
to expend effort to stifle any expression of his annoyed mood as he
wished the lord would talk about something important, something
they might need to know while on Xaliud. What further bothered
him was that Luxeniah's manner seemed to relate to Stephan an
awareness of this, as if he were putting effort into avoiding certain
subjects. Stephan would have preferred hearing about the meaning
of the reliefs he saw earlier or what their duties as Lord Luxeniah's
guard were supposed to be.

The others did not seem to mind the trivial nature of the knowledge they were being fed. Stephan was all too aware that Alexander
and Jessica both shared that common trait among those of their
personality types—they did not care nearly as much about truth or
knowledge for its own sake as about relationships and the contacts
they were making. Stephan often conceded to himself that this was
often the most advantageous goal to have. At this time, though,
Stephan felt that knowledge pertinent to their current situation
would be more useful since they did not even know whether the
relations with these people would prove advantageous. He remembered, though, his lower position and the Carn doctrine and decided to follow Alexander's lead.

Stephan broke from his ruminating thoughts and noticed, just then, how odd the sound of his boots sounded when striking the stones of the road they were on. The sound shared many of the same characteristics with the sound you would make when walking on concrete, but without the uniformity, which was most likely the result of the uniform shape of each stone.... He tore himself away from this thought as well and tried to think about what would be useful to learn about these lands.

Stephan then noticed Saul, who seemed to be ecstatic. His movements were quicker and crisper than those of the others. Stephan rolled his eyes. He could tell Saul was really taking in his surroundings and enjoying the experience like a child on their first day at a new park. The others did not seem to notice.

They passed by another farm. Stephan noticed fields and the similarity of the crops growing on them to the wheat of many English farmsteads. Other than this plant's greater height and size, the two were almost the same. He thought that it must have been this world's spring since the wheat in the fields were white and ready to harvest. There were workers here and there reaping the crop. The workers took notice and watched them pass by, but they never approached them or said anything. It must have not been a common sight for them to see a Geradian nobleman accompanied by some strangely dressed, smooth-eared creatures.

Stephan viewed other portions of that farm and witnessed that much of the livestock was also larger and much was smaller than those back in England. But then he saw a bull; at first, it looked to be unusually large, but it being so far in the distance past a barn, it was difficult to judge its size adequately. When Stephan's mind and eyes adjusted, however, he could not believe the size of the beast. It did not seem real, and an uncomfortable feeling dwelled inside Stephan.

Stephan turned away from the bull and the barn when he heard those in front of him walk off the road and onto a path heading in the direction of the cliff.

"This will be nothing but a slight deviation from the road to Geradia," Lord Luxeniah said as he gestured in the direction the path led, "a deviation through which could prove most illuminating."

After walking down the path for a few minutes, they came to a small clearing that revealed a tower positioned on the edge of the cliff. Two guards stood at its entrance, stoic and motionless, until they saluted Lord Luxeniah. When they entered the tower's foyer, Stephan saw a spiral staircase on the other side of the room leading upward and downward to the levels above and below. His survey of the tower's foyer was interrupted when a member of the King's Guard entered. He warmly approached Lord Luxeniah and they clasped forearms. Stephan could tell this Xalian was of the King's Guard because he wore a uniform similar, but more regal, to that worn by the two guards they had met at the top of the stairway monument.

"Welcome, sire!" the guard said. "I am overjoyed to be witness to your safe return to this realm. How may our humble post serve the kingdom?"

"Well met, Corporal. I require only what your post has in abundance: the grand view of the southern lands of the Coltrous that only this tower can bring and a warm, safe place to rest for the night."

The corporal gave a slight bow. "It shall be given; please, follow me."

The lord and his guard were then led up the spiral staircase to the tower's watch turret. There they took in the view of the southern lands below, which extended from the cliff's base outward toward the hills on the other side of the valley. The land was similar to what Stephan had surveyed earlier when they were on the pointed cliff near the arch. The ground and the trees in many parts of the valley were charred and there was that characteristic view of a land recently host to a battle.

"When was the previous attack?" Luxeniah asked, directing his question to the head guard.

"Not for several days, sire, which at this tower is a rare respite. We are expecting another any day now as the berserkers tend to strike when they think our guard is down."

"It appears as though in my year of absence, the frequency of assaults has increased."

After a momentary pause, the corporal continued, "That it has, my lord. These days bring greater trials for my men as we contend with greater numbers of intruders with no increase of men or arms. But still, in spite of this, my men fight with honor, gaining strength from their trials."

Lord Luxeniah looked troubled by the corporal's admission. "I will be meeting with the Council of Nobles shortly, and I intend on changing that shameful neglect."

The lord turned, stepped toward the railing of the spiral staircase, looked down into the foyer and down the stairwell into the underground levels. "Tell me, Corporal; does this post still have the finest cook in all the towers of the Hadriatic Cliff Fortress?"

The head guard brightened, and smiling, said with a little pride, "That it has! If it pleases his Excellency, we can descend to the mess hall now."

The lord was gazing at the sun as it was setting behind the mountains. "It would please me as it would please my guard, I am sure; we have been traveling all day and could use the rest." The corporal led them down the spiral staircase past the tower's foyer and into what was the bulk of the tower's structure, extending below the cliff's surface. They could see new perspectives of the cliff's rocky features from the windows as they made their way to the mess hall. They ate and laughed, enjoying the gaiety of a more relaxed atmosphere and feeling truly safe for the first time in what felt like quite some time.

Stephan was just about to lift the last spoonful of his soup to his mouth when the unmistakable sounds of alarm broke through, deep into the tower and into the mess hall. It was that primordial sound, as old as time itself, which anybody from any land could recognize instantly as a signal of something being amiss.

The guards on passive duty immediately stood and the whole room erupted as they all left in a hurry. As one was exiting the hall, he turned to the lord and said, "Sire, for your protection, please stay within the tower's walls!"

Lord Luxeniah stood and nodded gravely. When the guard left, the lord moved to one of the tower's windows, looking over a portion of the cliff where much of the commotion had originated. When the others followed, Stephan felt a premonition that they would be witness to something of significance soon. The air was tense and silent. The guards had all gone to their posts, some at the top of the tower, others on the wall, and a few were traversing the cliff itself, leaping from ledge to ledge, their weapons drawn.

The sounds of commotion stopped, and for many tense and long moments, nothing could be heard other than the disciplined positioning of the tower's guards on the cliff shelves. They seemed to be searching for something.

Stephan moved to the window to his left and looked down in an attempt to see if there were guardsmen on this part of the cliff. What he saw took a moment to register, for it was not a cliff ledge, nor was it a guard or anything he had seen, but when it became clear, it was a figure, his face shrouded in the dark lines streaking across it. He was looking directly at him, holding Stephan's gaze with his own. Stephan could not move or speak for a split second. When the arrestment wore off and Stephan was about to call out to the guardsmen, the marked figure crawled in an instant to stand on the cliff shelf below them. When the figure was about to leap up into the tower through the window in front of Stephan, a guardsman engaged the figure in combat lasting only an instant. There were brief moments when Stephan could actually see the attacks of the two engaged warriors, in-between furies of movement so intense and rapid as to appear invisible to any unseasoned eyes such as his. The two then stopped and held there. An arrow was now buried in the assailant's chest. The body of the Coltrous berserker went limp and fell backward, down the cliff.

Another Coltrous assailant leapt up onto the ledge and promptly vanished behind a wall as he fell into combat with the guardsman. Another berserker was about to creep into the shelf and ambush the already engaged guardsman when another of the tower's protectors fought with him.

As Lord Luxeniah and those of his guard viewed the fighting, the lord leaned in toward Alexander, gesturing to the combat. "As you can see, the Coltrous are fast and strong; they could be stronger than even my men, but they lack experience, knowledge, and above all, discipline."

After a moment, when they all were still trying to observe the fighting, Lord Luxeniah said loudly, "Look and behold the might of the Kingdom of Geradia!" Although all of the lord's guard could hear this, it was unmistakably directed to Alexander in a fraternity only leaders know. "No Coltrous berserker, in over a thousand years, has ever successfully penetrate our Hadriatic Cliff Fortress, try as they might!"

After the third berserker was dispatched, moments of apprehension for Stephan passed as the guardsmen checked for more of them. A few searched along the wall, strengthening the defense provided by those guardsmen who regularly traversed the length of the cliff. When it became evident the attack had ceased, the tension died down and the guardsmen returned to their respective duties.

Alexander addressed the lord. "They attack periodically?"

"If nothing has changed during the year of my absence, and it appears as if it has not, then they do indeed attack often. We do not know precisely why they do it, but what we do know is that they do not value life, as a living, experiencing being should. Even animals do not throw their lives away out of hate or revenge or to show their bravery, only those brutish things do so. Very few of them survive to flee, no doubt then executed by those who sent them."

Before long, the corporal came to them and addressed the lord. "It is most regrettable, sire, that a distinguished person of your prominence should be witness to such mundane and altogether ghastly deeds."

"Not at all," Luxeniah retorted. "In fact, it was my hope that such *mundane* tasks and duties would be ours to witness. The attack of the Coltrous berserkers was sure to be illuminating. It has been too long since I have seen it, and it was a primary experience for my

guard. Such deficiencies of knowledge of one's enemy are dangerous. Furthermore, I now have more to bring to the attention of the
Grand Council."

The head guardsman seemed genuinely relieved by this. "If I
may be so bold as to inquire, sire, when will the Grand Council
be meeting?"

"On the morrow, if I have correctly judged the time of departure
from the Earthen realm. We shall like to stay in the royal chambers
for the night because it will soon be dark and the castle is still a quarter's day journey north. We weary souls must rest at some point."

"But of course."

Lord Luxeniah showed a placid smile, but Stephan could tell it
was made more from obligation; the lord seemed to be acting in a
state of near fatigue. "I see nothing has changed in this past year in
regards to the excellence of our King's Guardsmen."

The corporal led them deeper into the tower, deeper into the cliff
itself, past the barracks and into a small hallway of larger and more
decorated rooms. It was clear these were the royal chambers spoken
of, and it was where they spent the night without disturbance by
any Coltrous berserker or infiltrator, or a disturbance of any sort in
what would later prove to be a rare reprieve of heart and mind.

Chapter 8

The Castle of Geradia

After a quarter of a day and after a good and peaceful night's rest, the High Ambassador of Geradia with his guard, the captain, the two lieutenants, and the private, were traveling along the road to the Castle of Geradia. They traversed the lush, green Geradian countryside without trouble, passing many more farms and manors along the way. In time, they entered Pepperwood, the kingdom's southernmost forest. The trees there were famous for their size, a fame not from a largeness of their trunks but from the length of their branches, many of which draped and sprawled overhead, weaving around each other to form a thin canopy. Before long, they passed through the thickest portions of the forest and into a wide clearing where a village was nestled.

A festival was then taking place in the largest clearing outside the village. Alongside the borders of this clearing ran Tucker's Brook with a line of trees bordering it at the higher point of soil. Children could be seen playing in the brook while old men smoked on their pipes as they sat on rocks close by.

Although the road did not pass directly through the event, it did wind closely enough for the attendees to see these passersby. At first, only a few of the festivals attendees here and there would stop and gaze at Stephan and the others, but when the bard's music died down, almost every engaged festival member became interested in the nobleman with his party of strange-looking creatures. Their oddly rounded ears and relatively darker skin caused them to stand out.

In the tense silence, Lord Luxeniah stopped. The others followed suit and faced the table where the main feast was being enjoyed.

Lord Luxeniah addressed the crowd. "Sons and daughters of the glorious Kingdom of Geradia, forgive our intrusion. It was not our intent to disrupt this happy celebration, but I bring an additional cause to rejoice." Lord Luxeniah gestured to the four standing beside him. "For this day has seen the arrival of the four written of in the ancient writings who will preserve both this realm and the realm from which they came!"

There was some applause and looks of genuine excitement among many of those attending, including those at the head of the banquet table, but there were many who were either clapping to conform or were not clapping at all. Stephan saw a slight look of consternation form and then quickly retreat from the lord's expression.

The Geradian nobleman continued, "And as there must be many here from the far reaches of the kingdom, it is my humble request that you take what you have learned this day and proclaim, as I have, this good news, that they may be at ease in mind and soul."

There was another round of applause, but it was somewhat more muted than before.

"We now go to this day's Grand Council. We beg your farewell as you continue with your day's merriment."

With that, Lord Luxeniah continued onward, the other following, toward the castle of Geradia, which was not within eyesight of the party and less than an hour's walk from where they were. Along the way, they entered another part of the Pepperwood forest that was thicker than the previous parts. In it were crudely constructed homes made from nothing more than beams of wood resting against a tree or the eroded part of a knoll. These seemed, from the rags on the bodies and the sparseness of the possessions of those who inhabited the crude houses, to belong to the most impoverished of the kingdom's inhabitants. It was surprising to Stephan and the others of the guard that these poverty-stricken Xalians exuded happiness and contentment in spite of their circumstances. This was a display foreign to those who were of Lord Luxeniah's guard and of the Earthen realm, to see a people content with their humble lots of making pottery, weaving blankets, and spoiling thread.

Although thicker in this area, the forest eventually thinned and gave way to a much closer and grander view of the castle. From the outset, Stephan could see that the stone edifice was heavily fortified. A gigantic wall separated them from its main structures with towers interrupting the wall periodically. Two turrets bordered the kingdom's entrance. Shouts came from somewhere high within one of them, announcing the arrival of Lord Luxeniah.

As the drawbridge lowered to allow them entry, Stephan caught the first glimpses of the lower parts of the inner structure's spires. In the following moment, he saw it—the symbol he did not know the name of but could recognize in an instant. It was almost always referred to as the ultimate symbol of hate, one of many symbols of hate that were illegal to name, write, or show some kind of manifestation of. It was even against the law to picture any of the symbols in one's mind. In grade schools all over the world, teachers taught their students the symbol only through description and were asked to imagine the symbol's shape, and while the image was fresh in

their minds, they were swiftly and severely punished for following
the instruction. Stephan could vividly recall his childhood instructor monitoring him, reading his facial expression and striking his
forehead with her ruler at the moment she knew he had achieved
conception of the symbol's shape in his mind. He could almost hear
her shrill, grating voice describe the shape simply as a vertical line
bisected by a line half its length at a point on the larger line somewhat above the line's midpoint. Stephan had often wondered if this
were the reason for the odd slant in the shorter of the two lines
which made up the lower case t, so that it wouldn't look too much
like the symbol. Other shapes were much more complex, involving
many times the number of lines.

Stephan, forgetting himself, foolishly displayed his discomfort
openly. He hurried to exert great effort to suppress these thoughts
and feelings. He looked at the captain, worried he might have seen
Stephan's violation of the Carn Doctrine, but instead, he found
relief in the sight of Alexander's similar struggle. He glanced at
Jessica and found the same. He observed Saul, whose look was not
of discomfort but more of surprise and defiant satisfaction. Stephan
felt disgust, yet another emotion to suppress.

Stephan tore his view from Saul and tried to admire the rest of
the architecture, which brought with it not the relief he sought, but
the horrible realization that the supreme symbol of hate was the
shape of many of the windows on almost all of the towers. He knew
with a sickening realization that he would be seeing the symbol many
more times during their stay in the castle. He was always taught that
those who bore the symbol were themselves evil. This confused him,
the treatment he and the others had received at the hands of the lord
as well as the guards at the Hadriatic wall's tower was nothing short

of magnanimous. He resolved to be cautious within the walls of Geradia, in case the other Geradians were hostile toward outsiders.

They continued on, passing the stoic guards posted at the kingdom's entrance, through the entrance to the castle square, and into the bustling activity of the early afternoon's trade. Stand after stand was set up throughout the square's market with droves of buyers and sellers trading at each one. In contrast to their last encounter with a crowd, this time very few seemed to care about their presence, save those close to them. Most in the market seemed more than willing to give way to the nobleman and the strange creatures accompanying him, giving only brief, puzzled looks.

They passed bakers, fruit stands, and blacksmiths before coming to the area in front of the entrance to the castle. A Xalian, dressed in an ornate royal cloak, stood in front of the entrance, engrossed in conversation with another similarly dressed Xalian. Both of their attires were of the same green and blue colors as Lord Luxeniah's robe. When one of them caught a view of the lord, he immediately broke off the conversation and walked quickly to meet them.

"My dear Cormin!" Lord Luxeniah exclaimed, greeting the approaching Xalian with an unmistakable familiarly.

"Sire!" The Xalian bowed to his knees and Luxeniah motioned for him to stand. When the Xalian stood, he said, "You have returned! How may your humble servant serve his long-missed master?"

Stephan was surprised when Cormin referred to himself as the lord's servant since he noticed how well dressed and well treated he was by his master. From what he had learned in school, Stephan always pictured the relationship between a servant and a lord to be much less cordial. *He is a servant to a nobleman,* Stephan thought, *surely a position of high repute among the servant class, but still.* The servant and his master spoke as they walked up the castle's steps and into the foyer.

After conversing for a moment about Cormin's wellbeing during the year of Luxeniah's absence, the lord said, "I apologize. I must quickly dispense with this reunion. However, my guard must be aided as pressing matters require my attention in preparation for the Grand Council." He looked at his servant. "Please show my enlisted and our guests to the royal library."

"Very well, my lord."

Lord Luxeniah left them, walking down the large hallway deeper into the keep of the castle.

The servant Cormin led Saul and the rest of the guard down a hallway that branched off to the right of the main foyer. As they walked, Cormin talked about the history of the castle's construction, its structure, and how the hallway they were then traversing led directly to the royal library. It was about this time—when they were passing a large, open door on the right—that Saul saw another building with colorful stained glass windows and ornate sculptures as its outer décor. As he continued to look on, no longer listening to what the servant guide was saying, he saw two robed figures enter the structure. When they opened the door to enter, Saul could hear, despite the noise of the people who populated the area between him and the new building, a faint collection of voices singing in a manner he had never heard before. The music was faint and was

abruptly cut off by the doors closing behind the two robed figures
entering the building.

Saul returned his attention to the group. He realized, being at
the back of the group, he could slip away without anybody noticing
his absence. With little hesitation, he went through the door, out of
the hallway, made his way through the crowd, and quickly reached
the building's tall, oak doors. He opened the right door just enough
to where he could ease himself in without making any noise and
quietly close it behind him. Luckily, the building's entryway was
barren of people and so he did not attract any attention. Although
physically empty, the entryway was filled with the echoes of voices
singing the unknown kind of music.

Saul continued down the entryway, following the source of the
heavenly sounds and coming finally to a large room with vaulted
ceilings. There was a group of robed and hooded Xalians, singing
in unison. Saul was reminded of the villagers back on Cult Island,
but these robes looked heavier and more ornate. The Xalians were
grouped together on an elevated part of the room. On the floor
was a line of robed figures kneeling with heads lowered in submis-
sion. Another robed, unhooded Xalian was walking in front of
those who kneeled, stopping at each prostrated figure one by one.
When he would reach one of them, he would extend his arm and
move it in the same way, over and over again. With the index and
middle fingers extended, he would move the arm downward, back
up, and then horizontally, bisecting the imaginary line made by the
first movement. The pattern made greatly resembled the supreme
symbol of hate. He then noticed the same symbol behind the group
of singing Xalians in wooden form.

Without thinking, Saul approached the line of kneeling, robed Xalians. He did not know why he had wanted to do so, but he found an opening in the line, entered it, and kneeled. Imitating the others, he bowed his head. He glanced over to see what else he was supposed to do and noticed the others interlocking their fingers and letting their arms rest against their legs. He also noticed them speaking to themselves in almost inaudible tones. Saul imitated them in this manner as well, to the best of his ability, all the while not quite sure whether what he was doing was right. He knew he stood out, being the only one without a robe, and the patterns of his private's uniform contrasted heavily with the basic colors of the others' robes.

Before long, the Xalian who had been making the ultimate symbol of hate approached Saul. He paused only briefly before making the sign with his arm, performing the same actions for Saul as he did for the others.

Saul felt a warmth in his chest and a kind of fullness, both of which he had not felt before. When he opened his eyes, he found his vision somewhat blurred by tears streaming down his face. He looked at the symbol that before, he was forbidden from even thinking about, and found that to him it was no longer a symbol of hate or a thing he could use to defy authority, but a thing whose nature was something else he had never known. At that moment, he vowed to find the true meaning and true essence of the symbol.

Chapter 9

The Royal Library

After Saul stole away to the cathedral, the guard of Lord Luxeniah, save for one, followed the servant of the nobleman further down the hall and into the Kingdom's Royal Library. Once there, the servant politely excused himself to attend to other duties, leaving the others in the foreign room. When he was gone, Stephan looked over the enormity of the library. Its several floors extended higher and higher up to a distant, stained-glass ceiling. Each floor had shelves and shelves of books, each shelf the height of two Xalians.

Alexander, after briefly looking over the room, turned to Stephan. "Lieutenant, you're on intel." Without waiting for any kind of response, he and Jessica ventured off into the depths of the literary labyrinth.

Stephan, being left alone for the first time in several days, at once felt a sense of relief. He was not used to being in any group of people for such an extended duration. He almost always found the experience draining. This was one of the reasons he had originally chosen intelligence and engineering as his specialties, as their working environments were usually quiet and solitary. The silence of the Royal Library reminded him of those places. He felt like he was now in his element.

He looked over the surrounding shelves and alcoves, trying to find among the many tomes where he should start, and what intel he was supposed to be gathering. The sheer size of the library would have intimidated most other people, but he was used to sifting through mountains of information. He searched for a few moments, scanning shelf after shelf to gain a sense of what knowledge each section had to offer. He then came to an anteroom, where the titles of the books revealed that they centered around the Xalian history during the time when the Xalians had first traveled to Earth.

He entered it and began scanning the tome's titles with greater scrupulosity. From what he saw, three titles stood out to Stephan: *The Prehistory of the Xalian Peoples*, *The Events Leading to the First Great Conflict*, and *The Four Heroes of the First Great Conflict*. The first tome was the thinnest, although still thick compared to what he had been exposed to while studying history in one of the required courses during his years of schooling. It was one of the only places where reading words on paper pages was still preferred.

In the center of the recess, a woman Xalian was busy placing books from a pile onto a shelf. Stephan continued to search the collection. He found a number of possible starting points. His search brought him closer to the Xalian woman, whom he assumed must have been a librarian. Being this close to her, he noticed more details about her appearance and found her surprisingly attractive. Her skin was milky white and her hair a dark brown, braided in a wide ponytail leading down to the base of her neck. When she noticed him looking at her, Stephan felt a flush of embarrassment and pretended to be looking not at her, but at the books beside her.

"May I be of assistance to you?" the librarian asked softly. Stephan did not know whether he was more surprised at the break in silence or the lack of the annoyance he was expecting to be in her voice.

He composed himself. "Yes, actually, I wish to learn as much as I can about a specific subject."

The librarian gestured to the books. "Well, you certainly are in the right place."

They both gave slight, uncomfortable smiles. "I suppose I am," Stephan said, becoming more serious. "More specifically, I need to learn whatever will prepare me to serve my superior, Lord Luxeniah, as a member of his guard."

The librarian beamed and breathed in deeply. She looked over the books to her right, and after searching for an instant, took a book from the shelf. "This should serve to be an excellent start." She handed it to Stephan. He received it and read the title on the book's cover, *The First Great Conflict: The Northern Kingdoms and the Coltrous.*

The librarian continued, "This should give you a general familiarity of the events leading up to, during, and following the First Great Conflict. If you have any further questions, there are more books that delve deeper into more narrow topics. If you need me to, I can stay around this area."

"I would like that," Stephan said, meaning the words in more than one way. He then sat at the table situated at the center of the alcove. Stephan read the book's title a second time and was impressed by the book's apparent relevance. *How did she know exactly what I was looking for?* he asked himself before opening the book.

As he read, it became clear from the archaic language that the rate by which he would be able to read would be significantly slower than what he was used to. Even with the diminished speed, he was still able to get through the first book in well under an hour, returning it to the librarian much sooner than she had anticipated. His brain was starved for knowledge relevant to his mission.

Stephan enjoyed each subsequent visit with the librarian and her displays of being impressed. As he read, he learned more and more about the common histories of both the Xalian and Human races. In the course of his research, it became clear that the monument stairway, specifically the figures carved into its walls, depicted many of the pivotal moments he was now reading of, and that his earlier assumption, that what he was viewing at the time was the reverse chronological order of the events, was correct.

The Xalians had originally been a brutish and primitive race drawn by some unknowable force to pass through the archway from Xaliud to the Earthen realm. The earliest accounts of their interaction with mankind involved lore of Xalians pestering and harassing farmers along the English countryside. Tensions continued to escalate until skirmishes and battles resulted. After one of these conflicts, four monks were searching the battlefield for the injured when they found four mortally wounded Xalians. The monks carried the Xalians to the nearest monastery where, over the course of months, they were nursed back to health.

While in bed healing from their injuries, the four Xalian warriors expressed curiosity in the ways of man and were taught English, religion, and culture. When they were fully healed and had learned all that would satisfy them, these four Xalians took what they learned to their still uncivilized brethren and shared with them the knowledge. Many found the ideas the four were relating to be of great worth and accepted them readily. To others, however, the ideas were the thoughts of sad and foolish weaklings, and they rejected most of the teachings outright.

For a time, there was peace and coexistence between the two groups of Xalians—those who had accepted the teachings and those who had rejected them. Eventually, though, those who would not accept the ideas left the British Isles and went to the Southeastern lands were they found ideas and ideologies more suited to their sensibilities.

Stephan remembered the relief depicting boats sailing across a sea in between two great masses of land. He also remembered the one with many Xalians learning from old hags, living in swamps and marshlands, receiving gifts of darkness and hatred.

He continued reading, learning about the ensuing war between the alliance between those who had accepted the teachings learned in the monastery from the monks and those who had not accepted the teachings and would later be known as the Coltrous. Stephan remembered the gaudy relief of historic figures locked in battle and made the connection between the event as it was described in the tome and the artwork on the stairway monument. The tome also related many accounts of the four Xalians having "the rare and gifted power to command the elements." Stephan skipped much of this material since he assumed the four were deified historical figures, and the powers merely part of the mythology surrounding them. He had read many similar exaggerations of ability written by ancient human historians about Earth's key historical figures.

When the war had run its course, the Xalian-Mankind alliance emerged victorious, despite the overwhelming numbers of the Coltrous hordes. The war would be known in time as the First Great Conflict. What was left of the Coltrous was banished to the region of Xaliud, south of the Hadriatic Cliff Fortress. The scene depicting a long line of chained Xalians, stretching from the Earthen Archway down the cliff, came to Stephan's mind.

In the next tome, the writer seemed to be depicting events from a much different perspective, even though this book was covering the same period as the previous books. Instead of relating the events surrounding the wars between the First Great Conflict, it instead described the political structures of the many Xalian tribes that would eventually merge to become the three Northern Kingdoms. Stephan read about how most tribes banded together under the leadership of one of two of the four original Xalian leaders. The formation of these merged tribes became, in time, permanent larger tribes, which were then deemed kingdoms. One kingdom took on the name of its first king Gerad, being dubbed Geradia. The other group of merged tribes became the kingdom of Durathia, being named after their leader Durath. The remaining tribes were those that had fought alongside the others during the war but chosen not to be included in either of the other two kingdoms. They were the tribes of Xalians who had originated from the mountains far to the north of where the other two kingdoms would be founded.

Stephan smirked a little when he read that they were unique in that they had the ability to tame the green dragons indigenous to the northern mountains. In the author's opinion, it was the only evidence that the Xalian civilization exhibited before the prior opening of the Earthen Archway of animal husbandry. Because of this unique and powerful mode of travel, these northern tribes were able to rout many of the Coltrous hordes in several key battles. Most Xalian histories and academic studies of the people agreed that the early animal husbandry exercised by the Northern Tribes greatly prepared them for the introduction of human civilization since no Xalian from these tribes opposed the new ideas. Although none resisted the general idea and utility of civilization, they did not take to it as wholly as those belonging to the other two kingdoms did. As a result, while still in the Earthen realm and in the time of peace after the First Great Conflict, they traveled east to visit other civilizations. According to oral accounts related by those traveling tribes, they spent most of their travels in the far eastern lands. The tribes returned after spending a substantial amount of time there to pass through the archway before it would close for a thousand years.

Stephan continued to read about the Northern Tribes and learned that they would eventually be called the Chromas, being a people who preferred to reside in the northern mountains beyond the barren lands. They never formed a kingdom, choosing instead to embody teachings from the many kingdoms and civilizations with which the many tribes had mingled. The tome Stephan was reading did not have much information on the Chromas beyond this early history. Apparently, contact between the Chromas and the Northern Kingdoms of Geradia and Durathia had dwindled over the ages. The reason for this was greatly debated, but the most popular theory was that the danger the green dragons in the northern mountains presented warded off any historian willing to make the journey. There was also a fair amount of disinterest in the Chromas due to their differing culture and religion. According to the original oral accounts, although the individual tribes had different gods they worshipped, almost all the tribes took on Eastern philosophies with an almost religious zeal.

After the fifth book in just under two-and-a-half hours, the librarian was struggling to produce additional research material that might aid Stephan in his mission. He placed a hand on her arm to stop her. "I won't be needing any more books. It seems as though I know now everything they have to offer me, but there are some fundamental points none of the books have defined or addressed."

"Perhaps I can dispel the confusion," the librarian offered.

"I have been trying to expand my knowledge of the geography of Xaliud in my mind, but I have not been able to read about any region east of Durathia or north of the Chromas tribes."

The librarian gave him a queer look. She then appeared as if she had come to some kind of realization and gave a lighthearted laugh. "Give me a moment." She went to a bookcase at the other side of the alcove and climbed up a ladder situated next to its entrance. When she reached a higher shelf, she produced several large, rolled-up sheets of paper and came back down and to the table in the alcove's center. There, she spread the sheets out and motioned to Stephan to examine them.

Stephan perused the unrolled scrolls and saw that they were maps. The one the librarian had displayed most prominently was of a land with vast mountain ranges surrounding it.

"This is a map of the Realm of Xaliud," the librarian explained. "Earlier, it slipped my mind that the mountains of the Earthen Realm are less numerous and that your homelands are not surrounded by them."

After studying the map for a few moments, Stephan had his own realization. "I read in one of the histories that historians from your kingdom have avoided visiting the Chromas in the north due to the presence of the dragons there." The librarian watched Stephan intensely, anticipating the epiphany. "There must be dragons in all of these other mountain ranges, those east of Durathia, those west of the portal, and those south of this southern region." Stephan then wondered whether Saul had been staring at one of these dragons, somehow being able to see it in the distance. He decided this was very unlikely because he would have noticed such a sight, having better vision than Saul did.

The librarian responded to Stephan's assessment. "Well, that southern region has yet to be explored, but for a different reason than the threat of any beast. It goes without saying that the mountain range beyond it has not been explored either. The mountains drawn on the map south of the southern region are drawn out of extrapolation and assumption. And you are correct about the dragons inhabiting every mountain range. They are drawn to them for some reason and block any inhabitation of those mountains, except of course for the mountains the Chromas tribes inhabit. The creatures in those lands tend to be weaker than those of other mountainous places. There most likely will never be a way. I have often daydreamed about what lies beyond them, but it is fruitless. There will never be a way to safely explore the surrounding mountains."

Stephan thought for a moment, mentally digesting what he had just heard, and trying to find a way to proceed to his next question. After a moment, it came to him. "Perhaps the four who have been written about will be able to explore those lands, those who supposedly will rise up and lead the kingdoms once again against the Coltrous." Stephan was paraphrasing one of the histories he had earlier read.

The librarian lit up at this statement. "Of course! It is a tale told to everybody when they are young children. You most likely did not read about it in any detail as it is something the historians do not consider actual history. In all, they consider it a myth. The tale is simple: Four leaders, not of these lands, will lead the kingdoms in a Second Great Conflict against the Coltrous. They will defeat four Coltrous leaders during this war. It is believed that although the first four leaders who led the Xalian-Man alliance during the First Great Conflict were Xalian, the alliance in the Second Great Conflict will be led by four from the Earthen Realm. The tale has fallen further from credibility largely due to the failed attempts of the Coltrous in attacking our lands. They are not seen as posing much of a threat, let alone being capable of launching any kind of serious invasion."

Stephan remembered the Coltrous attack they had witnessed the previous day and how futile the attack did seem to him.

"When I first saw you," the librarian continued, "some part of me had hopes you were the fabled leaders, but then I saw only three from your lands."

"Three?" Stephan was genuinely confused. He looked back at the library's entrance, realizing then that he had no memory of Saul entering the enormous room with them. He turned back to the librarian. "There is a fourth. But I'm not sure where he's gone off to."

The librarian appeared to be relieved to hear this. "So, there is hope after all!"

Stephan smiled at her enthusiasm and was genuinely encouraged by it. However, he wondered if the tale held any truth. There *were* four of them. He felt a sudden desire to speak to Alexander, so he politely excused himself from the library alcove and went back to the library's main floor. From there, he saw Alexander and Jessica across the large, expansive room. When he saw Stephan, Alexander motioned to a small room near to Stephan and they all entered it, shutting the door behind them. For the first time in a while, they were not in the presence of the lord and could speak to each other freely.

"What is your report, Lieutenant?" Alexander asked.

"I have read much about the history of the Xalians, specifically the period of time when they first came into contact with the human race." Stephan related to them all that he had learned regarding the monks who had saved the original four Xalians, the myth of their powers, and the rift between the Northern Kingdoms and the Coltrous. "It appears, sir, that Lord Luxeniah may believe we are the four foretold to lead the Northern Kingdoms against the Coltrous in this Second Great Conflict."

Alexander remained silent for a moment as his brow furrowed, giving Stephan the impression he was mulling over all that had just been related to him. He then looked up to Stephan, and then to Jessica.

"Considering all we have seen so far," Alexander began, "we will operate under the assumption that the fears of the lord are well founded. We've seen what these Coltrous have done, and Lord Luxeniah is the key to sanctuary from the UWI, so let's play along with this legend of the foretold four Earthen leaders until we are in a better position."

"Why don't we just go back and tell the UWI investigation board what we've seen?" Jessica asked.

"We need more evidence. If there is any chance to prove our innocence, it'll be here on Xaliud. If nothing else, we'll see if these Coltrous really are a threat to Earth."

Chapter 10

The Cathedral of Geradia

Lord Luxeniah entered the foyer of the castle's main keep where he had left his guard, having returned from completing his tasks, to find his servant pacing back and forth, as if something weighed heavily on his mind. When he saw Luxeniah, the servant approached him immediately.

"Sire! Oh, my master! I did as you did entail; I escorted those you entrusted to my care and guidance to the royal library, but it seems as though I may...." The servant hesitated.

Luxeniah looked at him sternly. "Well, out with it!"

The servant finally summoned the courage to continue. "One of them did not make it to the library." He was now looking down in shame. "I must have lost him. I looked and looked but could not find the Earthen anywhere."

As they had been talking, they were walking through the hallway leading to the library and were then just passing the doorway located across the way from the cathedral. The lord looked at the structure and then directed his attention back to his servant. "Worry not, my dear Cormin. I will check with the priests who are out and about. There is bound to be one who has seen a wandering man."

The servant gave a heavy sigh and continued onward to the Royal Library. Lord Luxeniah made his way to the cathedral's large, oak door and opened it. As he did so, the monks' chanting filled the entryway. He followed the sounds and came to the large sacrament hall where the blessings and rites were being administered by the high priest. He was about to approach him when he saw a supplicating figure in the line of others engaged in the same practice. The figure's dress was remarkably different from the rest, having no robe and being an Earthen private's uniform. The appearance of the foreign clothing starkly contrasted with Lord Luxeniah's ornate, green-and-white-striped robes. He was wearing the colors of House Luxeniah in preparation for the grand council.

The nobleman was taken aback by the sight of a man worshipping at the cathedral's altar. He had spent many nights during his sojourn in the Earthen realm trying to find religious observance in any place outside the brotherhood's island and outside the realms of terrorists. His searching always proved fruitless as the most comparable services he could find were humanist gatherings with the observers extolling the wonders of man's many achievements and attributing the source of these wonders solely to man's genius. The architecture of the structure these gatherings had taken place in and the symbology inherent in the structure's inner décor had been dominated by horizontal lines. To Lord Luxeniah, the humanist services had proved to be more disturbing and hollow than the complete absence of any religion he experienced in the vast majority of places. For these and many more reasons, he considered himself fortunate to see such a rare event. Being filled with the spirit of wonder and humility he walked forward and prostrated himself next to the man who had slipped away from the group to do what most men had not done anywhere for generations.

Saul noticed the lord's presence when Lord Luxeniah knelt next to him in the line of worshippers. Surprised, he did not know how to act and so stayed silent, continuing to perform the ritual, the purpose of which he did not fully understand but knew was right and desirable.

After some time had passed, Saul stood and left the line, and after exploring the strange structure, taking in the bizarre beauty of the colorful windows and other artwork, he came across an alcove. He glanced inside as he was about to pass it and saw a robed Xalian, sitting at a desk and strangely holding a feather pen, engrossed in writing with it. The Xalian stopped what he was doing and looked over at Saul, having sensed he was being watched. Saul did not look away; the sitting Xalian had a demeanor so entirely inviting that Saul felt comfortable as he walked into the alcove.

Saul stood in front of the Xalian, who was patiently giving the Earthen his full attention but did not say anything for a few silent moments. Finally, Saul asked, "What are you writing?"

The Xalian looked pleased with the inquiry. "It is...good news... to any who would read it."

Saul looked at the sheets of parchment on the writing table, not reading what was written on them but instead admiring the penmanship; he had never seen anything quite like it before. It had seemed silly at first that one would use such crude means for written communication. He had only rarely witnessed this means of writing, and when he did, it was only a basic note. After a few moments of observing the artistry of this monk, though, he thought the manner of communication could carry more significance than what he had originally thought.

"You seem to be," the Xalian continued, "a soul far removed from home yet closer to what he is looking for than ever before." The Xalian then rummaged through his writings, and upon finding what he was searching for, produced a small stack of parchment. He rolled up the pages, tied a ribbon around them, and handed them to Saul. "Here, take this. It will help you on your journeys."

Saul took the rolled-up parchment and placed the scroll in a pouch in the interior of his uniform.

What journeys? he thought.

Saul thanked the Xalian and returned to the large room he had been kneeling in earlier. Upon entering the room, he was met by Lord Luxeniah. The lord noticed something different about Saul and then admitted to himself, with a feeling of shame, that he spent hardly any time acquainting himself with the Earthen.

Together, the two left the cathedral, and when they had entered the library hallway, they were met by Cormin, who was escorting Stephan, Alexander, and Jessica back to the foyer. Alexander gave Saul a hard look, but at once subdued it in an effort to conform to the Carn Doctrine.

"He is found, at last!" the servant exclaimed. "And just in time too; the Grand Council is about to start."

Indeed, the lord thought, glancing over at Saul, *just in time.*

Chapter 11

The Grand Council

The king's hall was the largest room in all the kingdom of Geradia. Its soaring walls and lofty ceiling were designed with the intent to convey a sense of grandeur and awe to those who would visit the king there. Stained-glass windows decorated the walls and depicted, like the walls of the stairway monument, many key events in Xalian history. The king's hall had a long, rectangular shape leading to the king's throne. The throne, opulent in appearance, was gilded in many parts with plates of solid gold. It was also gilded in silver here and there while being decorated with royal jewels. On the day of the Grand Council, the king sat on the throne wearing the royal crown and holding a golden scepter.

Along the walls of the king's hall were stands of seats where the nobility sat when a council of nobles was called. A Grand Council could be convened only when all of the nobles were present. For the last year, only general councils had been called because one seat had always been empty. This seat was on the left stand and the nobles sitting immediately around it wore robes displaying the green and blue stripes of House Luxeniah. A general council was currently being held until the Grand Council could begin as the seat was still empty. Each noble in attendance, along with their aids, was dressed in ornate and lavishly striped robes, the colors of which reflected the colors of their own household.

In the center of the king's hall, a figure stood addressing the assembly. His robes displayed the striped colors of black and purple. In the design of the majority of them, the stripes were horizontally positioned at the lower parts and vertical on the higher parts up to a single horizontal stripe on the shoulders. The robes of the figure in the center of the king's hall, however, displayed horizontal stripes throughout the robe. Many in the right stands had robes sharing these colors and patterns, signifying the House Levine—the only difference being a gaudy display of emblems worn by the room's central figure.

The noble in the center of the king's hall who was addressing the general council of Geradian noblemen continued his oration. "My dear brethren, the Coltrous are not as much of a threat as many would have you believe. In fact, if I may contend, they are not a threat at all. They indeed may be ferocious and their attacks have been more common in the last few months; however, if we are to have hope in a peaceful reconciliation with our neighbors to the south, we must not—"

The oration was interrupted by the loud, echoing creek of the hall's thick, tall main door opening. Lord Luxeniah entered, followed by four oddly dressed creatures. Every eye in the king's hall was fixed on them. A vague sense of apprehensive curiosity flooded the assembly because all knew that, at last, the Grand Council could commence and the council would discover what the returning nobleman of House Luxeniah would relate to them concerning his sojourn in the Earthen Realm.

The nobleman whose oration had been interrupted turned to the entering group and extended, in an exaggerated manner, a welcoming arm with an open hand. "The good ambassador, and Lord of House Luxeniah, returns from the Earthen realm unkilled as it would seem." The assembly of nobles in the right stands gave a light chuckle at this. "I look forward with great anticipation to your report."

Lord Luxeniah nodded in response. Then nobleman addressing the general council turned to the left stands to continue his oration. "As I was saying, the recent Coltrous attacks, if they can really be deemed as such, cannot justify the expansion of our borders west. Any such expansion would just incite more attacks and doom any hope of peace with our brethren the Coltrous." The nobleman turned to the right stand, to the members of the stands sharing his robe's colors. "All of my house has pledged to oppose any attempt of territorial expansion." He turned to Lord Luxeniah and the others. "This matter will be closed for a time in light of Lord Luxeniah's arrival; let us begin the Grand Council—" The central figure turned to address the king on the throne, "if His Majesty permits."

The king nodded and the Xalian to his left spoke in a booming voice. "His Excellency permits the commencement of the Grand Council this day in the thousandth and first year of our lord."

The nobleman who had just finished his oration left the hall's floor, joining his similarly dressed kin in the right stands. Lord Luxeniah stepped forward and the four members of his guard followed him just as they had arranged before entering the hall. The lord positioned himself in the center of the floor, with the others at his side, in a way so that it was clear from his manner that he was addressing the entire assembly—the nobles as well as the king.

"My brethren," Lord Luxeniah began, "as the distinguished noble preceding me has revealed, I have indeed returned, having spent an entire year living in the Earthen realm among the Brotherhood of the Archway and even briefly among the Earthens." Murmurs spread among the assembly members. "Although I am overjoyed to now be with my kin in the lands of my youth and allegiance, I have learned a hard truth those here have yet to embrace. The archway is now open, that much has been clear, and it should be sufficient to prove the truthfulness of the ancient writings pertaining to… the Second Great Conflict of the Coltrous and the alliance of the Northern Kingdoms. The Day of Exodus is upon us!"

This final statement and its gravity caused most to whisper and murmur, the sounds of which filled the hall. The noise was growing in intensity until the king pounded his scepter on the floor. The noblemen fell silent.

"My stay," Lord Luxeniah continued, "in the Earthen realm has brought to my understanding the dangers which are now, as I speak, mounting and conspiring against us. Many Coltrous infiltrators have passed through the archway, sowing seeds of discord among the Earthens. Seeds which, if permitted to blossom, could mean the destruction of Geradia and our subjugation to the Coltrous hordes."

Upon hearing this, Stephan's mind produced a series of images: the terrorist leader he had seen during the Ghana mission, the privates who had attacked them on Cult Island, and the Coltrous infiltrator the lord had defeated by the portal. He recalled the slight hint of a red hue in their eyes and wondered about the possibility of a connection between these images and the infiltration Lord Luxeniah spoke of.

The lord of House Luxeniah went on with his report. "This is another fulfillment of what has been written of by scholars who had, in times past, read the writing on the wall and witnessed the fate of our realm. The time to act is now!" The lord's voice was now sharp and stern, with a piercing quality Stephan could not remember ever experiencing. "We must raise an army and send emissaries to the Durathians and to the northern Chromas tribes so that those peoples may start their preparations as well."

A nobleman in the left stands stood up sharply and pounded the surface of the wood beam in front of him. "The Chromas? Those heathens would never commit, even in the face of whatever imaginary danger the good lord thinks he has foreseen!" Most of the noblemen in the left stands nodded silently in agreement.

Lord Luxeniah turned to the interrupting noble. "The commitment of the Chromas was written in the ancient tomes. As for my *imagined* danger, the opening of the archway as well as the secretion of Coltrous spies and saboteurs in the Earthen realm are testament enough to this!" There was a stillness among most in the king's hall. The lord frowned. "What will it take?" he asked the entire assembly. "The arrival of two legions of the Coltrous hordes at the castle's gate?"

The last accusing question brought another uproar from nobles on both sides and took longer to subside in spite of the king pounding the royal scepter on the hall's floor.

"I have one more sign to show to those who would believe." The lord motioned to Alexander, who stepped forward. "I now present to the Council, Captain Bennet, the leader of the most decorated and skilled military unit in all the Earthen realm. The ancient writings tell of four possessing great talent and ability who will lead the alliance against the Coltrous in the Second Great Conflict and their origin foreign to the Xalian realm. I believe these to be the four."

In the right stand, the nobleman who had previously addressed the assembly stood to speak. "My dear Lord Luxeniah, I shall speak plainly. Your sojourn must have been long, for you do seem to have changed, choosing to ignore many of the niceties of this court—"

"I ignore the niceties of this court," Lord Luxeniah interrupted, "for they have blinded you all!" There was more murmuring from the nobles. Lord Luxeniah's voice rose to overpower it. "And if it appears that I have changed and been drastically altered, it is only the fervor of one who has seen the day of his demise and acts with the focus only the threat of death can bring!"

The noble who had been interrupted smirked at this, looking to the rest of the assembly, and then faced Lord Luxeniah again. "Let us speak according to our sight and not this passion that has so completely overtaken you. You have told us what you have seen, and now it is time for you to hear what *we* have seen. During the year of your absence, yes, we have witnessed the archway open as well as a *slight* increase in Coltrous attacks on the Hadriatic Cliff Fortress." He leveled a figure at Lord Luxeniah. "None of which have penetrated the fortress or resulted in any casualties, and with none before this day arriving from the Earthen realm! The Coltrous and the Earthens are both weaklings. There is no cause for alarm."

"It is good of you to bring to the discussion another point of strength to my assertion. I was there at the head tower for one of these attacks. True, none of the guards fell under a Coltrous blade, but the tower's corporal swears on his life there is something more to this and that he and his men grow weary in heart and mind by the attacks."

The opposing lord rolled his eyes at these last words.

Lord Luxeniah continued. "And before I end my report, let me remind you all of the sacred oath my ancestors took upon themselves of which I now bear. It is a sacred duty to watch over these lands and to act for its safety in any way I see fit and according to my conscious—to fill the cracks that may form in the walls of the kingdom's strength. Do I now seek to fill those cracks? Nay, I seek to fill fissures, even chasms that would let evil enter if I am not successful! Let the forsaking of my lands and the comforts of this glorious kingdom be the only true testaments of the truth of my words and the words of wiser men who foretold this day."

A heavy silence overtook the king's room. It was broken when the figure clad in black and purple stood again and gestured to the lord's guard, saying, "What say our silent saviors?"

Alexander took a step forward. He looked over the room, doing his best to exude strength while at the same time satisfying the necessities of the Carn Doctrine. After a tense yet appropriately timed moment, he spoke, "I am Captain Bennet, leader of Alpha Z, being, as you have learned, the Earthen realm's most accomplished military unit. Although I am not fully learned in Xalian ways, I represent the Earthen realm. I attest to the veracity of what Lord Luxeniah, whom I serve, has spoken of. We four of his guard have seen for ourselves the Coltrous attack on the head tower. As to whether we are the four who have been written of in Xalian lore, I cannot say. However, with all my years of military experience and training and with all that I have seen, the whole of my being tells me there is an attack on this realm mounting. All we can offer this kingdom in appreciation for the sanctuary so freely given by the High Ambassador is our best efforts to act in the interests of both our worlds."

A few more moments of silence passed, and during this time, Stephan was able to perceive the King's reaction to what had been said to be that of concern. It was not a grave expression of alarm bringing eagerness, but more of an inkling about some outcome that might come to pass.

The lord clad in black and purple gestured to Alexander with an open hand. "The ancient writings speak of the four who will lead the Northern Kingdoms having power over the elements. I would venture to guess they have not this power, and if they do not, how could they possibly be the four?"

Lord Luxeniah took a step toward the nobleman. "If you were truly acquainted with the ancient writings, you would know they say the four will find the power within in them *in time*, just as it was with the original four. We wield not the dark magic of the Coltrous, and so we must wait."

A nobleman sitting in the left stands, who was wearing the colors of a different house, stood up to speak. "This is all well and good, but let us consider the costs. What would have to be sacrificed in order for an army to be formed? Our kingdom has economic concerns, which when considered against—"

The booming crack of the king's scepter interrupted the nobleman's diatribe as well as the voices of other nobles who were beginning to raise their own concerns. All fell silent. The king, who had been quiet until this moment, spoke. In a voice powerful and booming, suitable for one holding such a position, he said, "I have heard many wise voices speak wisdom in opposition to each other. Surely, neither conviction can be doubted." The king stopped for a moment. He seemed to be deep in thought until he began to speak again. "When such a situation presents itself, the only wise course of action is compromise born of wisdom."

Stephan saw the reactions of the noblemen who all seemed genuinely surprised as they turned to one another and whispered about the king's unexpected statement. When the whisperings died down, the king continued. "Lord Luxeniah, you have presented your case well. However, if what you have said is true, and if the Second Great Conflict is indeed upon us, even an army with every subject of this kingdom armed and well trained to fight would be insufficient to withstand the Coltrous hordes, which would surely be at our gate. We, being in such dire straits, would require the aids of both our northern and eastern neighbors. Moreover, since contact with those peoples has fallen and dwindled, we would need an emissary capable of traversing such dangerous lands. Therefore, in a noble compromise of two opposing needs, *you* shall lead this emissary and your guard to the Chromas tribes and then to the Durathian kingdom."

Stephan looked at the lord and saw the slight widening of his eyes and parting of his lips—an expression of surprise well hidden to any but expert eyes.

A robed Xalian, another dressed in purple and black, walked up to the king's side and whispered something into his ear. The king's eyebrows arched. "Ah, yes, in addition to gaining the commitment of the other kingdoms, you are charged with the task of finding and obtaining the White Sword of Durath. For, as my distinguished advisor has so eloquently reminded me, the ancient writings also tell of the sword and its role in the Second Great Conflict. 'By its light, shall the dark clouds of the unyielding storm be dispelled and the way made clear.'"

The quote of the ancient wise man seemed to delight many in the right stands but, as Stephan could see, it brought Lord Luxeniah to an almost disparate state, the look of which was well hidden, as before. In an instant, this look changed to one of determination and he addressed the king.

"What your highness requires is fantastic but right. Tomorrow, I and my guard go to the lands of the Chromas and to the lands of the Durathians. We will find the White Sword of Xaliud wielded by Durath during the First Great Conflict and the northern kingdoms will again be united. We will send word after each of the enlistments. I humbly request a commitment to, after the first enlistment of the first kingdom, of the Chromas, the formation and training of the Geradian army so it will be ready for the conflict ahead."

The king nodded and gestured for his advisor to make note of it. Those in the right stands did not seem pleased to hear this part of the compromise or to hear Lord Luxeniah's resolve.

Lord Luxeniah looked over the assembly and then returned his gaze back to the king. "If your grace permits, we will retire to prepare for tomorrow's departure."

The king once again cracked his scepter on the hall's floor, the now familiar booming sound filled the room. "Go, my good Ambassador of House Luxeniah; may your path be clear and your journey swift. We will be ready to receive any word, and it will be my decree that all shall be fulfilled as promised."

Stephan looked at the nobles in the right stand, to those dressed in black and purple, and saw that their countenances had returned and they were now congratulating themselves on the impossibility of the task laid before Lord Luxeniah and his guard. As the lord was passing the others on the way to the hall's main door, Stephan caught his attention and asked, "Lord Luxeniah, who was that nobleman who was addressing the assembly when we entered?"

The lord looked to the purple-and-black clad group of nobles, still socializing and rejoicing in their victory. "That is Lord Landrin Levine. He is the most prominent of the noblemen of House Levine, a house which, from the beginning, has busied itself with the development of laws and theories. He and his kin seek to change this kingdom, some say for the better, others for the worse. He, in particular, has a particular disposition, almost a contempt, against most traditional beliefs. I knew he would oppose me, and although he now rejoices, it is we who have the chance for success." Lord Luxeniah turned back to Stephan. "Let us take that chance, for if we do not, I fear he very well may be the end of this kingdom and your world."

Chapter 12

Lord Levine's White Tower

After the Grand Council concluded and Lord Levine had completed the usual posturing and politics required of one so distinguished as he was, he retired to the White Tower. He stayed there when he had to spend the night in the kingdom, away from his estate, which was too far east to reach in any reasonable time. He was currently traversing the tower's staircase, which had a square shape, patterned after the tower's overall design.

As the lord ascended the steps, he passed several rooms, each branching out from the central stairway. These rooms were the quarters and offices of others with a similar proclivity to scholarly pursuits and who shared his vision of a renewed kingdom. As the lord passed by the apothecary, he could smell the fragrances of herbs wafting out into the hall. The philosopher seemed to be hard at work, mixing fluids and herbs in his flasks, creating new concoctions that would undoubtedly expand the kingdom's level of thought for the common subject.

Creating the future, Lord Levine thought.

Further up the tower's staircase, the alchemist's laboratory came into the lord's presence, along with its own scents and sounds. In the lab's confines, a group of philosophers attempted to work with the powder of Mylenian crystal and form it into new materials—materials he hoped could be used to trade with the Coltrous.

The next few offices were those of monks and scholars, whose works were thoughts of realms higher than the physical, philosophies to replace the stagnant, old ways he and the rest of the kingdom had been saddled with for over a millennium now. These were the only inhabitants of his white tower he ever spoke to, for they were the only ones intelligent enough and with the perspective requisite for his attention. He had his adjuncts, who were always more than willing, to deal with the lower people.

In this early evening, though, Lord Levine was too weary from the Grand Council and the infernal toil of debate to endure even their company. He was not weary so much in body but in mind and spirit, as was his usual state since that was where his talents resided, and nothing could tax him as what had happened at the Grand Council. The lord felt a sudden longing for that which did not exist—the utopia he and his followers would create where there could be no debate and his will would be unquestionably followed, not by his conquest but by the sole compulsion of his ideas. *Damn that Lord Luxeniah!* he thought. *He may yet threaten my plans!*

"Lord Levine!"

The lord groaned to himself as Figo, his most eager and sycophantic aid and student, approached. The lord had just passed by the study hall and had attempted to do so in an inconspicuous manner. "Wait, Lord Levine!" The small boy reached him and was now walking up the tower's staircase beside his professor.

Lord Levine let out an intentionally audible sigh. "What is it today, Figo?"

"My lord, I have the assignments all graded just as you asked!" Figo chirped, not noticing the lord's obvious lack of interest.

"Very good, Figo," Lord Levine said in a perfunctory tone.

"Oh, and I have some news!" This did not bring Figo any attention. "It concerns Lord Luxeniah!"

Lord Levine's head turned sharply to face his student. "What news?"

"It seems as though he has obtained entry into the royal armory. It also appears as though he will use the king's most prized weapons. You know, to be used by his guard, *the four who*—"

"I understand!" snapped the lord.

They were now approaching the top level of the White Tower, Lord Levine's own personal office and quarters. He was anticipating a quiet night to himself.

"May I join you, sire? We could discuss—"

"No! Now be gone!"

Silently, the aid handed his professor the papers and made his way back down the staircase to the study hall from whence he had come.

Lord Levine entered the top floor and walked into his study where he deposited the papers from Figo. The room was full of shelves, each full of books, mostly written by him or one of his acolytes, written of course under his direction. He passed by such titles as *The Dreams of Peace: Valor's Struggle in Geradia* and *A New Age, A New Realm*. As he passed, he ran his fingers against the spines of the tomes and treatises, feeling, in his mind, the wisdom they contained. *Creating a new world*, he thought, *requires creating new thoughts. Men create these thoughts, and they come from no other place.... I must remember to write that down.* He smiled slightly as he mused upon his genius.

After passing through the study, the lord entered his quarters, poured himself a glass of wine and collapsed into his chair. While he sat there, he could see the whole of the castle and most of the kingdom through a tall window. In his opinion, it was the best view in all of Geradia. *Fitting*, he thought, *as I should look over this kingdom in such a manner, as I am its only true guardian.*

He sipped his wine, thinking of what had been said at the councils that day and of his plans. He meditated on these things, all the while looking down at the ground far below the White Tower where he thought he could see the opening of a dark shaft at the base of another structure. He did not know where the shaft led, nor did he know why it interested him so much. He did not care. He just gazed and dwelled on his thoughts until he passed into a drunken slumber.

Chapter 13

The Ninth Dungeon

"The kingdom of Geradia is truly a place of light and strength," said Lord Luxeniah as he led Alexander, Stephan, Jessica, and Saul through the cathedral's entryway. "However, for as much light and virtue exist above, so much so is there darkness below."

They arrived where the lord wanted to take them—at the dungeon entrance located farther down the hallway Saul had wandered down when he had met the Xalian monk who had given him the scroll. The entrance was wide and arched with a large gate, barring entrance to almost all who passed. It not only provided a convenient place to read to the prisoners their last ceremonial rites, but it also provided access for the priests who would repeatedly visit them for their confessions. Two guards stood at the gate, and upon noticing Lord Luxeniah approaching, one immediately produced a key and opened it with a long, echoing creak. Beyond it, stairs led downward to another hallway with another gate at its end and with two more guards at its sides. Just as before, one of the guards produced a key and opened this portal, which was just in front of another stairway downward. This stairway led much farther downward. As they descended, the cathedral now above them, the walls of the dungeon became more and more cavernous. After a while, the floor they were walking on ceased to be tiled, and they found themselves walking on dirt. The way was lit by sparsely spaced torches on the walls. The light was dim throughout the halls and dimmer still within each individual dungeon cell.

Making their way through the cavernous halls of the dungeon, they passed cell after cell. Some could be seen to be occupied by prisoners, who showed little life as they passed by. The air was thick and dank. Silence filled the dark void, being interrupted only by the sound of their steps, the flickering of the torch fire, and the distant sound of water drops striking the surface of some dark, remote, underground body of water.

When they came to the end of the first hallway, Lord Luxeniah spoke for the first time since they had all entered the dungeon. "That first level is for those who break only minor Geradian laws. Theirs is usually a light and short sentence. This second level and those below are for those who commit more serious crimes. As you have seen, there are not many who have need of a stay down here." Stephan could hear the pride in the lord's voice.

They continued downward, from level to level, the lord describing whatever crime had brought the soul down to this lowly station, attributing the punishment to the glory of Geradia and its benevolence. On the second—theft. The third—assault. On the fourth—neglect of duties, and so on.

As they got to the lower dungeons, the air thinned and made it a little difficult to breathe. The air also stank with a putrid, pungent scent as if something had died in one of the cells and was left to rot. Strangely, when they reached the ninth dungeon, the air seemed to become more normal, more like the air on the surface. While the rank odor from the levels above faded away and the air became easier to breath, it still retained a strong musty quality.

In the ninth dungeon, there was only a small cluster of cells. "This hall is reserved for only the vilest of creatures!" The lord spoke louder now, as if he wanted somebody other than those of his guard to hear. He walked to the front of the farthest back cell. Facing the bars, the lord stood while maintaining some distance from the cell's bars. The chamber was dark, so much so that nobody, except it seemed for Lord Luxeniah, was sure whether there was even a prisoner residing within it. Stephan was about to give an inquiry on this when an arm abruptly jutted out of the darkness. It was stopped by the cell's bars, just before the lord's throat. The hand grasped frantically in vain as something inside the cell let out a blood-curdling shriek. The cry did not sound to any of them to be Xalian. A thin, barely visible outline of a figure emerged from the darkness, the apparent source of the arm.

Without speaking, Lord Luxeniah walked back to the stairwell, disappearing for a brief moment behind its bend, and came back down with the stairwell's torch in hand. As the lord approached the cell, the figure could be seen in full view in the torch's light.

"Behold Fabian, the third brother of the ruling house of the Coltrous," the lord said. Fabian, filthy and dressed in rags, held up his hand to block the torchlight as he retreated to the cell's corner. "I was pleased to hear, Fabian, that you had not escaped in the year of my absence. I would have hated to miss our visits."

"Is that so?" Fabian said in response. "I hardly noticed your absence." Stephan perceived the voice's sharpness and the precision of the words used. Stephan assumed from this small bit of information that Fabian, despite his pathetic state and wild-eyed, feral appearance, was quite intelligent.

"I have not come down to the lowest point of the kingdom of Geradia for banter, but to show my guard the darkness so they may know their enemy and better appreciate the light above."

"Your guard?" Fabian scoffed. "My brothers will have much joy in their torture and demise!"

"Your *brothers*, it would appear, still refuse to negotiate for your release! What familial relations could you possibly have to give you insight into their intentions?" Lord Luxeniah's voice now had a mocking incredulity in it.

Fabian scowled at this. To Stephan, the display was believable, but he detected an almost imperceptible faint hint of falseness in the expression.

The lord continued. "Now if you would be so intelligent as to give us the location of any Coltrous encampments in the barrens, I could see as to the shortening of your sentence."

Fabian let out a distinct, mocking laugh. "What need would I have for a shorter sentence? My own people will someday free me!"

Lord Luxeniah rolled his eyes and turned to the others. "I believe we have seen enough."

As they were leaving, Fabian yelled out after them. "And when I escape, you will be one of the first I kill! You and your pathetic excuse for a guard. All will be gutted like fish!" Fabian flung himself against the bars, spittle dripping from his mouth.

When the Geradian lord and his guard had ascended the stairwell and reached the above levels, far out of earshot of his screams, Fabian stopped. He grinned devilishly and walked to the darkest corner of his cell, which was where he went every night. In the corner was a shaft leading all the way up to the surface. He stared up the shaft and saw, in the distant square that was the shaft's opening on the surface, the starry night sky and a white tower. After an hour of fixating his gaze on the tower, he closed his eyes and slipped into a controlled reverie. The dream-like state would last for many hours and into the night.

Chapter 14

The Royal Armory

The next morning, Lord Luxeniah and his guard ate breakfast in the royal dining hall where they all enjoyed Geradia's finest cooking and light conversation with a group of nobles who had been eating there. As was the usual manner in these kinds of situations, Alexander took the lead in the talks slipping comfortably into the role of the fabled leader of the impending war. As he listened to the conversation and watched Alexander engage the noblemen, Stephan marveled at how the principles of leadership still held true even in this plane—that Alexander could gain favor so easily with people he had just met. Stephan was most impressed with the captain's expert ability to conform to the social mores of those to whom he was ingratiating himself, seeming to ignore all personal desires or having none other than to increase his stature with man or Xalian.

At the breakfast table, the conversation started with the topic of military tactics and the history of the Kingdom of Geradia, which led to the noblemen's innate curiosity about the "Earthen Realm." Alexander related to the noblemen the complex structure of what he called the "Earthen Governing Bodies," making sure to downplay the unitary and pervasive nature of the United Earth Initiative as it might appear, to these noblemen, to be very much similar to the

Coltrous Empire. He also made sure, in relating these facts, to make the "Earthen Governing Bodies" seem inferior to Geradia. The nobles all seemed pleased by what Alexander was saying. They also appeared, to Stephan, to be much more relaxed now than they had been during the Grand Council, for these noblemen were primarily seated in the left stands during the council and had seemed more passive and pensive during the assembly. Stephan did not remember many of them interjecting or expressing any developed opinion other than a suspicion of and disdain for the Chromas people.

After about an hour of pleasant conversation, the pleasantness saved by Alexander's expert maneuvering of the conversation around any topic directly related to religion as it was practiced in the Earthen Realm, Lord Luxeniah and his guard politely excused themselves and left the royal dining hall. They then crossed the castle's main hallway into one smaller, yet highly ornate in its décor. Stephan was reminded of the gaudiness of the royal robes of Lord Levine. There was also an abundance of flags, crests, and paintings, all relating to distinguished members of the royal family as well as major events in which they had played key parts. Stephan assumed that most of the events had taken place during or around the time of the First Great Conflict because he had learned, in his studies in the royal library, that there had been no major battles since that period in the Xalian Realm.

In between the room's items of decoration, stoic guards stood at their posts, giving no recognition of their passing as they neared the large doors at the hallway's end. When they had reached the door, the guards posted on its sides opened the entrance to the royal armory. As the interior of the room became visible, Stephan could finally see what was so precious as to require protection comparable to that of the king's own quarters.

"I present to all the Royal Armory," the lord said with an outstretched arm, pointing to the armory's walls and the plethora of weapons, suits of armor, and shields lining it. In the center were a few pieces prominently displayed. "As your Earthen projectile weapons have proved less than effective, his royal majesty has seen fit, in his infinite wisdom, to lend, from this room, whatever is necessary for our safe journey north."

The others wandered around different parts of the room, each attracted to differing types of weapons suited to each one's unique fighting style. Alexander went immediately to the broadswords. He perused them with instant and great interest. Jessica was near Alexander, but was examining one of the smaller, one-edged, curved swords. To her, they were pleasing to the eye, being elegant, and with one, she hoped she could gracefully defeat an enemy while preserving as much life as possible.

Stephan was on the other side of the room where the ranged weaponry was displayed. He picked up a crossbow, which at once caught his eye. After exploring the weapon's many features and facets, he looked over at the others. Alexander and Jessica were still in their respective places, but Saul, strangely even for him, was merely leaning against an empty portion of the armory's wall, seeming to express no interest in what the room had to offer. Stephan then noticed Alexander glaring at Saul while speaking to Jessica. Jessica's own expression told Stephan that she clearly shared Alexander's feelings.

Stephan redirected his attention back to the crossbow in his hand. Visually striking, it was obviously constructed with the best materials as well as the highest skill, but he found himself wondering how a crossbow could ever prove more powerful in combat than his sidearm or laser-rifle. Stephan felt the rifle strapped to his back with a surety that it would be far more effective than the crossbow in his hand. He then had the thought that perhaps the weapon would be more ornamental in function, serving as inspiration to the Xalian people they were meant to enlist. He thought of their encounter with the Coltrous infiltrator by the archway.

How could we ever counter that speed or that level of skill and strength? He dismissed the thought as soon as he had it and reminded himself that the only thing he had to commit to himself was the complete service to the command he was under. Thoughts like these often served as mantras for Stephan whenever he was in need of a new direction of thought.

A distinct sound, almost completely foreign to Stephan, interrupted his thoughts. It was the sound of something large slashing through the air. Stephan looked in the direction of the sound to find Alexander mock-fighting an invisible opponent with a broadsword. Alexander seemed more than pleased with the weapon as he handled it.

"Ah, it would have been my guess you would have chosen the weapon of Durath. He was the leader of the alliance during the First Great Conflict and wielded this sword for the first few battles," Lord Luxeniah said. He then looked curious. "You wield it well, as if it were yours."

Alexander held up the sword, admiring the blade in the light. "I would hope so. I spent most of my spare time at Oxford in practice. I never thought I would have the chance to put the skill into actual practice."

"Nor should you have, it being such an ancient weapon in your realm."

The lord looked over at Saul, who was still leaning against the wall in the same passive position as before. To Stephan, Saul seemed to be standing with an air of contempt. However Saul might have appeared to Stephan, Lord Luxeniah seemed pleased with Saul's choice, or lack thereof.

Lord Luxeniah then looked to Jessica and the slender, curved sword she had chosen. "Such an elegant weapon that one. It was wielded by the Duchess of House Taldera."

"It just seemed like the right choice," Jessica said as she ran her fingers along the sword's curved blade.

"Indeed, fighting with such an elegant weapon should serve to balance the brute force of the captain's choosing."

To Stephan, Jessica seemed to interpret the lord's words as if he meant her combat abilities to be merely an accessory to Alexander's. Stephan noticed her employing the Carn suppression and Jessica showed an expression of gratitude instead.

The lord continued to Stephan. "You seem to now have two weapons of use while the others have but one."

"My...the weapon I currently have, the one I brought from the Earthen realm, may run out of ammunition, depending on how often it will be used," Stephan reported.

"Then you have acted most prudently. However, will the load of both weapons cause too much weariness over the course of our journey?"

"I don't believe it will, sire, and if it does, I can always discard the...lesser of the two."

The lord seemed pleased by this. "The mind of man never ceases with the outpouring of wonders." He put his hand on Stephan's shoulder. "Yours might be our greatest asset yet." Stephan gave a slight but genuine smile.

Finally, Lord Luxeniah walked over to Saul, who was still leaning against the armory's wall. As the lord neared him, Saul opened his eyes and looked up. The nobleman stood in front of Saul with some space between them. In an instant, the lord was in a maneuver's final position, now directly in front of Saul. His arm was outstretched as if to deliver a punch to Saul's chest, but the arm was apparently parried by Saul. Jessica and Stephan could not help but stare, slack-jawed, amazed by the speed by which Saul reacted, considering the speed of the lord himself.

Lord Luxeniah let out a loud and hearty laugh, which to Stephan seemed to have an element of relief in it, and walked away to peruse the rest of the room and its artifacts.

Chapter 15

The Village of Elk Lake

In the office of the royal notary, a scribe sat behind his raised writing table. It was his duty to perform the most important and crucial notaries. At the waiting bench across the room sat Cormin, the servant of Lord Luxeniah, who was waiting for the scribe to begin his work. This scribe particularly seemed to enjoy taking his time. Cormin bore it with noble patience.

The scribe finally stood to retrieve the tools of his trade: the quill of a royally bred eagle and the ink. Cormin stood and approached the elevated writing table, for although he had heard of it, he had never actually seen a document written with the kind of ink about to be used.

The scribe returned, placing the items carefully and ceremoniously onto the table, and sat. He then proceeded to unroll the royal parchment, made from the finest wood found in all of Geradia, and placed four smooth stones on it, one on each corner of the parchment, to keep it open while he wrote. Then came the opening of the ink bottle, the golden ink already visible through the glass. As the bottle's top was removed, a fine trail of shimmering gold dust formed a trail leading from the bottle to where the bottle's top was placed on the writing table. After a moment, the trail dissipated.

The scribe took his quill, dipped it into the golden ink, and placed the quill's now golden tip on the parchment to begin the king's epistle to the Northern Chromas tribes. As the quill moved across the parchment, each letter written was luminescent, giving off a golden, shimmering light. Cormin knew enough of this practice to know that the luminescent quality of ink used to write the epistle would make any attempt at a forgery impossible.

"This decree is to the Chromas, is it not?" asked the royal scribe.

"It is," replied Cormin. "I am to bring it immediately to Lord Luxeniah."

"Ah, it would seem as though he wastes no time. Was not the Grand Council but one day past?"

"Yes, it was." Cormin watched the scribe write, impressed at how the artisan could continue on in conversation while writing such an important document with such precious and valuable ink. Although the clauses the scribe would be using to compose the epistle must have been so well known from its constant repetitive use, not to mention the years of intense legal study, the expertise being demonstrated was no less than astonishing to someone of Cormin's humble status.

The scribe's writing hand reached the end of the last page. He then rolled up the parchment, sealed it by dripping maroon wax onto the page's edge, and pressed it with the royal seal. The scribe handed Cormin the scroll and the servant examined the seal in more detail. It depicted a lion, body contorted, wrapping around a crown's left side with an elk opposite him, whose body was twisting around the crown's right side. *A balance of offense and defense.* Cormin had once overheard the brief explanation of the crest's symbolism during a conversation his master was having with another nobleman. The inclusion of the elk and what it symbolized was a revolutionary idea at one point in Xalian history, with offense being the only means of military conduct, as well as the only means to accomplish any aim.

"And now for the Durathians' invitation into chaos." The scribe wrote the second epistle, which was much like the first in form and length, yet included differences due to the larger population of Durathia and the particulars pertaining to a respectively larger army. When the scribe finished his task of composing the epistle and sealing it with the maroon wax and royal crest, he blew on the seal and gave it to Cormin. The servant gave a polite goodbye, bowed, and left the scribe's alcove to deliver the scrolls to his master.

Lord Luxeniah, Alexander, Stephan, Jessica, and Saul were standing in the hallway near the castle's entrance. Surrounded by a large crowd, they gave their goodbyes to all kinds of people who had come to bid them farewell. There were a few noblemen present, who seemed to be the only heads of state who truly believed in the cause for which Lord Luxeniah and his guard now embarked. There were also a number of higher royal craftsmen, scholars, and priests, most seeming to have more of an academic interest in the events or a curiosity born from reading of such events described in the ancient writings. The remainder of the people there, almost the entire crowd, were ordinary peasants and tradesmen. By their earnestness, one could tell they had the most genuine interest in the group's departure and success, having been raised on fables and songs telling of the events in the ancient writings.

As they left the hallway, the people, mostly those of the lower classes, cheered and wished them good fortune on their journey. As they passed through the market, more shouts of praise were given from random tradesmen who could not leave their stands to attend the formal farewell gathering. After passing through the market, they traveled along the castle's eastern side path, through the town behind the castle still inside the kingdom's walls, and left the kingdom through the postern gate.

Heading in the direction Stephan had previously designated as being north, which was remarkably close to what the Geradians actually considered north, Lord Luxeniah and his guard traveled along the road leading to the Northern Bridge. After crossing the bridge, they would have to brave the barrens and its long stretches of desert, or travel east and through the Riverwoods. The latter was impractical, as it would add far too much time—time they could ill afford.

Lord Luxeniah had warned the others before they left that the barrens might be the most perilous of all the lands they would traverse on their journey, not because it was void of all life, but because it was common land, and roving bands of the Coltrous would most certainly pose some kind of danger. Before the bridge and the desert of the common lands, they would need to pass through the Village of Elk Lake. The lord told the others of a blacksmith who dwelled there who was always willing to provide lodgings for him and his traveling companions.

Although he listened to the lord's words, Stephan could not get his mind off the part about the roving bands, so he concerned himself instead with his immediate surroundings. He took in the landscape and observed the agricultural life of the farming peasants they passed as they traveled through the Northern Lands of Geradia. The farms were similar to those they had passed when they were traveling on the road that led parallel to the Hadriatic Cliff Fortress, but they were smaller and more numerous. Those who worked the farmland also had other professions. The party caught glimpses of their performance from time to time: a blacksmith shoeing a horse in his barn; another at his anvil crafting a tool or a weapon; or a carpenter building or measuring to make alterations to an existing structure. They continued on the path throughout the day, passing farm after farm.

When the lord and his guard reached Village of Elk Lake, it was late in the afternoon, that time of the day when the sun is low in the sky, getting ready to set. Upon entering the town square, a crowd came into view as they walked around the corner of a building. In its center, a Xalian was visible to them since he was raised above the others by something he stood on. He spoke with outstretched arms, but the cold demeanor of the townsfolk gave reason to believe that they were not taking to the speaker's message. The figure, the object of the crowd's cold attention, was dressed in the recognizable black-and-purple-striped colors of House Levine, but with an unfamiliar design.

The group reached the outer edge of the crowd. "That is Liot," Lord Luxeniah explained. "As you can see from his attire, he is of House Levine. Although not a member of the nobility, he wears the colors as one of his fanatics and spews Lord Levine's lies!"

"The teachings of my master are sound!" Liot exclaimed loudly, his arms still outstretched as he spoke. "In order for our glorious kingdom to ascend to a higher state, sacrifices must be made! Read his words and you will see the wisdom of relinquishing your arms for the greater peace!"

The smirks, folded arms, and slowly shaking heads of those in attendance were the only replies to Liot's words.

"Without your arms," Liot continued, "you will never again provoke the Coltrous to attack." This caused many of the towns-people to utter cries of anger and groans of disgust.

Stephan was sincerely confused by what Levine's zealot was saying. He did not see any sound reasoning in the statement. When he looked around, the faces of the townsfolk displayed a similar confusion among some and a sort of irritability among others.

Just then, there was a boisterous voice from outside the crowd.

"And by what means would we oust the likes of you from this town?"

The crowd laughed at the insulting question. Most turned to see the source and saw a tall, large Xalian. They parted respectfully to let him through the crowd. "Oh, do not mistake; house cats could easily drive you away, but a black-and-purple-striped horde of your kind descending upon us to nag and badger in a manner as to put our own wives to shame—we must protect ourselves!" The crowd laughed again, more loudly this time.

The Levinian was visibly perturbed, like a peacock whose feath-ers had been ruffled the wrong way. When he spoke to give his retort, his voice took on a haughty, academic quality. "The ancient fascination with the sword is an oppressive and incendiary patriar-chal tool. It must be put to an end!"

"Who is more fascinated with a horse—the owner or he who covets it, spying on the owner as he uses the horse and attempts to con the owner out of the animal?"

The crowd again laughed and many voiced their agreement with the sentiment. "If what you say is true," the large Xalian continued, "then we should also give up our quills and books, for they are mightier, starting more wars than the living swords of your imagination."

"Enough of this!" The Levinian fanatic picked up his books and walked briskly through the crowd. "I see that reason has no power over the minds of clinging vermin!" As he passed through and then out of the crowd, a couple of villagers threw eggs and vegetables at him, his black and purple robe becoming more and more tarnished.

When the noise from the crowd's jeering the Levinian and praising the tall, large Xalian had died down, Lord Luxeniah approached the man of repute.

"Well done, Fortus!" The large Xalian turned to the lord. "It seems as though your position here has only grown!"

Lord Luxeniah and Fortus clasped right arms. "Ah, your lordship praises me too highly! I am but a humble blacksmith who defends his home from those who might take it away."

"It is good to see the fire of your spirit, which grows increasingly rare in the world!"

"How can it be used to serve your lordship and…." He motioned to the others.

"Oh, forgive my rudeness. These are the members of my guard and his royal emissary to the Chomas and Durathian peoples. Perhaps we can become better acquainted as new friends over a fire. All we need is a place to stay for the night before we continue north."

"As I have said many a time before, you and yours are always welcome to the warm fire of my home!"

Later that night, after purchasing supplies at the market, they traveled to the homestead of Fortus, which was not far north of the Village of Elk. He showed them their lodgings and described them, with pride, as being more comfortable than the town's inn. After settling in, they spent most of the night sitting around a fire just outside the blacksmith's homestead, conversing about the Grand Council, the Coltrous infiltrator, the berserkers they had encountered, and their quest. They also talked about the various parts of the north they would have to pass through in order to complete their quest, their discussion dwelling on the Vile Gorge as it would be the final and most likely greatest obstacle to overcome.

"Where will your journey take you next?" Fortus asked as he stoked the fire's flames with a stick.

"We will head north, past the Elk Lake Forest and over the Great Ravine on the North Bridge," Lord Luxeniah said, staring at the fire, transfixed.

"I would not use the bridge, my lord. It has not been used or maintained for ages."

The lord did not seem surprised by what was said. "I thought that might be the case; there has been no trade with the north for many generations. In any case, the bridge would surely be a place for the Coltrous to lie in wait to attack. There are also bandits to concern ourselves with." Lord Luxeniah looked to those of his guard who had been patiently listening to what had been said. His look stopped on Stephan. "Lieutenant, you are a man of sound mind. How would you go about finding a way out of this quandary?"

Stephan was surprised by the unexpected question, so he took a moment to think critically about the problem and its possible solutions. He cleared his throat and said, "Well, my first thought would be to find another bridge, but even assuming there is another, if the northern trade route has been inactive for so long, it is unlikely any other bridge would not be derelict as well. The same would apply to the dangers presented by possible bands of the Coltrous and bandits to any crossing of the other bridges."

Stephan poked the wood in the fire, pausing before continuing. "My next thought would be to construct a makeshift bridge or strengthen the existing bridge, but this would not eliminate the existing possible threat from the Coltrous or the bandits. The only way to proceed and bypass these dangers would be to take a route that would not be anticipated by our enemies. I would search down at the bottom of the Great Ravine in a place affording adequate cover from any dangers from the ravine's higher levels. With more information, a more thorough analysis could be given."

Stephan looked up, not certain whether what he said had been said well or whether it was useful. He found the others intently looking at him.

Lord Luxeniah turned to Fortus. "What did I tell you; these are the finest the Earthen realm has to offer. They are the hope of both our worlds!" The lord's enthusiasm then faded, and he appeared concerned as he stared once again into the fire.

Fortus noticed the change. "My lord, what cloud of mind has overtaken you?"

"A grave concern, as daunting as our quest to unite the kingdoms is on its own. We must also find the Sword of Durath, that White Sword of White Light. It is required by the king, and he is in the right; the ancient writings do speak of it."

Fortus brightened when he heard the lord mention the sword's title. "I know of that sword! Not just from the legends, as any child does, mind you, but from one who has actually been in the presence the sword!"

Lord Luxeniah's eyes widened, intrigued by the blacksmith's words. "Who is this you speak of?"

"He is Gilgamesh. I met him once in the eastern woods where no Xalian ventures. He lives out there as a wild man of sorts. He is not violent, nor is he like any other of this world. He has lived a strange life, being at one point an heir to a noble house. This house once possessed the sword. It was, as you can imagine, a highly sought-after artifact. Many a guard died protecting it from thieves. Gilgamesh always suspected they were hired by other noblemen. The house's duke decided that it should be possessed by no man house, so he had his monks encase it in Mylenian crystal and hide it in faraway lands."

The lord looked hopeful. "Did this man, this Gilgamesh, divulge the whereabouts of the sword?"

"He did not know where the sword now rests. He fell from the grace of his parents by rejecting the life he had been given, choosing instead to give himself to the forest to commune with its majesty. As a result, he was not privy to the sword's final resting place."

Lord Luxeniah looked dejected until Fortus spoke again. "He did tell me of a poem he learned later on, from one of his father's servants, which reveals the sword's location. He only knew the second half but shared it with me. For the life of me, and no matter how many times I repeated it to myself, I cannot now remember enough of the poem to recite it. I can recall hundreds of others, mind you, but not this one! However, what remains in my mind is that the poem was about a lion and its white, luminescent claw, which shown brighter than the sun. The claw is on the lion's left paw. When the wild man first told me of the poem, I did not know why he did so. After some time and some of my own searching, I came to the realization that the lion's claw in the poem is the sword. The lion, however, is the shape of the underground labyrinth, making up one of the many tombs north of Durathia. Which one it is I do not believe any man knows."

Silence hung in the air as they all contemplated what was said. Lord Luxeniah finally spoke. "Well, we have a new quest! We will search the tomb of Durath. It makes perfect sense it would be hidden there."

"Most likely, my lord, but the location of Durath's resting place has shamefully been forgotten, and searching the many tombs could take many months, years even.... I do not say these things to burden your mind; I only...."

"All is well, Fortus; better to know now so we may find the way to the sword."

After a few moments of silence, Fortus excused himself, having additional work to finish before retiring for the right. From the fire, the blacksmith went to his forge. Before long, the sound of his hammer and its metallic clang could be heard by those who were still sitting around the fire. The noise of the pounding of metal was heard most by Alexander. For the others, it was merely more ambient noise. When the fire's heat grew too great for his liking, Alexander got up and walked around the area outside the fire's warm aura and into the woods. As he walked aimlessly in the darkness of the night, a restlessness he could not understand began to consume him. When a chill began to join it, he returned, but not to the fire to rejoin the others; instead, he went to the area just outside the forge. There he wandered around, hearing the now louder sound of metallic pounding and the hissing of hot metal being submerged in cool water, often followed by the sound of the billow being pressed and its air being blowing into the hot coals to give them more heat to heat the steel.

Alexander stopped pacing and stood outside the barn, continuing to listen to these sounds while imagining the process unfold. When the sounds stopped, Alexander forgot himself and the possibility of violating the Carn Doctrine and followed the undeniable urge to walk into the forge of Fortus. He entered and found the blacksmith doing something unexpected.

The blacksmith held a green crystal, much like those he had seen here and there throughout the countryside. This color of crystal became slightly less rare as they traveled farther north from the Castle of Geradia. It was just like those by the Archway being transparent, but instead of being mostly clear with opaque blotches, it was green.

Fortus turned to Alexander, but instead of showing any hostility at the interruption, the blacksmith beckoned with a motion of his hand to observe his work. Alexander approached the forge and Fortus then held the green crystal in his outstretched palms and stared at it with a strange intensity. Alexander was not aware of the reason for this, and for some time, the blacksmith seemed just to stand there and stare. After some time, though, Alexander noticed that the green crystal had become smaller. When he looked closer, Alexander could see that sparkling, green dust had formed where the crystal had been resting on Fortus's open palms. The blacksmith cupped his hands, depositing the dust from one hand into the other, forming a small pile, and with his now free hand, he placed the crystal on his worktable.

The blacksmith looked to Alexander, who must have appeared confused for Fortus said, "Few know the secret of the crystal because they do not know the crystal. How can one divulge his secrets to any but those who know him?" To Alexander, Fortus's manner of speaking seemed more archaic than his usual tone. It reminded him of the way Lord Luxeniah spoke when quoting the ancient writings during the Grand Council.

The blacksmith continued, "I show you this not for your benefit but for the sake of our two realms. I can tell you have been doing a type of this most of your life." Alexander did not know what he meant, but he nodded anyway.

Fortus took the green powder in his cupped hand and moved it over a red-hot, metal slab. As he did so, he poured in a small stream of the green powder onto the slab meant to become a sword, until about half of the sparkling green powder had been placed on the metal. When the powder hit the metal's hot surface, there was a small but brief reaction. The blacksmith then turned over the metal slab and repeated the action until the other side was also coated with the powder. Fortus then continued to pound the metal. Since it was mostly formed into the intended shape of a sharp blade, it did not take much time to complete its formation by smelting it in a barrel of water by the anvil. When he pulled the finished sword out, now without the amber hue it once had, Alexander could see a faint coloring it now possessed. Alexander suspected the weapon now had a quality beyond a mere green coloration.

Fortus held up the fruit of his labor so that it would catch the light from the fire, and it glinted. "He now knows more than he would have, and the sword will now be true in its strike," Fortus said as if quoting again from some ancient writing to confirm Alexander's unspoken suspicion. Instead of asking how it was possible, he just stared at the sword, seeing something in this particular blade he could not explain.

With the sword, Fortus turned toward the other end of the workshop and motioned to Alexander to follow him. He obeyed and they walked over to one of the haystacks that covered that side of the forge. He then lifted a fold of the hay to reveal many swords, all seeming to be imbued, most of them with the powder from the green crystal. Others had a blue tint and one a red. They appeared to be imbued with the powder of other kinds of crystals he had not yet seen. Fortus placed the newly forged sword in with the others and let down the fold of hay, concealing the metal so that it once again appeared to be a simple pile of hay.

Alexander looked over the other haystacks, realizing there must be hundreds of swords hidden. Fortus walked over to a section of the floor where, when he moved some small piles of hay off of it, it became clear that it was wooden. He reached down to pull up a square of the floor, revealing a hidden cellar underneath. In it, Alexander saw more swords and hiding places for them. Fortus placed his index finger on his lips and then whispered, "The lord you serve may feel an obligation of loyalty to report this to his king, and I would not want to cause a conflict of any sort within him. What I have here does not stand against any of the king's decrees, but Liot and more of his kind might persuade the king to form such a decree if they knew what I have done here."

"I understand," Alexander said, not completely comfortable with the secret but remembering the Carn Doctrine and how it required one to be tolerant, even of the questionable activities of those belonging to the realm when one was in a foreign land. "I see the wisdom in this." A silent moment passed before Alexander spoke again. "May I ask a favor?"

"Of course, if it would further the cause for which we fight."

Alexander left the forge, and in a few moments, he reentered, carrying the royal sword that had been gifted to him by the king to be used on their journey. He presented the blade to Fortus, who upon seeing it in the firelight, seemed to recognize it immediately, and as he took it from Alexander to examine it, he said, "This weapon has a royal history. It was used during the First Great Conflict!"

"The king gifted it to me. There may be more support for armament than it may appear. It would further our cause if you would imbue it so that it would…strike true."

Fortus looked disappointed, almost sad at the request. "I cannot; the sword is far too old to be forged again and imbued. It is fine enough now for combat, but I cannot. There is also a decree that no artifact of history be altered by any means, especially by imbuement."

Alexander suppressed any expression of his feeling dejected and silently berated himself for attempting something so foolishly against common sense and against the Carn Doctrine.

Fortus, sensing what the Earthen leader was thinking and feeling, said, "I would not give so much regret for innocent deviations. You might find them necessary in the coming times of war. The true path may not always be clear." He gave the sword back and brightened. "Take heart; you will not need the imbuement; at least you do not need it yet."

Alexander nodded, outwardly accepting what was said by the Xalian, but inwardly seriously doubting the sentiment, especially the portion regarding deviation. He then politely excused himself and went back outside to the fire that was being put out by Saul.

The others were cleaning up the various utensils and dishes used during their meal. They then retired for the night, each ready for the next day's travels. They slept reasonably well in the loft above the blacksmith's forge, being warmed throughout the night by the warmth of its fire.

Chapter 16

The Guardian Elk

The morning after their stay at the homestead of Fortus, Lord Luxeniah, Alexander, Jessica, Stephan, and Saul enjoyed a generous breakfast provided by their host. Following the meal, they departed, traveling north as they continued on the path leading to the bridge over the Great Ravine. Throughout the day, Stephan noticed more and more the sparseness of farms and the increase in abundance of the green crystal which they had only uncommonly seen before.

By the early afternoon, the road started to wind to the east and they came upon a sign pointing in that direction reading "North Bridge," and below that, in smaller print, "The Great Ravine." Soon after the sign, they came upon a small path, which led from the main road northward and somewhat to the west toward the ravine.

Upon direction from Lord Luxeniah, they made their way, winding through the forest thick with foliage. It was difficult to see far while traversing the trail until they came upon a clearing with a lake in its center. The trees all around the lake had a green light painted on them. Stephan surmised that it was the light that trickled in through the cracks in the forest canopy and was refracted by the many patches of green crystal common in this forest.

Each of the lord's guard had an impression that they should stop a ways from the lake. Lord Luxeniah continued toward a portion of the body of water where it narrowed. Lord Luxeniah stood close to the water's edge, facing the opposite bank.

The lord spread out his arms and closed his eyes. Although he could not see his face, Stephan felt a distinct impression that the lord was putting great effort into focusing his concentration. It was similar to what he had experienced in the caves when they all were traveling to the Earthen Archway. After some time had passed, leaves in the distant could be heard rustling as if something very large was approaching. Stephan then saw what at first looked like moving, leafless branches above the leafed one above the opposite bank. It quickly became apparent, however, that they were not branches at all but antlers, which became even more evident when the snout and then entire head of an elk poked through the foliage. The elk's neck and hooves then appeared, follow by the rest of its body, until the whole of it stood there in the water, its eyes locked on Lord Luxeniah. Stephan thought he should be more alarmed and should want to shout out to the lord to be careful of the danger the beast might pose, but there was no urgency within him or with the others from what he could gather. Like many of the creatures they had seen in the Xalian realm, the elk's size varied from any he had ever seen. But while there was only a somewhat noticeable difference in many of the other animals, this elk towered over its Earthen twin.

For a time longer than what Stephan would think would be comfortable, nothing was said. Lord Luxeniah's arms were still out-stretched. The elk stared at him. Finally, the lord lowered his arms.

Without any indication or warning, an unfamiliar voice boomed in Stephan's mind, but not so loud as to cause him pain. "Many seasons have passed since last we have met, Lord Luxeniah. Why have you summoned me?"

"Elk Guardian of the North…" The lord's voice could now be clearly heard in Stephan's mind, "we travel north to the Chromas tribes. Times have darkened and the fates of two worlds are in peril." He then related to the Guardian Elk the details regarding the Grand Council, the events written of in the ancient writings that had already transpired, and the king's decree to visit the other two Northern Kingdoms in order to unite them all against the Coltrous. "Now it seems as though we have a barrier to our progress. The Northern Bridge, I have been informed, is deteriorated and fraught with danger. Is there another way?"

The Guardian Elk stood still for a moment without thinking to them and then looked to the west. After returning his gaze, he thought to them, "Take the path which is in my mind and you will surely find a way over the waters. However, beware those who are covered in the skins of beasts, for they are at times present in these lands. They cannot dwell here long as they are speedily driven away either by my kin or your kind. Nevertheless, once you leave these forests and the land of your birth, there will be none to guide or protect you."

"Your wisdom," Lord Luxeniah thought to the Guardian Elk, "will be protection enough."

The Guardian's gaze then drifted and he looked into the distance. "There was a time when my kin could match the strength of your kind. It was then when we lived in perfect balance. None have seen those times but those who came long before. We now look over these lands and must exist between you and your bloodthirsty brethren."

"We seek to restore that balance and once again establish peace in this realm."

With that, Lord Luxeniah gave a formal farewell before he and his guard made their way to the path the Guardian Elk had in his mind. As they walked around the lake's shore to the path's head, Saul, who was at the back, stumbled. Although he did not fall, Alexander heard it, turned toward Saul, and looked at him as though he were a child, with condescension and contempt. Jessica's expression mirrored that of Alexander's as they both smirked at him. When they turned to continue to the path's head, Stephan could see Saul shaking with rage at the expression. For a moment, Stephan thought he was about to witness another outburst, similar to the one that had caused Saul's previous demotion, but his posture relaxed. The contortion of his face melted and he looked calm again. In the many months, long months Stephan monitored Saul, he never saw him regain his composure so quickly after being that angered. *What could have caused such a change?*

Many moments had passed since the nobleman and his guard left the lake. The Elk Guardian stood still in the water, feeling a sort of peace and tranquility while he remained there. Secure in the midst of the groves, he raised his head, the leaves rustling softly as his antlers brushed them. As he stood there, he pondered the things he had learned and what was written in the ancient writings regarding the Second Great Conflict. Just as his mind was about to reach the apex of his meditative trance, a distant rustling and crashing noise through the leaves above him interrupted his reverie. He opened his eyes and looked upward. The foliage moved with every sharp crashing sound until he could see a ball of fur falling, bouncing from branch to branch until it hit the ground. Upon impact, the ball split into two squirrels. After being stunned for a moment, they started tussling and swiping at each other playfully, laughing and giggling. A crushing sound, with the quaking of the earth knocking them to the ground, stopped their fun.

The two squirrels quickly got back up and saw a massive hoof planted like the trunk of a tree in front, almost in between the two.

"Fit Wit and Man Maul!" sounded the booming voice of the Guardian Elk. "I did not save you from that badger to witness this utter wasting of your time and talents!"

Man Maul, the gray squirrel, stood wide-eyed and mortified, and stammered as he said to his friend, "Are we going to die? I-Is this what happens when you die?"

Fit Wit, his friend the red squirrel, gave Man Maul a look. "*Just calm down.*" He stretched out his tiny, squirrel arms, displaying the white fur of his chest and stomach. "Oh, Guardian Elk of the Northern Forest, forgive our transgression. We are but humble and lowly creatures, servants interested in the day's events—"

The booming voice of the Guardian Elk sounded again, interrupting the squirrel's mock plea. "I know what it is you two were doing. It is what you do each and every day, which is to waste time!"

"My lord," Fit Wit took a step forward. The hoof lifted and gave a small stomp and Fit Wit took a step backward. "We were merely curious. Surely you can understand, considering the grave nature of what has and will transpire!"

The Guardian Elk looked off into the distance in the general direction where the Geradian nobleman, with his guard, had traveled. He turned his head downward, back to the two squirrels. "If you sorry excuses for subjects of this forest are so curious about the nobleman and his strange companions, I have a great quest for you."

Both Man Maul and Fit Wit almost leapt with joy as Man Maul blurted out, "We love quests! How shall we serve thee, my lord?" The gray squirrel was excited by the notion of a new quest for he, at that instant, had the previous quests the Elk Guardian had charged them with in mind. They were small, fun quests, usually in the vein of delivering a message to the fox prince of the south or gathering nuts and other foods for the less fortunate rodents. They were tasks Man Maul thought of as being above the daily menial labor they often shirked.

"You both shall be charged with a quest of the utmost importance. You are to follow Lord Luxeniah and those who accompany him and to aid them in whatever dangers come their way."

Fit Wit and Man Maul stood there, silent for a moment as their joy evaporated. Fit Wit blinked twice. "My dear guardian, those treelings? It is—"

"Silence!" the guardian's voice almost shook the squirrels back to the ground. "I am not yet finished. In addition to following them, you are to stay completely out of their view. The *treelings*, as you are so fond of calling them, are not to know of your existence!"

Both of the squirrels stood there, looking dumbly up at the guardian, not knowing what to say. Man Maul clutched his tail while stroking it and curling the fur around his fore-claw. Fit Wit opened his mouth to protest while opening his hand to gesture some profound thought that would counter the guardian's wisdom, but no thought could be formed in his mind. He closed his hand and mouth, looking to the ground and trying to think of an argument. When he thought he had it, he opened his mouth and hand again only to find that nothing, again, had formed in his mind. This continued a couple of more times until the Elk Guardian lifted his hoof again; the squirrels cowered.

"Perhaps you two would prefer I feed you to the badger? Or recommend you to the labor camps, which would surely do you both a lot of good!"

Both Fit Wit and Man Maul reacted instantly and in unison. "No, no, no!" Fit Wit looked at Man Maul, who put his tail back behind him and said, trying his best to sound enthused by the guardian's decree, "We accept the quest, your highness." After a pause, Fit Wit elbowed him. "And trust in your infinite wisdom."

"My wisdom may be without end; however, my patience for you two is about to expire. Now go!"

In an instant, the red and gray squirrels were off in the direction the guardian had before turned to face.

Minutes into their traversing of the terrain, jumping from tree branch to tree branch and from rock to rock, they picked up the unmistakable scent of creatures whose scent was always accompanied by another—the strange smell of the fur and skin of other animals. Most squirrels would be appalled by this pungent scent, but neither Fit Wit nor Man Maul were. There were many things about them other squirrels and beasts did not understand or particularly like. Their manner of speaking, their manner of acting, and their preferences, just to name a few, were mostly unorthodox. This might be why they were chosen and why they then did not mind leaving the forest of their birth and childhood so much.

Chapter 17

The Gray, Ornery Owl

The path the Guardian Elk had shown them in his mind led northward and farther to the west. After many twists and bends, the path headed downward, down to the bottom of the ravine with portions of the path dropping off, where the group would have to climb down. After a few hours, they reached the ravine's base where the ravine's river raged before them. On the other side of the river was an entrance to a cave a quick climb up from the opposite bank. Since the current appeared so powerful and the river too precarious to swim across, they stood there for a moment, appraising the situation.

Every member of the emissary stared at the rocks calmly, trying to find a way across, considering the options at their disposal. Would they use their rope and somehow make a temporary bridge from one boulder to another? Or would they chop down some trees and achieve a similar end with wooden beams? All were contemplating these possibilities with military precision except for Saul. Stephan noticed from the corner of his eye that he was impatiently fidgeting, not so much that one untrained in monitoring would realize, but Stephan was so trained and so he noticed.

"This presents quite the predicament," Alexander proclaimed and turned to Stephan. "Lieutenant, how would…" As Alexander was speaking, Saul's fidgeting became more pronounced until he burst and loudly interrupted the captain. "It's so obvious!" As he said this, he moved his body into a stance that indicated a readying for movement and then ran forward past the others to the river's edge and jumped, seeming to fly through the air. He jumped higher than Stephan had ever seen him or anybody jump before. He finally landed onto the nearest boulder jutting out of the river's powerful current. He then jumped again and landed on the next boulder.

Noticeably perturbed, Alexander readied himself and ran forward to the river's edge, making his own leap to the first boulder, which he almost completely made, except for a quick dip his right foot made into the river's waters, which he quickly pulled out. When Alexander made his second jump, Saul was almost to the opposite riverbank. This time, although he completely made the jump, he still appeared, from what Stephan could gather, annoyed.

Jessica, Stephan, and Lord Luxeniah each made their own successful jumps, and soon, the whole emissary was on the other bank. From there, they all made the quick climb to the cave's entrance where they were free to sit and rest a while in the shade the cave provided and to wonder how they had been able to perform the incredible feat they had just performed.

Fit Wit and Man Maul made their way throughout the Northern Geradian forest at a furious pace. When they reached the part of the path that descended downward, they climbed a tree where they could get a good view. Through the trees, they saw the point of the ravine where the treelings from the south were to cross. Here they found with great disappointment that they were already on the other side of the ravine; the squirrels had missed their chance to sneak into their bags and ride along with them.

"How are we going to cross now?" Man Maul asked between heavy, deep breaths.

Fit Wit looked to the east where the dilapidated bridge could be seen in the distance through many leaves and branches. "I guess we could cross the bridge."

"But the Guardian Elk said it was dangerous. The treeling from the south, the nobleman, he too said it was—"

"I know!" Fit Wit snapped. "I heard them, too! But we're small and light, so it wouldn't be as dangerous for us."

"I still don't like it." Just then, Man Maul saw the treelings disappear into the cave above the opposite bank. "Look!" Man Maul pointed and Fit Wit saw them too. "If we go over the bridge, there might not be a way down into the cave. And it would take forever!"

"Let's look for another way then." While looking around for another way across the Great Ravine, Fit Wit saw an owl landing on a branch just outside an owl's nest far above them. He motioned to Man Maul to be quiet and pointed up to the bird of prey. Man Maul ran and hid inside a close by knot on the tree's trunk. Fit Wit, after seeing the display of cowardice, rolled his eyes and climbed up to the tree's trunk, toward the owl's nest.

"Fit Wit!" Man Maul whispered as loudly as he could as he poked his head out of the tree's knot. "Owls eat squirrels!"

Fit Wit stopped climbing and turned to his frightened, timid friend, "I know, but I have a plan!" After a moment of silence, Fit

Wit saw that Man Maul was not going to come out on his own. "Oh, come on!" Fit Wit then scurried down the trunk of the tree to Man Maul's knot and said, very deliberately in his tone, stressing each word carefully, "be—a—warrior!"

When his friend had said these words, they ignited a memory in Man Maul's mind he had tried very hard to forget. It was from Man Maul's childhood when he had been training to be a hunter. He and several other young gray squirrels were being taught the fundamentals of hunting and fighting. Each had a position and place they were supposed to be and a task to perform. As the long day dragged on and as all the other young squirrels seemed to be thriving in these new challenges, delighted in the scurrying, foraging, and biting exercises, Man Maul had no other desire than just to sit on one of the branches and play with twigs and leaves. When his father saw this, he kindly leaned over to his wife and said, in a thick, gray squirrelish accent, "Ehhh, I don't think Man Maul's going to be a warrior."

Man Maul broke his mind from the reverie and hesitated to go up to the owl's nest, but with the shame of the memory fresh in his mind, he gathered his courage and joined Fit Wit. Together, they climbed the trunk to where the owl sat perched, facing away from them. The owl was eating, slurping up the last of his meal, a rat's tail disappearing into his beak. The bird grumbled to himself something about there never being enough to eat.

As if to respond to the owl's murmuring, Fit Wit said, "I know where you could get more!"

The owl turned sharply, his eyes glowing in the dark of the knot. He lumbered out of his nest toward them.

"A lot more…" Fit Wit said with feigned confidence.

When he was in front of him, the owl looked Fit Wit up and down. "I could eat you now, although you do not look like you would be much of a meal." The gray owl chomped its beak. "But it is better than nothing."

"Wait!" Fit Wit yelled, his arms extended and hands open. "Why eat us when there is more waiting for you, much more than we two, scrawny rodents?"

The owl's eyes narrowed and Fit Wit saw that he had the bird thinking. Man Maul was bug-eyed, shivering with fright, and holding his tail for comfort as he often did.

"Where?" the owl squawked loudly.

"If you take us with you, I'll show you. I know where some treelings have gone, and they are always carrying meat since they eat it, you know?"

There was no response from the owl for some time. Man Maul spoke up to break the silence. "W-we would want only the berries from the pouch!" This was not technically a lie; they would gladly eat whatever berries the treelings had.

"You'd need us to get the meat for you," Fit Wit said and then pointed to the owl's wings. "You're not equipped to rummage through their packs."

The owl seemed to take umbrage at this, lifting up his head and puffing out his feathers in a prideful display. He shot back at them. "You better not be lying to me!"

Without waiting for a response, the gray owl flapped his mighty wings, lifting himself up. Fit Wit and Man Maul felt the violent gusts of wind and braced themselves against them. The owl's powerful talons gripped them, rendering them completely immobile. They were then in the air high above the forest's canopy and moving fast.

They circled for a while without direction. Fit Wit was confused by this until he realized he had not yet told the owl where to go. With a great struggle, the red squirrel wrestled free an arm and pointed to the cave's entrance on the other side of the ravine where the treelings had entered. Upon seeing the squirrels' tiny arm pointing, the owl swooped down into the ravine. When they were below the elevation of the cave, he banked up to lessen his speed. Over the ground, just outside the cave's entrance, the bird flapped his wings to float in the air, and squawked, "Where are they?"

"They're near, just inside that cave!" Fit Wit was now yelling over the wind from the owl's wings and pointing to the cave's entrance in front of them. "Let us go and we'll show you where they are!"

The owl's talons opened and the two squirrels spilled out onto the ground. They quickly got up and Fit Wit gave Man Maul a familiar grin that usually meant that he had a plan so be calm and play along. They walked into the cave alongside the owl. Fit Wit saw, just inside the cave's entrance, a fissure, just large enough for two squirrels to fit inside.

Fit Wit pointed into the darkness of the cave. "Just beyond that bend."

The owl walked faster and greedily toward the promised meat, but he knew not to fly and make noise because the treelings might become aware of his presence. Fit Wit walked slower and slower, Man Maul following suit, allowing the owl to walk farther ahead. This succeeded in creating distance between them.

Fit Wit motioned to the fissure. When he was certain Man Maul understood his plan, they turned back and ran for the fissure's tiny entrance. The owl heard behind him the pitter-patter of little squirrel paws. He turned, suddenly noticing the escaping rodents, and let out a loud, indignant squawk. He took to flight, quickly closing the distance between himself and the squirrels. Just as he was about to catch them, the squirrels slipped into the fissure and the owl's claws clasped nothing but dirt and rock.

The owl let out another squawk, louder and more indignant than before, being amplified by the compact nature of the crevice in which the two squirrels were now hiding.

"You deceived me!" the owl bellowed in bitter anger.

Neither Fit Wit nor Man Maul could respond since they were both on the fissure's floor, rolling around and laughing uncontrollably. When they could control themselves, they stood up.

"I will get you both for this!" the owl wailed.

Fit Wit shrugged, wiping the tears from his eyes. "You know, for an owl, you're not very wise!" They would have burst into laughter again were it not for the deafening sound of the owl's piercing screech filling the fissure. The noise was so loud and so filled with rage that the two rodents ran at once in fear, farther into the darkness of the crevice and in the direction of the treelings to continue their quest.

Chapter 18

The Blue Crystal Caves

Stephan, along with his fellow officers, Lord Luxeniah and Saul, had only rested briefly at the mouth of the cave before entering. They were concerned with the ever-present and ever-looming threat of the Coltrous bands and infiltrators who infested the common lands north of the Great Ravine. Now deep inside the cave system, Stephan hoped the nobleman knew his way and that they were heading north toward the northern Chromas tribes.

As they traveled, Stephan was growing wary of being underground. He felt like they had been subterranean often lately. Despite this feeling, though, this underground experience was proving to be unique not only due to the nature of their journey north to the Chromas but also due to the deep blue hue that lit the cavern around him. Common in the cavern were blue crystals. This new type of crystal seemed to emanate the light. This was puzzling to Stephan because he knew the crystals of other colors were not themselves sources of light. He had spent enough nights outside around the crystals to know that, and unless these blue crystals had the unique quality of being luminescent, there must be some other explanation.

The distinct noise of the flapping of wings echoed throughout the cave, interrupting Stephan's train of thought. The sound seemed out of place since it was too deep and full to be the sound of a bat's wings. He thought, though, that the noise could be as distant as the cave's mouth, an appropriate place for some other winged creature to enter. Another noise confirmed these suspicions when a distant screech echoed from what seemed like a similar distance. *A spotted, long eared owl,* Stephan concluded.

Just then, the lord stopped. He raised his hand, motioning to the others to do likewise. A distant and quiet sound broke the silence. It was unmistakable—boots striking the ground as if a formation of men were marching. These sounds were more aggressive than almost any other kind he had ever heard. At first, it was only the sound of a small formation. Then the noise grew—the sound of more and more boots striking ground.

Stephan looked to the lord, whose demeanor was unusual for the noble Xalian because his countenance was that of one who was alarmed and unsure what to do.

Fit Wit and Man Maul had been scampering through the cave, trying to catch up with the treelings. They were both surprised when they turned a bend and saw them merely standing there, not moving or talking. It was when the pitter-patter of their paws striking the cave floor had ceased that Man Maul noticed the distant, growing noise. Fit Wit saw his friend's reaction. "What is it?" he whispered.

"Many treelings," Man Maul answered. "Many large treelings are coming this way fast, and they don't seem very nice."

They looked around for any place to hide and found above them a fissure, much larger than the one they had hid in to avoid the owl. They got inside one of its crevices and then felt safe. Notwithstanding the feeling, the charge of the Guardian Elk to look over and protect the treelings weighed heavily on Fit Wit's mind. He could tell Man Maul bore the same burden, but he was at a loss as to the manner by which they could help.

After thinking as hard as he could, Man Maul made a face at Fit Wit, a face he had made many times. Fit Wit recognized it instantly. Man Maul had an idea.

The sounds of the approaching formation continued to grow and were now accompanied by shouts, instantly recognizable as being those of the Coltrous. Stephan and the others looked around frantically for a place to hide, for they all knew they would be no match for the number of approaching berserkers. The search was unfruitful until Stephan heard the sharp crack of a stone hitting another, larger stone and rolling to the ground. The sound caught his attention because it was out of place. It sounded as though it had fallen from a height higher than the cave's ceiling. Stephan turned to see where the sound had come from, but he could not locate it.

Above the sound's origin, Fit Wit and Man Maul poked their heads out from inside the fissure. "It's not working," Man Maul said. "Only one of them looked and he'll never see this hole!" The two squirrels went back up to their own hiding place within the fissure. Man Maul had another one of his looks.

Stephan walked over to the noise of the stone's impact, not quite sure why he was so interested in it, when he heard a deep, moaning sound coming from above. It seemed to be the sound of air passing through some kind of expanse. He looked up and saw nothing but darkness as the light from the blue crystals did not reach that area. He stepped on a rock, extended his arm upward, and found that there indeed was an empty shaft. It seemed to be a large enough of a place to hide. As he entered it, Fit Wit and Man Maul scurried inside a small crevice. "I told you my deep throat singing would do the trick," Man Maul whispered as he poked Fit Wit's side.

After finding the hiding spot, and marveling as to their good fortune, Stephan looked toward the others. He did not want to call out; the band of Coltrous infiltrators would surely hear him. In another moment of good fortune, Alexander just happened to be looking in the general direction because he was searching for his lieutenant, so Stephan motioned to the captain. Upon seeing the signal, Alexander gave the signal to Jessica and motioned to Lord Luxeniah to follow him. Saul noticed the activity of the others and followed.

When the others had joined Stephan and he had shown them the fissure, they each entered it. It was large enough to fit all of them as the expanse continued much higher, seeming to continue forever. They would have climbed, but the act of their climbing might dislodge a rock, and if one struck a Coltrous, it would surely inform them of their presence inside the fissure. Silently, they waited as the sounds of the band of Coltrous infiltrators was deafening now. They passed by below, like the rushing current of a flood. When the last of them was gone and the last of the sounds of marching and the shouting of orders faded into the distance, they all remained still, each of the lord's guard waiting to see what Lord Luxeniah would decide.

Silence filled the fissure while waiting for the lord's decision. It was broken not by a sound, or even a voice in their minds, but an impression felt by each one of them individually to continue climbing the fissure for the caves were no longer safe.

The Geradian nobleman and his guard climbed for almost an hour, stopping now and then for some kind of rest while taking care not to make a noise. As they were ascending, they came upon a part of the fissure where light shown through small cracks. The cracks were large enough, however, to peer through and see a large chamber. Inside the space, many Coltrous infiltrators were handling various parts of mech armor suits, parts Stephan recognized, having worked on the design, construction, and maintenance of many such suits. He could tell, however, from the crude assembly and damaged nature of the parts, that the Coltrous workers would never get any of the suits to work at even a diminished capacity. The thought did occur to him that perhaps the workers were not trying to assemble the pieces, but rather, were studying them for some reason. Stephan dismissed this thought almost as soon as he had it for he knew of no purpose they could possibly have for the knowledge if they were not assembling the components into full suits.

Another impression could be felt by each of the members of the guard, a distinct feeling as if the result of hearing a voice, to continue upward as lingering too long might reveal their presence. As they continued climbing upward, Stephan saw a small component lying near one of the larger cracks. It was a seeker, a module of the suit's visual system. Thinking he might gain some insight to the activities of the Coltrous workers and their purpose there as well as being overcome by a strange curiosity, he reached into the space, grabbed the eyepiece, and placed it into his pocket. He thought he might also use the part because it was modular in design and would work without being attached to a mech suit.

For almost another hour, they climbed. In time, the quality of air changed, coming alive and moving, a clear sign to Stephan that they were nearing the surface. After a few more moments of climbing, faint morning sunlight filled the fissure. They reached the surface, and all, except for Saul, collapsed onto the rocky ground, breathing deep gulps of air. While the others rested, fatigued from the prolonged climb, Saul climbed to the highest point of the rocky surface and away from the others. In spite of his struggle for air, Stephan noticed Alexander shooting fiery darts at Saul with his gaze as he passed.

At the top of the rock formation, Saul took in the surrounding terrain. Behind their position, the land was starkly different from the forests of Geradia. It was much more arid, the land being dominated by sand dunes with dry, dying trees dotting the landscape here and there. Saul shifted his gaze toward the land northward, which was much of the same until the terrain stopped at a mountain range in the distance. As if seeing it himself, Lord Luxeniah said, "That is our destination." He got to his feet, and after struggling to climb the rock formation, joined Saul at the top. "We must make those mountains before noon, or risk the wrath of the sun."

Chapter 19

The Chromas

When they felt rested, the officers of Alpha Z, Saul, and Lord Luxeniah traveled north throughout the morning. They walked in silence, much like their climb through the fissure earlier. At certain times, however, when the way seemed clear and safe, the lord would think to them what he knew about the Northern Chromas tribes, the mountains in which they resided, and the dragons that inhabited them. He thought to them about how the mythical beasts were the weakest of all known kinds of dragons, and, for this reason, were the only known kind ever to be broken and ridden by any Xalian. Ancient writings told of knights proving their valor by battling them at the base of the Chromas Mountains, and despite the weakness of the green dragons, most of the knights were never heard of again.

The terrain on the way to the Chromas Mountains was as arid and dry as it had appeared to be from the rock formation and the sand dunes. The unstable sand formations made the journey all the more difficult and prolonged.

The sun had risen high above them before they were within sight of the base of the mountain. It was late morning by the time they approached it. They were at the top of a particularly large dune when Lord Luxeniah stopped. He turned and looked behind them toward the direction from which they had come. The others stopped as well, and looked back to find the object of the lord's gaze. The lord then closed his eyes and got on one knee, apparently to feel the sand with his hand. After a few moments, the silence was broken by a quiet, beeping noise. Lord Luxeniah's eyes opened sharply. He stood up and turned sharply toward the source of the sound. Stephan was wearing a device of some kind on the side of his head. Part of the device hung from his ear, and a transparent eyepiece was covering his right eye. A few, distinct flashing lights could be seen in the eyepiece.

A chirp sounded from the seeker Stephan wore. "There are about…fifty approaching objects, most likely Xalian," Stephan said, appearing pleased with his own resourcefulness.

Lord Luxeniah glared at Stephan. "Tell me you did not take that from the chasm when we stopped climbing in the fissure to view the Coltrous infiltrators!"

Stephan's stomach dropped and he took the seeker off at once. He could not answer the lord, but when he realized what the Lord had been dreading, he thought, *How could I have been so stupid?*

"They tracked us with that, you fool!" The lord seethed before snatching the seeker from the lieutenant's hand and throwing it to the ground. Stephan was taken aback by the lord's sudden brash demeanor. "Quickly," Lord Luxeniah said, running toward the base of the mountain range, "we need cover."

As they ran, they could hear what the lord had felt before. It was the sound of marching, the sound of many boots striking sand. There were scores of them—a troop much larger than the band of infiltrators they had nearly encountered before in the blue crystal cave. When they finally reached the mountain base, it was too late to try to escape up the trail in time to reach any kind of cover. The trail wound up the mountain for some distance before it turned the first bend to provide any kind of cover. They instead hid behind a few boulders away from where the trail started, but still at the foot of the mountain range. Lord Luxeniah hoped whoever was pursuing them would assume they had gone up the trail and would pass them by.

As they hid, a dust cloud approached in the distance. The dust cloud and the sounds accompanying it continued to grow louder and louder until both stopped at the top of the large dune where the seeker was left. Lord Luxeniah peered out of a crack between two boulders to see the troop of Coltrous fighters standing in a line. The tallest of them stood out not only because of his height, but for being the most well-equipped, wearing actual plates of armor, unlike the others who wore skins. From his more ornate attire, one would readily assume he was the leader. The towering figure crouched and picked up the seeker dropped by Lord Luxeniah. In his hand, there was another device, and he looked back and forth between the two. The lord then recognized him by his armor's appearance, being laden in black and gold, as being of the ruling house of the Coltrous Empire.

Those of Lord Luxeniah's guard felt what he was thinking, getting the general idea of who the menacing figure was. They also felt his assumption that he and his men must have been following them by detecting the location of the mech suit's seeker. Stephan's face became flushed with embarrassment and shame. *I should have assumed they could track the part!*

By then, the Coltrous troop was approaching the location of the trail's start, and just as it appeared as though they would go on the trail and pass them by, they stopped. The well-armored leader stepped forward and spoke, his voice echoing slightly from inside the helmet. "Lord Luxeniah!" the leader called out. "I know you are there!"

How could he know? The lord's thoughts filled Stephan's mind; he then felt the lord remembering the legendary ability of the youngest of the brothers of the ruling house of the Coltrous to track his enemies by some unknown, supernatural power or sense. *Perhaps the seeker did not give away our position but merely indicated that somebody had crawled through the fissure.* Lord Luxeniah wondered whether the legend was true. The lord shuddered to think that a member of Coltrous nobility had penetrated this far north of the Hadriatic cliff fortress.

Stephan thought that he should go out and give the others a chance to escape. As he was intending to leave the hiding place behind the boulder, he had an impression of Lord Luxeniah's thoughts, *Stay; I will go out to meet them.*

Before Stephan could protest, the lord stepped out from behind the boulder and onto the sand, his sword drawn. He stood alone, facing the scores of Coltrous fighters and the well-armored leader in their center. A distant vulture's screech sounded in the vast, empty desert.

The leader of the troop of Coltrous infiltrators broke the silence. "I know you are not traveling alone; where are the others? Hiding as you were behind those rocks, no doubt."

"Concern yourself only with me," the lord replied.

"They are of my concern when they steal from my workshop—an actionable offense for sure here in these common lands. A Geradian lord should know these things, Lord Luxeniah."

"You have me at a disadvantage. You know my name and I know not yours or how you know mine."

"I am Ferekin of the ruling house of the Coltrous Empire and my sources are my own. From my sources, however, I know you are a nobleman of the kingdom of Geradia and that you seek to unite the three kingdoms of the Realm of Peace so that those cowering Earthens can lead an army to defeat my people during the Second Great Conflict."

From the corner of his eye, Stephan saw Alexander move, shifting his stance slightly as if wanting to step out from the safety of the boulder when Ferekin said the words "cowering Earthens."

The Geradian and Coultrous leaders stood there again in silence, the air dry and still.

It was Lord Luxeniah who broke the silence this time. "What is your intent in pursuing us?"

"You travel with curious company who would be of value to our people. My emperor would surely be pleased by the sight of a great Geradian locked away in our dungeons along with four Earthens. Tell me," his voice took on a mocking quality, "are they the four of the ancient writings who will lead the Northern Kingdoms against the Coltrous hordes?" Ferekin gave a hearty laugh, which was without mirth.

Lord Luxeniah ignored the question. "Perhaps a trade is in order. Surely your emperor would be pleased at the sight of his younger brother free and back in his empire."

Ferekin gave another loud, mocking laugh and then said, "You Geradians know nothing of our ways. Fabian will be freed soon enough, when we invade your lands and take possession of the entire

Realm the Peace. How then would it behoove us to trade when we could have the whole of it?"

The lord held up his sword. "It would behoove you to avoid death by my blade or by the hand of any of the members of my guard. How little you know of their strength!"

At this, Ferekin only gave a cruel smirk. He then opened his mouth to speak when Lord Luxeniah suddenly looked up. He then ran, in haste, back to the safety of the boulders.

Confused, the Coltrous royalty was about to look up at what commanded the Geradian's attention, but an explosion on his right sent many of his men flying through the air. Now when Ferekin looked up, his vision was obstructed by the smoke from the explosion and the cloud of sand it sent into the air. Such eruptions continued as more and more Coltrous fighters were sent flying. As the chaos ensued, Ferekin signaled a retreat. He turned to find that his signal was made in vain since his men were already fleeing in the direction opposite the foot of the mountain range.

Lord Luxeniah and the others hid behind the boulders, listening to the carnage, and waited for it to end. When the screams and the fiery explosions became more distant, the lord and those of his guard looked up, unsure at first whether they would do better to run up the trail or stay in relative safety. Finding the attacks concentrated solely on the Coltrous, they stayed. When the dust was almost completely settled, a green dragon broke through and flew toward the retreating Coltrous infiltrators. Almost at once, another three green dragons, with riders, followed the first dragon through the clouds of sand, still swirling in the air, and joined the first green dragon in pursuit.

Another green dragon came through the sand clouds above, but it did not join the others in finishing off the rest of Ferekin's men. Instead, it, along with its rider, landed in front of the boulders behind which Lord Luxeniah and his guard were hiding. Stephan's heart almost stopped when he got a closer look at the mythical beast, the existence of which he had never believed for an instant. It was covered in green scales on its belly and neck while sturdy plates shielded its back. Its large claws, on the extremities of muscular legs, dug into the sand, and even larger spikes dotted much of the neck and back in a row interrupted briefly by a leather saddle.

As the rider dismounted, the lord left the boulders, and those of his guard followed suit. Stephan assumed the lord knew there was no ill intent in the rider, and he mused as to whether there had been some kind of higher communication between them that would bring the lord to that conclusion. Stephan looked to the distant battle and caught glimpses, through the distant clouds of sand and smoke, of one of the dragons carrying and then dropping from a great height one of the Coltrous fighters. The body flailed as it plummeted to the ground.

The dragon rider walked over to meet them. When he stopped in front of the Geradian emissary, Stephan expected a spoken greeting; instead, he heard a voice in his mind, *It seems as though we arrived at just the right time!* The rider, who was dressed in green robes, the same green as the dragon he rode, gave a soft, friendly smile.

Indeed, you did! The voice of Lord Luxeniah now filled their minds. *Without your aid, we surely would now be in chains under the tyranny of our enemies, not to mention the sun!*

The rider's smile widened, clearly pleased; the smile standing in stark contrast to the background scene of carnage in the distance.

To Stephan, it underscored the rider's tolerance for such situations, appearing to be unphased and, therefore, a seasoned warrior.

When my men return, the rider thought to them, *we can take you to our home*. When the rider thought to them, it became apparent to Stephan that the thoughts were accompanied by much more than the literal meaning of the words, but with it, impressions and inklings that seemed to accompany and surround the words. Although he could not know what the others experienced, what accompanied the rider's thoughts, at least in Stephan's mind, was the general direction they would be traveling. With it, there was the sense that their destination would be high in the mountains. It occurred to Stephan that this was similar to how the tone of voice of somebody talking, as well as their mannerisms, would communicate more than the literal meaning of what was being said.

Before long, the other riders returned from their pursuit of the Coltrous. Each landed, and altogether, there were five dragons, each able to carry one passenger. Stephan wondered how they knew to send five or whether it was a matter of convenient coincidence. After mounting, one member of Lord Luxeniah's guard behind each rider, they took flight and flew through the air. The riders wielded the dragons with great skill, so much so that the ride was safe and comfortable for those who were their passengers.

When the green dragons with their riders and new passengers were far in the distance, Ferekin emerged from under a sand dune. He had been completely covered during the attack from the force of one of the dragon's fireballs. As he stood, he felt a sharp pain in his leg. Limping as he went, he headed south back to his base to heal and clean the char off his armor. He would then replenish his numbers and find Lord Luxeniah again.

High above the Chromas Mountains, the dragon riders caused their green dragons to ascend higher and higher. Before entering the clouds, Stephan surveyed the land below and saw the forests of Geradia in the distant south. He was surprised by how far they had come since leaving the land of Geradia. He saw the lands eastward and to the south. Covering the lands was a vast forest, with many rivers winding through it. He knew the forest would be a barrier between them and the Durathian kingdom when they finished their visit with the Chromas. Stephan also saw an area south of this forest covered by canyons and valleys. The wind whipped his hair, and the smell of moisture in the air filled his lungs as they entered the clouds. Once in, all he could see was a thick white mist until they broke through to the clear blue sky above. The clouds they had just passed through now appeared to be a vast, pillowy floor.

Above the clouds, the Geradian emissary and the Chromas dragon rider flew. In just under an hour, they descended again back into the clouds, continuing until they broke through back into the world below where the cities of the Chromas tribes stretched out, dotting the many flattened mountain tops. From the sense each of them had gathered from the head dragon rider, they knew the largest of these was the capital city and their destination. They landed on a patch of land that seemed to be kept clear for the purpose of harboring and maintaining the dragons. When they reached the ground and dismounted their respective dragons, Stephan noticed that they were close to a large building. It was one of the largest in the city from what Stephan had seen as they were approaching. He also took note of the distinct nature of the architecture; the buildings were made more out of wood, and they contrasted with the stone structures of the Geradian kingdom. Most were decorated with broad, wooden arches that flared up at the ends. The members of the emissary were now walking, though, to a larger, dome-shaped building. The ground they were on was a dirt path that eventually led to a lonely stone walkway leading to the prominent building.

When they neared the structure's entrance, two more Chromas came out to meet them. Each gave a generous bow. *Welcome to the land of the Chromas,* one of them thought to Lord Luxeniah and those who accompanied him. *We are honored to finally meet those from the southern lands. The Kingdom of Geradia and the Chromas peoples have been separated for far too long.*

The words in Stephan's mind came with the distinct impression that the Xalian addressing them was one of high prominence and one whom they could speak to about matters regarding the whole of the Chromas people or even those regarding the whole of Xaliud. Lord Luxeniah reached into his pouch and produced a cylindrical wooden case. He then proceeded to open it and took out the royal decree written in the golden, luminescent ink. The light from the luminescent ink could be seen radiating out from the scroll's ends. One of the Chromas representatives took the decree and thought to them, *I will take this to my superior immediately.*

Your kindness and generosity is much appreciated, the lord thought to the representative. *Not only yours, but that of your riders who saved us from certain capture.*

The representative responded, *We have been watching you and your companions since you reached the surface. We started out some time after you and your guard reached the surface after climbing up through that fissure.*

Stephan noticed the shocked look on Lord Luxeniah's face, mirroring his own surprise, and wondered how what the representative said could possibly be true. As if to answer his question, the Chromas Xalian thought to them, *We have our ways of receiving and giving thought over long distances. However, we usually watch only the lands just south of these mountains, lest our enemies get the better of us. It was strange that our monks felt the need to extend their range farther.*

The look of surprise on Lord Luxeniah's face gave way to a look of excitement, *Could you give thought to someone as far south as the kingdom of Geradia?*

The Chromas representative paused and furrowed his brow as if in deep thought, as if considering the question, *An interesting thought. We have never attempted such an extension of our reach. Our interests almost never lie there. However, perhaps with your aid, it could be done. Do you wish to deliver a message?*

Yes, replied the representative, *but we have pressing matters, the particulars of such are detailed in that document.*

The representative turned and walked toward the domed building. Lord Luxeniah and his guard followed him, and they all entered through the structure's large door. The Chromas turned and gestured to the document in his hand. *Is this decree meant for only one's eyes, or may it be unsealed, perhaps by one as lowly as myself?*

No, no, the lord thought to the representative. *The matter at hand concerns all Xalians and even those who are Earthen. So, by all means, open it.*

The Chromas placed his forefinger underneath the scroll's top layer of parchment and carefully broke the seal. He then unraveled the parchment and read its contents. As he read, Stephan could see his face grow more and more concerned with the apparent realization of the impending conflict. When it appeared as though he had finished reading, he looked up at Lord Luxeniah, his eyes wider and more alert. *We must visit the Grand Vizier at once!* He turned and walked at a faster pace than before. They were at that time making their way down a vastly spacious hall with an upper level. Both levels were adorned with large scrolls hung on the walls, with weapons between them, as well as painted portraits of what must have been prominent Chromas historical figures from a foregone age. Stephan remarked to himself that the appearance of that room, although not as gaudy, and much different in artistic style, resembled the Geradian armory in many respects.

Near the end of the hall, they reached a staircase. After ascending it, they continued down a much smaller hallway. At the end of this hall, an ornate door stood, as if guarding a prized treasure. Stephan noticed that there were no guards posted to protect whom he assumed would be the Supreme Vizier they would soon be meeting.

The representative opened the door and they walked into what Stephan thought would have been a palace hall similar to the Geradian king's hall in which the Grand Council had been held. Instead, they walked into a much smaller room. In its corner was a large, opulent desk and a Chromas Xalian sitting at it who appeared to be the Supreme Vizier since he had servants ready to obey his every whim standing on both sides of the room.

The Chromas who had led them to the room approached the sitting figure of importance. The others stopped and stood at what they assumed to be a respectable distance away. As the Supreme Vizier stood to meet them, Stephan got a better look at his ornate attire. Like the noblemen in the kingdom of Geradia, he wore layers of robes, but they were a different kind. Instead of being draped off the shoulders and dragging on the floor, they were more form fitting, the gold-embroidered white outer robe held close to the black inner robe with a thick belt.

A traditional greeting and acceptance was made between the representative and the Vizier. It was followed by a bow to the Geradian nobleman and those who served him. The Supreme Vizier acknowledged each of them warmly, and his greetings were returned with equal but uncertain bows.

How may I be of assistance, the Vizier thought to them, *to those who have traveled so far?*

Did he also monitor us in the desert? Stephan thought as discretely as he could.

The Chromas who had led them to the Supreme Vizier's office handed the Supreme Vizier the parchment. When he unraveled and began reading it, the illuminated text shined and lit his face, even in the already well-lit room. As he read, the reaction of the Vizier did not take on the same look of alarm as that of the representative. He seemed to be more contemplative of what knowledge was being offered him, as if to consider its implications. Then, without speaking, he walked over to the bookshelf on the room's wall, adjacent to the desk. He pulled out a book, opened it, and read. The Geradian royal decree rested on the left page of the book, now nestled in his right arm. He appeared to be comparing the two.

It was wise for you to come to me, the Supreme Vizier thought to them without turning, *I just so happen to be quite familiar with the ancient lore surrounding the events of the First Great Conflict.* He continued to search the tome, comparing it to what was written in the Geradian decree. In time, his countenance brightened and he tapped the book with a soft thud. *That is it!* He thought this to them, turning to face those who had been patiently waiting to find out what he was searching for. *It is in here, the location of the tomb in which the white sword of Durath resides.* After the Chromas leader said this, his manner took on a concerned, puzzled look. *I only have the location of the tomb. It is found in a poem, and I have only its first half. The page it was written upon was found long ago, but the rest of the poem must be on another.*

This time it was Lord Luxeniah who brightened. *This is no concern of ours,* the Geradian lord thought to the Supreme Vizier, and with it, impressions of their visit with Fortus. *We have learned of the contents of the second half of a poem, most likely that very poem you now have. We know the location of the sword within the tomb's interior!*

The Supreme Vizier seemed pleased by this. *Well, other than the acquisition of the ancient sword, it appeared as though all there is left, other than the convincing of the Durathians, is to convince the other viziers to commit. It should not prove to be too difficult, especially when they read the royal decree!*

The Supreme Vizier walked back to the others where Lord Luxeniah and he clasped arms. To Stephan, both appeared content with the unfolding of events. Those looking on also seemed pleased by what had transpired.

They left the distinguished Chromas leader, who had preparations to make because he, along with Lord Luxeniah, would be visiting the other viziers throughout that day. Stephan and the others exited the large domed building and entered the courtyard. They walked to its end, taking in the design and beauty of the cloister. Upon reaching the edge, through the arches they could see the marketplace down the streets with the shops along its sides and the calm, quiet demeanor of the Chromas people inhabiting the city. After some time there in the courtyard, it occurred to Stephan that their hopes in uniting the Northern Kingdoms just might be well founded and their efforts not wasted.

Several days passed, during which the Geradian lord, as well as his emissary, received some much-needed rest. The Chromas city they were staying in had more than enough in the way of sights, sounds, and scenery to keep them occupied for the extent of their stay. Lord Luxeniah spent much of the time visiting the other viziers who, as the Supreme Vizier had predicted, understood quickly the nature of their shared situation and believed strongly the Geradian nobleman's contention concerning the daunting dangers the Coltrous presented. This was due not only to the presentation of the royal decree but also the accounts Lord Luxeniah gave of all he and his guard had experienced so far. The minds of the viziers were especially clear and receptive to the images that accompanied the lord's thoughts. In spite of this great understanding on the part of the Chromas nobility, Lord Luxeniah found that although they were quick to commit and prepare for the Second Great Conflict, they were unfortunately unwilling to leave the safety of their mountainous home to lend any aid until they could, in some way, sense that the fabled Day of Exodus was indeed upon them.

On the third day of their sojourn among the Chromas, and after making frequent requests during that time, Lord Luxeniah was able to convince one of the Viziers to grant him the assistance of four Chromas monks in reaching somebody in Geradia with their thoughts. With them, the lord ascended a mountain by the Chromas capital city, and near its peak, he entered a temple. There was some danger in the climb because they were far away from the safety of the city. Lord Luxeniah had made the dangerous trip gratefully since the difficulty of what they would soon be attempting would be eased by both the altitude and remoteness of the temple.

Once they reached the temple and entered, the lord noticed that the building had a dome shape, similar to the first Chromas structure they had entered upon their arrival three days before. The main difference, however, was the size, since the temple was much smaller, clearly intended for limited use by relatively few. It consisted only of one room with tall, vaulted ceilings. The monks who accompanied the lord went to the center and situated themselves into four parts of a circle, leaving a space for Lord Luxeniah. The Geradian lord had been nearer to the temple's entrance, admiring the structure's architecture and the attention to detail its builder must have had during its construction. Upon noticing the beckoning gazes of the waiting monks, Lord Luxeniah quickly walked over to the circle. Upon entering it, the lord immediately felt something enter the circle. It was something invisible, part of which seemed to Lord Luxeniah to be flowing through him and part seeming to flowing through each of the monks.

The holy men drew their swords, and the lord followed their lead, drawing his own. They all lifted them up, the points almost meeting at a point above the center of the circle. Lord Luxeniah was the only one unfamiliar with this ceremony, but he understood enough of its purpose. With all of their power united, they might be able to communicate with one of inhabitants of the White Tower of Geradia. The lord needed to get word to the king and the other noblemen of the willingness of the Chromas to commit to battle with their own condition. The lord was wondering what he would do if this did not work. The prospects would not be good since the obvious solution of riding a dragon south, or even sending a courier, would never be possible due to the intensely reclusive nature of the Chromas people. Lord Luxeniah knew all too well that only the approaching threat of annihilation would force them from the mountainous abode.

When all of their swords were pointing to the same point above the circle, the monks closed their eyes and the lord followed their lead. At first, he did not know who in the White Tower should be the object of their thoughts, so he attempted to reach a monk who might possibly be visiting. He also hoped his thoughts might even extend to the cathedral where the Geradian clergy would more likely be, but the reception might not be strong with the throngs of other thoughts emanating from the other minds, crowding the space around the cathedral. As he concentrated, he could sense the minds and thoughts of the monks who must have known his thoughts and intentions for their thoughts were also directed to the White Tower. Lord Luxeniah was impressed by the speed by which the monks sensed his thoughts as well as the clarity of their understanding.

While standing there for what could have been many hours, they sensed all the while the thoughts and senses of the people between them and the white tower. At first, after a long time of complete silence and vacant minds, they sensed a group of roving hunters making their way across the barren lands to the river forests in the east. After a longer silence, they sensed the thoughts of some passersby who were having a late afternoon stroll through the Elk Lake forests, their minds centered on the shared hope of perhaps catching a glimpse of the legendary and elusive elk of the forest's namesake. Lord Luxeniah and the four monks together pushed farther and farther, extending the range of their thoughts past many towns and villages, including the Village of Elk Lake. They pushed past the farmlands to the south of the towns and villages where the thoughts were simple, yet powerful, and the minds pure. Farther and farther they pushed, the limits of their endurance about to be reached when a torrent of thoughts flooded their own minds as they pushed into the kingdom of Geradia, the most populated part of those lands. Then they reached and focused on the White Tower, which provided a reprieve with its relatively few inhabitants. Not only were there fewer of them, but these thoughts were much more focused. It would be a simple matter to find a mind who would be open to Lord Luxeniah's message if there were one meditating or even spending a few moments in quiet rest.

They kept searching, the monks following the Geradian lord's lead, yet carrying most of the mental and emotional load necessary to extend the reach of their thoughts this far south. For a substantial amount of time, nothing was found until finally a quiet and open mind came into focus. It was not a mind the lord recognized immediately, and it, in a confusing manner, did not give strong impressions along with its thoughts.

This is the High Ambassador and Lord Luxeniah. The lord paused but received no response, so he continued. *I am reaching you from the Chromas Mountains with a dire message which must be given at once to the king and the noblemen of the land.* Again, no response for a time until finally a thought, which did seem vaguely familiar to Lord Luxeniah. Although he could not be certain who it was beyond the weak notion that it belonged to one who was young. *I understand,* the young mind finally responded. *Forgive me. I am as student of the mental arts; I am inexperienced.*

With whom do I have the pleasure of the exchange of thought? Lord Luxeniah asked.

I am Figo. I study under the tutelage of Lord Levine and would gladly deliver any message immediately to him…unless you would like to communicate directly to the lord.

No, no, there is little time enough for pleasantries; just deliver the message I will relate as soon as you can. Relate it directly to the king first and nobody else; do you understand? The student said he did, and the Geradian lord then told him about all that they had experienced since they had left Geradia, including their encounter with Ferekin, the commitment of the Chromas, and even the riddle revealing the location of the White Sword of Durath, with much of the actual experience communicated as impressions to accompany the thoughts. Lord Luxeniah hoped the bit of knowledge regarding the location of the White Sword would do much in motivating the King as well as the noblemen to commit resources in raising an army to counter the Coltrous.

A moment of silence passed after the lord had finished saying all there was to say before the young student responded. *All is received and understood. The lords and the king will know before the day's end!* With that, Lord Luxeniah gave a formal and quick parting statement, being satisfied by the vibrant quality of Figo's thought. He was also eager to end the communication because he was ready to collapse from the ceremony's incredible strain.

Exhausted, Lord Luxeniah opened his eyes and collapsed to his knees, dropping his sword with a loud clang as it struck the temple's marble floor. He breathed heavily, and although his eyes were open, he did not see his surroundings. His vision began to return. After a while, the pangs of his exhaustion waned and the beads of sweat ceased to pour down his face. He was able to see the monks. They were looking him, seeming concerned. Although visibly tired, they did not give the lord the impression that they were nearly as drained.

Impressed by the monk's show of great resilience, the lord stood and thanked each of them one by one, bowing while thinking thoughts of gratitude. Lord Luxeniah then remembered, after he had expressed his gratitude, the half-day long climb down the mountain which lay before him. After realizing he was lacking the strength to complete the small journey, he turned to the monks and thought to them collectively, *Is there a place I may rest?*

In the kingdom of Geradia, in the White Ivory Tower, Lord Levine sat slumped over in the chair in which he often dozed off. His eyes opened softly, as if emerging from a deep sleep, and as the red glow receded from them, he pondered the strangest dream he had ever had, the events of which were already fading from memory—some nonsense about Lord Luxeniah and his rabble of a guard in some ridiculous set of circumstances clearly not within the realm of possibility.

Shaking off the impressions and feelings that accompanied the fruitless dream, he stood and walked over to his wine stock to pour himself another drink, which he immediately took back to the chair. He then sat down to nurse himself with the nectar. He did this all the while looking down at the shaft, which was what he always gazed at and what he had been gazing at when he had fallen asleep earlier in the late afternoon.

As the drink took hold of his mind, he slipped into the familiar reverie—the dreams he could have while still awake just before falling asleep. He would think joyful and hopeful thoughts of a new era of Geradia. This time, however, he had the hopeful thought that the era would shortly be upon him. He slipped away, the nearly empty goblet falling from his hands to the floor, its red contents spilling lightly onto the rug the chair sat upon. The red stain of the wine was much darker than the red hue that had returned to Lord Levine's eyes just before they fell shut.

While Lord Luxeniah made his trip to the temple high in the mountains north and to the west of the Chromas capital city, the rest of the nobleman's guard had taken the time to rest. Alexander, Jessica, and Stephan spent the day strolling around the city's market, perusing the Chromas goods sold there. Although they had no Chromas currency or gold pieces, nor anything to barter, they were recognized as Earthen and received a free set of meals. This did not happen nearly as much as it had happened in the Geradian lands, but Stephan thought a possible explanation was that these people had rarely, if ever, encountered the Coltrous since the First Great Conflict a thousand years before. So they would not care as much about the four mythical figures come to fight in a great war. Stephan imagined that the recent encounter the dragon riders had with the easily defeated band of Coltrous only served to distance the minds of the Chromas people from the threat of the Coltrous aggression.

These thoughts were only a few of those that occupied Stephan's mind, for even when he was at rest and relaxed, his mind was still searching with the insatiable appetite for knowledge and the analysis of it.

When Stephan realized that his thoughts were, as usual, distracting him from the reality surrounding him, he looked around to see Alexander and Jessica were as they were before, perusing the wares of the merchants of the market. Stephan, sighing quietly to himself, turned his attention to a sudden upstart of commotion coming from a crowd in the market's center. The crowd was surrounding whatever was causing the spectacle. Stephan could see that through small spaces between some of the people in the crowd there was a sparring match. Two Chromas martial artists, who must have been experts to draw such a crowd, were sparring vigorously. Stephan was about to walk over to get a better look when he noticed Saul in the crowd, appearing to be watching the match. Stephan was surprised he had not seen Saul sooner considering the strangeness of his attire amid the other members of the crowd. Any interest in the match Stephan might have had departed as soon as he saw Saul and his plain private's uniform. He walked instead back to be around Alexander and Jessica, most likely to slip comfortably into another of his reveries—another never-ending stream of thoughts and analysis of those thoughts.

Saul stood in the midst of a group of Chromas Xalians, who were all silent, not speaking as they tended not to, but also not thinking thoughts openly as Lord Luxeniah and the Supreme Vizier had done so freely before. He was also aware of the presence of the other members of the emissary who were shopping at the surrounding market tables. This was only distantly in the back of his mind since he was now devoting the lion's share of his attention to the sparring match. He was engrossed by the warrior's display of technique. Although most of it was foreign to him, he did recognize some of the movements that either originated from or coincided with ancient practices from the orient. This was not a complete surprise to him since he had learned from the Grand Council that the Xalians had been in contact with what they had termed as the Earthens a thousand years before. What was unexpected was the Oriental influence; he had expected a completely medieval European culture, as he had seen in the Kingdom of Geradia.

The two Chromas fighters continued as the audience looked on intently. Their movements were quick and precise. At times, Saul could not see the attacks, and he was reminded of the infiltrator Lord Luxeniah had fought near the Earthen Archway and the incredible speed of the lord's attacks when he could only see in between attacks when it was necessary for the two fighters to pause. The techniques these two warriors used were much different, though. Other than the fact that they were engaged in hand-to-hand combat while the lord and the infiltrator had been wielding swords, many of their strikes were accompanied by waves of heat. Saul could feel the warmth from the strikes and see the light bend in the space around their fists where the heat emanated. He wondered where the heat came from and felt a great desire to learn its source.

Saul continued to watch the sparring match, and he noticed that the attacks of these fighters could also be seen much more often. Saul thought it was because these fighters were either not fighting as hard, this being an exhibition fight and not a death match, or they simply lacked the speed and skill of the infiltrator and the Geradian nobleman. He did not dwell on this point because his thoughts were directed toward a decision he would have to make that he knew, vaguely in his mind, would both please and infuriate the other members of Lord Luxeniah's guard.

When Lord Luxeniah returned the next day, after spending the night in the mountainous Chromas temple, he looked for the members of his guard, first in the dome building the Supreme Vizier had so graciously allowed his visitors, including him, to stay in while visiting his city. When he did not find them there, and finding all but Saul's belongings in their rooms, he looked throughout the city until he found Alexander, Jessica, and Stephan eating noodles in one of the market's several prominent restaurants. They seemed bored and almost depressed until they noticed the lord and greeted him with an enthusiasm suppressed to a level appropriate, according to the Carn Doctrine.

Where is Saul? he thought to them. Stephan assumed the lord was keeping some Geradian form of the Carn Doctrine in adopting the Chromas way of speaking by thought. The question, though, only produced puzzled shrugs from Stephan and Jessica, with a complete indifference from Alexander.

Wait here, the lord thought to them. *I will return shortly.*

Lord Luxeniah left the others to finish their meals and went to find somebody who knew where Saul was. He thought about the representative who had brought them to see the Supreme Vizier in the first place. He was unsure, though, where the representative was at that moment. He thought to make his way back to the dome building where the Earthens had been staying for the past few days to look for him there, but he doubted the representative had returned to the building in the last few minutes.

Where could he possibly be staying? Lord Luxeniah thought as he walked. He was about to ask some of the local Chromas concerning Saul's whereabouts when he heard among the cacophony of the city's bustling activity the distinct sounds of two people physically fighting. The lord knew, however, that it was not a true fight due to the regularity and order of the thuds of fists and palms striking clothed arms and torsos. The sounds were a promising lead to the lord for reasons he was not fully conscious of, so he went to seek out the source of the sounds of training. He walked once again past the shops that bordered the marketplace and down the space between a blacksmith's smithy and a stable until he came to an open area where he found Saul and a Chromas Xalian. It seemed as though they were training, which surprised Lord Luxeniah. He thought back to when they were all in the Royal Armory and how Saul had refused to select a weapon. Although he knew of Saul's liking for hand-to-hand combat and the martial arts, he had not anticipated Saul becoming a pupil under the tutelage of any Chromas Xalian.

The training continued for a few moments until they both stopped abruptly. Saul bowed and the master reciprocated. Saul then noticed the lord, but in keeping with the Carn Doctrine, did not speak but simply looked at him. The lord could sense Saul's thoughts, which he knew were intentionally directed to him. The thoughts brought to Lord Luxeniah another surprise and a worry that would accompany him for quite some time thereafter.

Chapter 20

Parting Paths

On top of a ledge, just removed from a path leading from the Chromas city of their recent sojourn, which wound down the Chromas Mountains and into the forests at the foot of the mountain, stood Lord Luxeniah, Alexander, Jessica, and Stephan. There they enjoyed the view of the lands below from their vantage point on the ledge. The forests below stretched out as far as they could see between them and the Kingdom of Durath. All that could be seen in the lands, other than the never-ending forest, was a small fishing village and a vast network of rivers, the source of which was the large mountain peaks, farther to the east.

The lord told them they were part of Bloodfall Mountain. He spoke of the peaks, being named after the mountains' faint red glow, visible only at night, and only visible if one looked intently for the glow. According to legend, the glow came from the presence of red crystals covering the mountain. They had seen some of them sparsely here and there in the lands surrounding the Chromas capital city. The lord had said that the Geradian philosophers surmised that the faint red glow was a result of the moon's light passing through the crystals and its cumulative effect. The Geradian priests, however, swore by the honor of the kingdom that the red glow was due to the evil of the mountain, which was why no Xalian had or ever would venture to its heights and live.

Despite the beauty and majesty of the view before them, their collective mood was not of a similar vein. Before the short lecture on the geography of the lands in view, Lord Luxeniah had told them of his finding of Saul and of his learning of Saul's decision, which all knew could not be changed. He was determined to remain in the Chromas city to receive the training only the Chromas could give. As when he had learned of this news, the evening before, Lord Luxeniah was concerned because the ancient writings told of four who would unite and lead the Kingdoms. The lord sighed. All had gone so unexpectedly well to this point.

Alexander had reacted to the news not fully surprised but with disdain, which he could all but completely hide from those around him. The thin veneer of professional and clinically dry acceptance did little to hide his true reaction. Jessica and Stephan had reacted in a similar spirit to Alexander with the same farce of professional decorum. Lord Luxeniah had told the others about the promise Saul had made to him to attempt to catch up with the others once his training was complete. Contrary to the lord's hopes, it did little to assuage their anger.

They were all ready to embark on their descent down the Chromas mountain range and into the seemingly endless forest on their way to the Durathians, the final kingdom of the Realm of Peace, when Saul appeared on a ledge farther up the mountain and closer to the city. Stephan saw him from the corner of his eye and ignored him at first, but then turned to him, not realizing the glare he was giving. From the other corner of his eye, he saw Alexander and Jessica, also looking at Saul, with their own looks of contempt. Saul continued to stand there in spite of the unspoken hostility he was receiving without speaking or signaling to them. He then reached into a pocket in the breast of his private's uniform. His hand reappeared, holding something too small and too far away for Stephan to make out. Saul then held the object up next to his head for a moment before throwing what was in his hand to Stephan. Stephan could see in the brief moment before reaching his own hand the object's irregular shape, the main bulk of the item trailed by a thick string. Stephan caught the object, curious what it was and why Saul had thrown it to him. He opened his hand to find, in horror, the object's true nature and shape as being a wooden manifestation of the symbol of hate—the symbol he had been taught from a young age was the source of all suffering in their world; the symbol, the commonality of which, previous generations had caused by their foolish and irresponsible embracing of it.

Stephan quickly glanced over to Alexander and Jessica, relieved to find the object of their attention had shifted from Saul to Lord Luxeniah before Saul had thrown the symbol to him. Although he knew he should destroy the symbol at once, or at the very least drop it right away, Stephan did not. He instead held the hateful thing with some kind of sick, morbid fascination. He then pocketed the hateful symbol, with the attached string of beads, in his own uniform's pouch, out of his, and more importantly Alexander and Jessica's, sight.

The others were descending from the ledge, and Stephan started to follow. As he was leaving, he gave Saul one last glare, this one being intentional. He had cared, moments before, if not by pure practicality, about Saul's decision to stay, but he did not, at that moment, and in many future moments, care about what would become of the former Alpha Z officer.

Over the next several days, Lord Luxeniah, Alexander, Stephan, and Jessica would make their way through the forests. Located in the midst of them were many fishing villages dotting the way to the Durathian Kingdom. Having found the walking treelings safe in the protective care of the Coultrous, and not wanting to be eaten by any of the dragons, Fit Wit and Man Maul had made their way, over the past days, in an easterly direction along the base of the Chromas Mountains. The squirrels of the Geradian forest were now less than a day away from the path the treelings were on. They could have headed north to reach them sooner, but Fit Wit insisted that if they continued east, their path would pass close by one of the most legendary places on Xaliud and they could not possibly pass up the opportunity to visit it.

As they traversed the forest, leaping from branch to branch along no beaten path, they were both elated to be on their way. While traveling east from the place where the treelings flew off on the dragons, they had time to take many breaks where they met many other animals, most of which were not what they could call kindred spirits. There were almost no creatures of rodent size and the smallest animals they had come across were unfriendly to say the least.

Before long, Fit Wit and Man Maul neared their small journey's end. It was now within their sight—the place of legend Fit Wit and Man Maul had both heard of as young squirrelings during bedtime stories—the largest and tallest tree on Xaliud. As Fit Wit looked up at it, it towered over him, its branches seeming to extend upward to the heavens. Shortly, Fit Wit was on its roots, leaping from one to another until he arrived at an area where the space between the two roots was wide and the ground there flat. He paused, his tiny squirrel heart beating even more rapidly than usual, partly from the pace they had been maintaining, and partly from the excitement of finally visiting the tree he had heard so many tales about and had spent so many sunsets of his youth trying to find on the horizon.

After stopping on the flat ground between the roots, he looked back to find Man Maul nowhere in sight. In a few moments, though, he could hear his companion's familiar wheezing and panting. Fit Wit ran back to the root he had just jumped off of and climbed onto it. From there, he could see the struggling gray squirrel.

"You're thinner than I am; aren't you in better shape?" Fit Wit jeered at his friend with mirth in his voice.

In between the wheezes and coughs, Man Maul replied, "I don't see the point of visiting this tree. Shouldn't we be following the treelings? The Elk Guardian said—"

"The Elk Guardian said," Fit Wit said, interrupting his friend, "to *watch over* the treelings. What better way to do so than from the tallest tree in the world?"

Unable to argue with Fit Wit's usually superior logic, Man Maul watched Fit Wit run up the tree's many cracks and knots. Man Maul started to climb himself, and he made it to one of the lowest knots near the roots before collapsing. Fit Wit heard the change of noises Man

Maul was making and looked back. The little red squirrel furrowed his brow in disappointment. "C'mon, Man! We're almost there!"

To this, Man Maul gave a halfhearted flip of his paw. "Okay, Fit. Just a few minutes to rest, buddy." He then brought his tail around against the root and placed his head on it to rest.

Fit Wit saw his friend's lack of progress and ran back down to Man Maul's side. He then swiped at Man Maul's ears, a way Fit Wit often used to motivate him, which his childhood friend always hated. Fit Wit said, "No! There's no time to rest. If you want to quit, then you can just die right here!" With that, Fit Wit ran back up the tree's trunk. Annoyed, and still tired, Man Maul slowly got up to his feet. He was dreading the unavoidable climb. As he trudged his way up the tree's trunk, moving as slowly has he possibly could, his eye was caught by a trail of ants who were anxiously engaged in the work of carrying food six times their size up the trunk he was now about to climb. In a moment of whimsy and curiosity, Man Maul ripped off a nearby leaf from its stem and placed it on a part of the trail of ants where there was little being carried. These ants seemed to the gray squirrel to be all too willing to carry the leaf. His curiosity piqued, Man Maul collected several more and placed them onto and around the first leaf. After placing a few more leaves onto the pile, he smoothed it out and found he had made a moving bed. With great hopes, Man Maul then carefully stepped onto it so that the ants would believe that the weight being added was food from their fellow comrades. As he sat on the moving bed of leaves, he waited to see if the ants would believe his farce. When there was no change in the movement of the line of ants, he laid back, put his paws behind his head, and relaxed. As he lay there resting, the gray squirrel had a thought, chuckling a little to himself, *These little ser-*

vants of mine are not just serving myself, but in reality, they are serving the Kingdom of Geradia, if you think about it.

Fit Wit noticed once again the absence of his friend and came back down from the higher parts of the trunk. He was ready to give Man Maul another, more powerful swipe, when he saw Man Maul lying on a bed of leaves, being carried by a line of ants.

"What are you doing?" Fit Wit demanded.

"Climbing the tallest tree in the world, just like you wanted," Man Maul said, responding with his eyes shut and paws still behind his head.

"You can't do that! It's cheating!" After there was no response to what he had just said, Fit Wit was about to climb back up the tree's trunk, but then he had an epiphany and instead grabbed a few leaves, figured out how Man Maul had made the moving bed, and placed his own bundle of leaves. He then placed them, one by one, on a portion of the line of ants where there was no food being carried, and laid down onto his own moving bed.

Man Maul, not hearing what he was expecting he would hear associated with Fit Wit climbing the tree's trunk, but instead, hearing the rustling of leaves, opened his eyes and saw his friend below him on his own bed of leaves. "Cheating?" he asked.

Fit Wit, who was now also lying down relaxed with his own paws behind his own head, simply shrugged in response. "Meh."

Up the tree they went, or rather, were carried, and after a long climb, they were at the hole in the tree where the ants would enter, it being the entrance to their colony and near the tree's top. By this point, Man Maul was asleep. He was awoken by the ant's attempts to pull the leaves that made up his bed, along with him, into the hole. Alarmed and a little annoyed, he hopped off his bed. He then woke up Fit Wit, who had also fallen asleep on their trip. Fit Wit yawned and stretched his arms while getting off his own leaf bed. The ants who had been carrying him noticed the lack of weight and flipped over the leaves in their hands. After shrugging over the lack of food, they continued onward into the hole.

Man Maul and Fit Wit finished their ascension up the trunk, which did not take long, they being so far up the tree where the trunk decreased in size and so close to its top. They quickly reached it and continued up one of the branches to get a better view of the whole valley. Fit Wit had been forcing himself not to look. Even though he was exhilarated to finally see the many lands of Xaliud from the tallest tree in the world, he did not want to spoil the experience with an inferior point of view.

When they had gone most of the way up the branch, and when the branch had shrunk to a bunch of twigs and stems unable to support their weight, they stopped and took in the highest view of the northern lands. They saw the sand dunes and waste places of the barren lands to the west. They saw the Northern Geradian forest of their births, and they could see even as far as the Geradian castle, to the southwest. They saw the Great Ravine, which stretched all the way from the southeast to the southwest, ending near the cliff where the Earthen Archway stood. They looked and beheld the Chromas mountains to the north, and they even thought they could see the capital city through the clouds. Finally, they looked to the forests to the east and southeast and saw them stretching all the way to the mountains that bordered the lands of the Durathian kingdom.

Man Maul, upon looking to the mountains north of the forest, pointed, "Look! It's Bloodfall Mountain!"

Fit Wit looked at the mountain peaks. "That's where the Behemoth lives," he said, his tone taking on a newly serious and grave tone.

"Oh, yeah! I sure hope the treelings don't venture that way.

"Naw, they won't; they're going to the Kingdom of Durathia!" Fit Wit pointed to the south and eastward, the castle barely visible on the horizon just as the Geradian castle was.

Man Maul pointed to the rivers that passed through the forests to the north and eastward. "And they'll have to cross those rivers." The rivers Man Maul was referring to originated at Bloodfall Mountain and continued southwest, the river splitting into many, covering a large part of the forest. Most of them then converged at the mouth of the Great Ravine, forming the Great Waterfall. Some of the rivers, though, went east into the lands of Durath. None, however, continued in a straight course; they wound and twisted all the way.

Fit Wit listened to what Man Maul had said as he admired the appealing shapes the many rivers made and the breaks in the forest that mimicked the shape of their paths. His gaze then came across the river villages, which dotted the forest along a line close to Bloodfall Mountain but not at the foot of the mountain range.

"I wonder if they'll pass through one of those villages," Fit Wit mused, partially to Man Maul, but mostly thinking out loud to himself. He then thought about the nature of those who inhabited those villages and worked in the rivers around them. He was dwelling on the tales of how ill-mannered and unhelpful they were when he came to a startling realization requiring immediate action. Without saying a word, Fit Wit ran down from the high branch he and Man Maul had been sitting on while overlooking the valley below.

"Where are you going?" Man Maul yelled.

Without looking back but only turning his head, Fit Wit yelled back. "C'mon; we have work to do!"

Man Maul scurried to catch up to his friend.

Fit Wit continued. "They will have to pass through the river woods!"

At first, Man Maul did not know the significance of this statement. He felt like it should be obvious to him, but then he quickly caught on to what Fit Wit was getting at. "I know just the guy for the job!"

Chapter 21

Bloodfall Mountain

Saul stood on a rock at the top of a hill just outside the Chromas capital city and gazed at Bloodfall Mountain in the distance. This was his favorite place to rest after a long day of training with the Chromas martial arts masters. While he stood there, he viewed the steep cliffs of Bloodfall Mountain range, watching as the sun dipped behind the horizon. The mountain peaks would glow red in patterns of falling streaks.

He pondered a decision he had to make that night. The next day he would leave the Chromas, and he needed to choose between catching up to Lord Luxeniah and the others or continuing his training on the cliffs and peaks of Bloodfall Mountain. The more responsible choice was obviously the former, but when he looked upon the mountain range, it seemed to call to him.

The sun, now lower in the sky, drew close to the horizon. Saul imagined himself climbing higher and higher up on the mountain's side, continuing his training in solitude. He wondered if he was strong enough to withstand the mountain's harsh environment.

He reflected primarily on the previous days of his travels as well as the lessons and techniques he had learned in the Chromas capital city while among the Chromas peoples. His training had been challenging, during which he pushed his body, mind, and whatever else was part of his being to unknown limits. Throughout the trials and the pain, his master's thoughts lived in his mind, and they imparted to him the techniques he would have to learn in order to fight in the way he had seen the Chromas fighters sparring on the day he had decided to stay behind. He had been taught the techniques of fighting and the ways of thinking that enabled him to manipulate the heat around and inside him. He remembered the moment he had first done it—how his understanding of fire had been radically altered in that moment as he became part of the fire instead of the traditional view he had always clung to—a view of fire as being dangerous and something to avoid or to handle with great apprehension and care.

How have I been able to do this? he thought to his master on the third day of training. *How have I been able to reach this level in so little time?*

Many times the master would remain silent when Saul would think to him a question, but in this moment, the instructor responded, *You have been training for a far greater amount of time than the mere days you have been in this city. I have looked into your mind as far as you have let me, and I have seen your world. When one trains there, one is only mindful of what actions he has seen himself take in the pursuit of strength. What your kind fails to see is what came before and what will come later. In these past days, you have not grown so much stronger than you have before but have awakened a fire that was already there, deep within.*

Saul did not understand all of his master's thoughts, but he continued with the training, hoping the words would make sense in time. At first, the heat was used as a way to expand air, adding force and power to his blows. Eventually, however, the heat he was able to produce grew until he could cause objects to be engulfed in the flame from his being. When this practice was mastered, he ascended to higher levels of skill and made small flames that were able to exist without an object to engulf, with the potential to strike a target with explosive force. He had obliterated many training dummies and, on one occasion, even a grocer's cart in the process of its mastery.

Each time Saul had created fire, the thought that he could do it and the power to do so had come to him in a moment of great effort and laborious work. It seemed to him when he would have this thought that both it and power came to him independent of his own actions—that it was being gifted to him. It certainly never, at any moment, was power he could perform on a whim or at will, even with a great deal of effort. When the power was within him, though, he would then have full control of the fire from within. When he had come to this realization, his master thought to him notions that he could not put into words, but were similar to thoughts he had had before when he had failed to achieve a desired outcome but had accomplished something else instead. It was a strange thought, but he had noticed the same event occur in the lives of others. He noticed it very often in those he was training. Sadly, their frustration at not achieving the desired aim was hardly ever even tempered by this realization Saul would share with them about their unintended accomplishment.

Saul not only saw this happen in the lives of his pupils, but in the lives of many others, even his superiors back on Earth, when they would attempt to inspire their subordinates. They almost always failed in the attempt. Saul remembered other times when the very

same officers would discipline a subordinate with the aim of correcting undesirable traits, only to fail and flame the trait's intensity.

These vivid memories helped him understand more fully the
undefinable and vague notions his master had thought to him. They
taught him that a man could never truly attain any sought-after
prize, and that any prize worth having was gifted in the course of
doing another action. Saul took this to mean more specifically that
the randomness of the ability he gained to manipulate heat and
create fire only seemed random, and that the ability was gifted to
him. Also, if he continued on the right course of action, additional
abilities could be gifted to him.

This reverie, although joyful to Saul, was something he knew
was merely a series of assumptions, which may or may not have
been true. Outside the realm of his own experiences, he had no way
of verifying its accuracy, as he was trained to do many times in his
life. In order to find out whether it was, he would have to act on it
and live according to the ideas, and then it would become obvious,
over time, whether these were lies he was telling himself or whether
they were indeed true.

After his master had taught him these principles, Saul had continued training, and in time, it became apparent that he had reached
the summit of his abilities, or at least the summit in terms of what
new ability that training environment could help him achieve. When
Saul had reached the apex, both in manifesting fire and in physical
technique—heights he thought he would never reach—he thought
his master would be proud and pleased with the progress. He had
hoped his master would hail him as being the foretold Earthen hero,
one of the four who would lead the Alliance of the Realm of Peace
and the Earthen forces against the hordes of Coltrous threatening

both worlds. He even had a moment when he imagined the crowds of Chromas people thinking thoughts of praise and adulation to him.

Looking back, he felt foolish, as reality did not exist in accordance with his lofty and vain imaginations. His master, upon witnessing Saul's first manifestation of a projectile of fire, reacted not with pride but, strangely, with apprehension. He had learned of his master's feeling not through direct thought but by sensing an impression his master had involuntarily shown, although he more than likely was not trying to hide it. Although he learned of the master's attitude, he did not know why the Chromas teacher had this fear or what he could possibly be afraid of. Saul never did ask or learn of its true nature.

As he now stood, watching the red streaks of Bloodfall Mountain grow in brightness, Saul recalled the sense of dread he got from his master's thoughts, and along with them, random images of the skeletal remains. At the time, he did not understand the meaning of the images, but as he now looked upon the foreboding spires high in the distant mountains, he thought they could be the remains of those before him who had attempted to ascend the peaks of Bloodfall Mountain only to perish in the effort. Along with these images, Saul got the vague sense that those who once were, were nothing now and were far less than nothing, but also forgotten. Within the torrent of images and impressions within Saul's mind was the thought many of the Chromas held as legend. The thought was of one who did survive, who did not return but dwelled near the mountain's highest peak. Over time, he became warped, both in mind and body, into some kind of beast, and on some quiet nights if one listened intently, he could hear the bestial cries of whatever was living there echo in the distance.

Saul had seen many strange and fantastic things since passing through the Earthen Archway and encountering the Coltrous infiltrator, such as the incredible speed at which the lord and the infiltrator had fought. It was just one of a myriad of happenings he had witnessed that he could not even begin to explain. In spite of all of them, he still found the tale of the lone, mutated Chromas survivor somehow living alone on the highest mountain peak too much to believe. He also had the nagging notion that the images of the skeletal remains were merely the manifestation of irrational fears of an overprotective master. Surely they were not images from actual memory but were from his master's imagination, for it was impossible that his master could have possibly seen the place where all who attempted to climb the mountain died. He resolved, however, to be on his guard if he chose to climb the peaks for whatever might be up there—man, beast, or anything else. He found the allure of furthering his strength and skills by training in such a hostile environment almost too much to resist.

A strong gust of wind whipped Saul's now unkempt, long hair, giving pause to his thoughts. Before Xaliud, he had kept up a somewhat comely appearance. He did not know why he felt a need to do so. Saul thought that perhaps it was the presence of officers, with their stifling standards. Whatever the case, since they had left Earth, he had not felt the need to cut his hair and let it grow. The knife he could have used to cut his hair remained unused in a hidden pocket. The Chromas did not seem to mind the hair; it was common for their warriors to keep their hair wild.

In addition to the change in appearance the growth of his hair had brought, he also wore the traditional Chromas clothes of a warrior. The Chromas martial artists often wore it with the symbol of their master stained on the back portion. The clothes were black with red lettering, a drastic improvement from the dull, bluish color of his private's uniform. He had refused any change in attire at Geradia, and he did not know why he had the desire to refuse. He found it strange and coincidental that he should find the gi he now wore such a welcomed change in attire, as if he had been pre-destined to refuse the change in Geradia, there being a better change in store for him.

When this path of thought reached its end, Saul felt a strong need to leave the Chromas capital city and head toward Bloodfall Mountain. Although he thought the mountains to be the ultimate training ground, he felt the shame he often experienced when he was doing something he was conditioned to think was a waste of time. He had experienced the sensation again and again while train-ing over the past days, or even when he would stop to take in the views before him. The shame he felt was only an unusually high peak of what was already a high plateau of the experience. He was supposed to be with the others, to aid in the uniting of the Northern Kingdoms and the defeat of the growing Coltrous horde and its ap-parent threat to both Earth and Xaliud. In spite of this resistance, he knew somehow, for a reason he was not consciously aware of, that he would soon be on the right path. Whichever one he chose, he would find a way to rejoin the others and finish the duties for which Lord Luxeniah had originally enlisted him.

At times during the past days, he would try to conceive of a way he could possibly catch up to the others after his training. He knew the Chromas would not leave the safety and seclusion of their moun-tainous home, and he knew nobody lived in the peaks of Bloodfall Mountain who could possibly provide any sort of transportation.

He always dispelled these thoughts as soon as he had them. If nothing else, he could catch up to the others by traveling both day and night, surviving on less sleep than the standard amount the captain would surely be enforcing as per the regulations of the UWI initiative. Lord Luxeniah had also thought to him the general location of the Durathian kingdom, and he was sure he could find it if he persisted in traveling in its direction. If this did not work, he knew he could travel directly to the Geradian Kingdom and meet the others there. Even with these thoughts of comfort, it was the fear-eliminating thought techniques his master in the capital city had taught him that dispelled most of his gnawing doubt. He had always had an unusual resistance against the emotion, avoiding the use of it as a means of motivation, but the techniques he learned were much more effective, serving to solidify his original resolve.

Saul could now see the fullness of Bloodfall Mountain's glow. The light was so faint that most would not be able to see the red streaks, but his eyes could. To him, the peaks lit up the red in the obscure pattern of falling streams. His master had once thought to him the origins of the red glow—it came from the moonlight passing through the red kind of crystal, the same kind as those they had seen before in other parts of Xaliud. There was a faint but common thought that the red crystal had an aura about it, and that those within its presence would be affected by it. It was widely held that those who ascended the mountain and never returned were driven to madness and eventually death, either starving or dying in some other gruesome way.

Saul's thoughts and memories vanished as the reality of the choice he would soon have to make hit him. He retrieved from inside his gi the scroll given to him by the Xalian in the cathedral.

He read it for a while, not understanding much of the archaic Xalian use of the English language, but feeling anyway that he was gaining something important from it. The thought then came to Saul to go to sleep. He would trust that the decision of whether to climb the mountain or head toward the Kingdom of Durathia would come to him by morning.

Saul returned to his quarters and laid down to sleep for the night. Before slipping into a slumber, a distant, bestial cry sounded from somewhere near the mountain's summit and rang into the dark abyss of the night.

Chapter 22

The Workers of Beaverton

Fit Wit and Man Maul had been traveling all the previous night and day. They were both becoming exhausted, which, by both red and gray squirrelish standards, made them quite the sloths. Man Maul, the one most often accused of this, was feeling the greatest degree of exhaustion, but he was leading the way. He felt he had to lead since it was his acquaintance they were about to visit, and he was tired of yelping out directions between bouts of gasping for air.

"Who is this guy you keep saying we need to meet?" Fit Wit asked in between his own gasps for air.

"He's an old friend. You've met him. He used to build dams in the Northern Geradian forests," Man Maul replied.

"Gunther the beaver?" Fit Wit asked incredulously. "When did he move?"

"Recently, a few moons ago; he said there was more work in the Riverwoods, but I suspect it had more to do with the selection of ladies."

"Oh, yeah, he always said he wanted better tail!" At this, Fit Wit laughed uproariously.

"Fit Wit!" Man Maul said, chastising his friend. "Kiss your mother with that mouth?"

"What? Tell me you don't remember him complaining about his lady friend's tail, how the fur on it was all ratty?"

Man Maul fell silent for a moment and then said, "Okay, yes, that's exactly what he said. Notwithstanding his adventurous attitude in the ways of romance, he's got to be the best dam builder around!"

"Man Maul! *You* watch *your* mouth."

"I'm talking about the river dams beavers construct! We'll need him to build some so that the treelings can cross."

"Oh…why don't we just ask Gunther and his workers to build bridges; they'll take less time."

"It would, but remember what the Elk Guardian said; we are to stay out of their range of attention. They cannot know we are helping them. Felled trees conveniently placed for their convenience would be too obvious. It has to look natural."

"Wow! You know Man Maul, you actually came up with a good idea for once!"

"Shut up, piss ant!"

"Piss ant? That doesn't even make sense. You're weird!"

"*You're* weird!"

"*You're* weird!"

"*You're* weird!"

"*You're* weird!"

And so, the bickering between Fit Wit and Man Maul continued in this fashion for many farsees, the common way of measuring distance among all the animal kingdoms, until, at last, the two squirrels' conversation was interrupted.

"I can't believe you! I don't know why I even hang out with you!" Fit Wit exclaimed, retorting Man Maul's last insult.

"Because, if I didn't you'd…." Man Maul stopped short, in mid-insult, when his gaze stumbled upon a group of beavers engaged in some organized effort along the bank of a river. He and Fit Wit made their way through the beaver workers, who seemed not even to notice the small rodents weaving in and out of the traffic of workers, who were busy carrying stacks of sticks and branches to a pile next to the river. There was an area clearly designated as the place where the wood, the squirrels assumed, to build this particular dam would be stacked.

They were heading toward the center of the worker's activities where a larger, sturdier looking beaver, who seemed to be in charge, was barking orders to the workers. His commands were somewhat inaudible until they got close enough to where the string of his words were not drowned out by the noise of the workers surrounding them. A strip of bark hung from his mouth, and when he would shout at the workers, it rapidly flipped up and down.

"Ey! Make sure to separate the twigs and da branches!" the head beaver yelled to one particular worker beaver, whose response was too quiet to be heard by Fit Wit and Man Maul. The head beaver replied, "Just use ya best judgement...if ya don't 'ave to chomp it, it's a twig!" The head beaver looked as if he was going to further the point, pointing at the small pile of twigs and branches the worker inquired about aggressively, when he saw the squirrels approaching him.

"Man Maul!" The large beaver took a couple of steps toward his squirrelish friend. "What brings you and ya furry little frien' here to dese humble operations?"

"Furry? Little? *Who*? We've met before!" Fit Wit shot back. Man Maul gave him a look and then turned back to Gunther.

"Gunther, my distinguished and successful friend, how the heck are you?" Man Maul asked, seeming to Fit Wit to be gushing in a toady manner as much as possible.

"Eh, can't complain. The operation is going decently, as decently as one operation can go," Gunther said before he raised his voice so that as many of the workers as possible would overheard him, "considerin' da help!"

Man Maul laughed too hard at this, and Fit Wit joined in, deeming the sucking up to be necessary.

Gunther seemed to notice the lack of sincerity in the jovial farce and looked at the two squirrels stone-faced, stopping them. He then asked, "You never answered 'da question, Curly." "Curly" was a nickname Gunther had given Man Maul years before on account of the curly locks on his tail, an obvious reference to his habit of curling the fur on his tail when he was very nervous.

"Well," Man Maul hesitated, not knowing precisely how to word his request, "See…the thing is…."

Fit Wit fidgeted and struggled for as long as he could bear before blurting out, "We need you to build some bridges for us in the form of dams!"

The head beaver looked taken aback by the sudden outburst and turned to Man Maul with a look that seemed to say, *Is this so?* Before he could answer, a worker interrupted.

"Hey, boss! Hey, boss!" the worker shouted.

"Hold on," Gunther said to the two squirrels before him. He turned to the interrupting worker beaver. "Ya? Wat da ya want?" Gunther shouted back.

"Can I get some bark strips?" By now the worker was close enough that he no longer needed to shout.

"Strips?" Gunther turned to a pile of various kinds and amounts of wood near his feet. "Eh, we don't got any."

"I want more strips."

"Ya, ya, well, I already said we don' 'ave any stripes, so wat do you wan' instead?"

"Ginger chunks. I wan' ginger chunks."

"All right, hold on; I might have some chunks." Gunther checked a different pile a little farther away. "Ya, we got chunks, but we only got hazel!"

"Damn it!"

"I mean, they're good an' aalll. But if we had like, like cinnamon chip or sumptin'."

The worker turned, and as he was walking away, shaking his paws in the air, he said, "Ohhh, don' even get me started. Don't even get me started!"

When the worker was gone, Gunther turned back to Man Maul. "You'll 'ave to escuse my friend, 'is manna's aint wat you'd call," Gunther held up his paws and touched the lowest claw to a higher one in a display of daintiness, "refined. Now, what was your liddle friend so consumed wit as to tawk out a turn?" Fit Wit gave another scowl at this second mention of his stature.

"What my friend was trying to say," Man Maul said, more clearly and confidently than before, "was that we humbly request your help."

"Oh, yeah! Sometin' to do wit a bridge or whateva."

"Exactly!" Man Maul said, excitedly pointing his pointer claw at the river. "See, we have friends who cannot cross those many rivers without great difficulty and danger!"

The beaver leader looked in the general direction of the rivers with a look of mild confusion as he considered the project. "Wat, are they lame or sometin'?"

"Sort of, see they are…." Man Maul hesitated, gulping before he started again. "They are treelings."

The worker beavers within earshot of Man Maul immediately stopped and stared at Man Maul, not believing the squirrel would bring up the topic.

"Treelings!" Gunther shouted, not as loudly or angrily as Man Maul was anticipating. "Why would I help any of der kind? I've seen 'em huntin' my kin!"

"Oh, no, no, not these treelings!" Man Maul exclaimed, not quite sure whether what he was saying was completely truthful or not. "These treelings are on a quest sanctioned by the Elk Guardian himself! In fact, we've been charged with our own quest to help them in any humble way we can."

Just as he finished saying this, the sounds of a sudden commotion coming from the general direction of the river caught Man Maul's attention. He looked toward the sound to see a couple of beaver workers dragging a fish from the river onto the bank where it thrashed around violently. The fish was large, so much so that it took two more workers to subdue and kill it. Gunther laughed heartily. "Dos treelings wud surely need our help. They wouldn't survive long against dos tings! Tell me more about dis eh…quest. You have intrigued me."

"Oh, it's the most important quest a treeling, or any being, could possibly be on! They are on a quest to save the world!"

"Two worlds, in fact," Fit Wit interjected.

Gunther looked a little disappointed and waved his paw dismissively. "Aw, wat do I care fa' the world, or even fa' two worlds?"

Man Maul thought for a moment but fell silent, unable to think of any way to convince the head beaver. Just as he was about to give up, Fit Wit said, motioning to their surroundings, "You know, if the treelings fail in their quest, this whole place will be crawling with them!" This seemed to catch Gunther's attention, which had been directed at a strip of bark he had been chewing on that was now in his hand. His head turned to Fit Wit sharply, his eyes wide with a deep concern.

"Wat? Crawling… dis place…*treelings*!"

"Yes." Fit Wit was now wiggling his claws at Gunther, his own eyes wide, like he was telling a child a ghost story. "No beaver would survive."

A few of the workers around them stopped what they were doing and gaped at Fit Wit. Their boss laughed heartily and slapped Fit Wit on the back, almost knocking him over, and he spoke loud enough that his workers would overhear. "Oh, my friend, ya sure do know how da crack quite da joke!" The workers, seemingly satisfied by this, went back to work, most keeping one eye on the strange squirrel as they did.

Gunther looked at Fit Wit, eyes now narrow in a look of uncertainty of what he was looking at. His gaze then turned to Man Maul with the same unsure look. He finally turned to the half-completed dam, the beaver's current project. The head beaver performed some calculations to himself, touching his lower claw with his higher ones, one at a time.

"I guess I can leave some of my guys here to finish up and expand to some other rivers. We'll 'ave to build dem at a minimal scale." As he said this, he extended only his pointer and lower claws and brought them closer together.

In response to this, Man Maul excitedly exclaimed, "That's great! Can you start right away?"

"Yeah, yeah," Gunther said, still giving Man Maul a suspicious look, as if he were not quite convinced of the truthfulness of what he was told about the possible future of Beaverton. "Don't worry 'bout it; I'll start right away. But der's one point you've failed to sufficiently clarify: where are we to build dese all-important bridgedams?"

"That should be easy to figure out." Man Maul could see a scowl about to form on the beaver's face and quickly added, "F-For someone of your extraordinary talents that is." The brewing storm receded. "All that is needed is a way for the treelings to travel quickly from Riverton to the Kingdom of Durathia."

"The Kingdom of Dur…"

"Durathia," Man Maul finished for his beaver friend. "It's southeast from here." Man Maul turned to look and pointed in the direction that seemed to be correct, according to what he witnessed from atop the largest tree in Xaliud. "In that direction."

Gunther's demeanor shifted from one of doubt and suspicion to one of resolution. He turned to his workers. "All right, listen up!" Every beaver worker stopped what he was doing and looked at his boss. "Anyone carrying something, finish up wat ya doin' an' follow me! The rest of yas, finish da bare bones of dis dam an' and den proceed to follow us!" When the workers carrying wood did finish their individual tasks, the head beaver walked across the skeletal, half-finished dam with a long line of beavers following him. Man Maul gave Fit Wit a look that seemed to say, *I didn't mean right now.* The beavers were heading north toward the area east of Riverton.

Fit Wit and Man Maul both assumed it was where they would be starting, which pleased the squirrels since it was at least generally in the right direction.

The rest of the beavers continued the construction of the dam with a new beaver barking orders with his own strip of bark hanging from his mouth, flipping up and down as he shouted.

Being forgotten and ignored, Man Maul and Fit Wit sheepishly excused themselves, making their own way across the half-completed dam-bridge to catch up with Gunther and his troop of beaver workers. After all, how could such a massive undertaking as these beavers were about to undertake possibly be completed without the guiding eyes of individuals as distinguished as Fit Wit and Man Maul?

Chapter 23

Death Mountain

Saul collapsed onto the only part of the ledge not covered in jagged, piercing rocks and heaved heavy breaths. He rolled over, still heaving, and lay there, enduring the burning pain in his lungs and limbs. He knew, from the kind of agony the previous days had brought, that lying down would provide no relief from pain or exhaustion. He chose, however, to at least try to meditate with the vain hope of dislocating himself from the anguish. He tried to dwell on whatever progress he might have made during the past days. When he had started to climb Bloodfall Mountain, Saul had experienced all of the normal difficulties generally associated with climbing a rock face. Finding a place to sleep, finding food, or even finding a way up some of the particularly high and steep cliffs were only the initial obstacles.

As he ascended the mountain's treacherous side, the environment became increasingly hazardous. The hostility the mountain inflicted on him was mostly non-physical in nature, but there was something about its spires, ledges, and peaks that both drained and antagonized his soul. Even the sun seemed different; while it used to merely peek out from in between the cracks of the cliffs and come out to beat him down with its heat, it now was an enemy, spying on him, waiting for the right moment to oppress him with its heat.

Physical threats from the mountain would become his reality when Saul would encounter a mountain goat or a rat, which were always hostile and suspicious since they would sneer from a distance.

When Saul climbed farther up the mountain, he left these physical threats behind as the presence of the creatures dwindled until they became nonexistent. Saul assumed it was due to whatever was causing him the anguish, which would have affected the creatures as well if it did not ward them off completely. He thought he might have entered the domain of the mountain his master thought to him as being *The place where nothing can grow and all who enter die the worst death.*

Night brought with it its own terrors because sleeping only produced the specter of nightmares, and when Saul would awake in the middle of them, there was the fear only night can bring. Although the creatures had dwindled in number so that Saul had no reason to fear anything of the night, the apprehension of being mauled to death by some rabid beast never completely left him. It was fear that brought a surety that around the bend or just above him there would be a creature, unimaginably savage and fierce, that would surely kill him in an instant and without warning.

The foregone days had become fraught with a burning hate for all things within Saul's heart, along with the many bitter memories that plagued his mind so intensely he could not concentrate on his training or anything else. In this state, he was becoming more and more fixated on past offenses inflicted upon him. Ancient memories surfaced from what before had seemed like a distant foregone age; they became fresh in his mind as if they had all just occurred just then and at once. They were thoughts and fears held as forgotten, but they were, in reality, festering deep within the dark recesses of his mind. The normal stream of one of them occupying his mind at a time gave way to a torrent of thoughts and impressions. Normally to Saul, pain, anguish, and humiliation could be something to become accustomed to so that one could barely feel it or at least bear it in a hopeful resolve. Now, though, on this mountain, he was being crushed into a corner, and the only thing he could do to save his own life was to lift the imaginary crushing weight, weighing a thousand times what even his exceptional strength could lift.

In spite of this and other calamities, Saul pushed on, climbing to new heights and training under new, difficult conditions. He was not sure, but he could swear the force pulling downward on him was real. There were times when he was certain his skin and flesh were being stripped off of his bones. The intensity of these pains and the anguish continued to mount, pushing and pulling him down as if multiple beings had gotten a hold on him, working for his demise. There were many times when he could barely move. During these bouts, he would almost pass out, but the relief would be denied him.

I'm being tortured by this mountain. It was the first thought, emerging from the torrent of unwanted memories and feelings, he could call his own in however many hours or days since his last. He had the thought while performing one-armed pushups. While on the mountain, he could not do very many, but it did not matter what part of his training regimen he could do; the haunting, un-relenting specters of the mind came, and it seemed as though no amount of training, meditation, or even suppression of thought would bring any measure of relief. It was as though he was barely staving off an onslaught of enemies, about to be overwhelmed when his strength was sure to break.

Saul finished his training session and started to climb to the next ledge. From where he was, he could not see it, but he hoped it would come and that he would not collapse from exhaustion before reaching it. After a long climb and after the pain of jagged rock all but piercing the skin of his palms, the ledge came into view. He almost fell several times before reaching it and was sure he would not have the strength to pull himself over the ledge's edge, but in a miraculous surge of power to pull his body up the cliff, he grasped the cliff's edge and began to lift himself up. As he did, Saul thought of the higher reaches of the mountain's peaks, heights he surely must be reaching soon, considering how long he had been scaling the mountain's cliff.

Filled with some semblance of hope, Saul at last brought himself over the ledge and rolled onto it. He lay there on his back, eyes closed, the hope for a respite not being realized. In fact, if there was any change at all in his state of mind and body, it was the increase of the mountain's hostility toward him. He opened his eyes, turned over, and tried to rise to his feet, but collapsed instead to his hands and knees. As he stared at the ground beneath him, he realized something he knew he should have realized moments before. His vision was growing dark and smaller with a black shroud closing in, consuming the field of it from the outside inward. He could feel a tighter grip of the mountain's downward pull on him, and the onslaught of thoughts assaulting him gave way to a sickening morass growing deep in his chest. It was as though the hordes invading his mind had stopped to triumphantly watch him sink.

With great effort, Saul forced his head up. Although the darkness shrouding his vision had made progress closing inward, there was still a portion of it where he could see clearly. As he directed it toward the area around him, all he could see was death and decay. The bones of those who had come before him were strewn all around him. The skeletons were contorted and twisted in a struggle before their individual deaths.

One lone, remaining thought occupied Saul's mind; the thought he was certain would be his last. It was the memory of his master's warning, thought to him before he left the Chromas capital. The thought was one of this very event. His master warned him of a specific point at which those who attempted to scale Bloodfall Mountain would fail and be defeated by its power.

I am going to die, Saul thought to himself, the mountain giving him one more moment of clarity before death. In an instant of desperate hope, he looked up and tried to stare at the sun, whose light now was barely visible. And then, for a moment, the darkness was gone. In its place was nothing but the brightest and purest white light he had ever seen. After a moment passed, he could see an outline of a shadowy figure, the intense brightness of the light behind him preventing any detail other than the contours of his outline to be seen. Saul could tell, though, from the shape of the outline, that the man was robed, tall, and had long hair, much of it resting on his shoulders. Saul felt some reprieve from the misery he had long been experiencing by the man's presence, which seemed to be driving away a portion of the darkness and pain.

Saul gazed longingly at the shadowy stranger, unsure if he was looking back at him. After a long moment and in desperate hope, Saul cried out to the figure, "Please, help me!" As soon as he had uttered these words, the intense light and the man vanished. Saul was alone, on the ledge, with the skeletal remains still strewn about him. Although it was the same ledge as before, he could see it clearly, with no more darkness clouding his vision and no more misery burdening his soul. There was still the downward pull of the mountain, but it was familiar, and he felt he was accustomed to it. It was only a minor challenge to overcome now, and he found that his mind was free from the former harassing and invading thoughts. He stood up, feeling light from the sudden relief. He looked at where the ledge ended at the base of another cliff and experienced the urge to continue his ascension up Bloodfall Mountain. The thought seemed absurd to him since he had almost died, but there was the familiar pull inside him. It had been propelling him since he had first met his master, before his deciding to stay in the Chromas capital city, and it was now there and stronger than ever before. He *had* to climb.

Saul placed one foot on a rock at the cliff's base, the other into a small crevice, and started up the mountain once again. As he did so, he resolved then to not only exceed those who had come before him, but to reach the mountain's top and to exceed, in skill, any who would ever climb the mountain.

Chapter 24

The Riverwoods

Stephan stood on the bank of a river within the Riverwoods. It was the first they had come across since entering the endless forest. Its current was strong and its appearance formidable. Also on the bank stood Alexander, Lord Luxeniah, and Jessica. They had been traveling to the Kingdom of Durathia every day, for most of the day, for a period long enough to make the lord give signs of nervousness. Although the lord did not make the cause of his worry known to the others, Stephan assumed the signs were most likely due to concerns of whether they would make it back to the Kingdom of Geradia before the beginning of the Second Great Conflict. Until now, the way had been trouble free, allowing them to travel swiftly and with little inconvenience or impediment to their progress. This had been the case until they had reached the wide rivers and dense foliage of the Riverwood forests whose thick branches and bunches of trees covered any previously cleared path.

When they first reached Riverton, they found themselves in a village of fishermen. At the sight of the settlement through the trees, they all experienced mutual relief, anticipating some kind of warm reception, food, and lodgings, with even some guidance through the difficult terrain. Upon arriving, however, they were only greeted with lukewarm company as they dined at the local inn. They were then shown to their uncomfortable straw beds within their cramped quarters. When they had attempted to inquire as to alternate paths or the possibility of hiring a guide to aid them in braving the seem-ingly endless forest that lay before them, the innkeeper shrugged in cold indifference. Early the next morning, they awoke, feeling rested merely in body, and promptly left, eager as a group to leave the vil-lage as soon as was possible to continue on their way.

Upon their departure from the Chromas capital city, they had taken the shortest and most direct path in the direction of the mountains Lord Luxeniah knew bordered the area of the Kingdom of Durathia to the south and east. He had seen no advantage in trav-eling any other way because the vast forest seemed uniformly dense. And now they were presented with another problem, a problem that completely stopped their progress. The river before them would not be the insurmountable obstacle it was now if it were not for its incredible current as well as something Stephan had witnessed when he had seen a fisherman, just outside the Riverwoods village, take incredible precautions to avoid any contact with the water when boarding his boat. Stephan informed the others of what he had seen and the conclusion he had come to: something dangerous was in the water so they should not step in any part of it.

In order to find out what dangers dwelled below the river's sur-face, Alexander had his broadsword drawn with the pommel on the ground and the blade pointing up. He held the blade carefully between his index finger and thumb as he placed a chunk of deer meat on the blade's end. Alexander then gripped the sword by its handle and held out the sword into the water with the meat held securely on its end. Within a few seconds, the sword's submerged end jerked in violent bursts, as if something powerful was trying with all its might to rip the meat from the blade. Alexander gripped the sword more tightly with both hands and brought the blade back out of the water to reveal two fish furiously gnawing on the meat. As he lifted the blade, one of the fish fell back into the water. Alexander then brought his sword's tip closer to him in order to get a closer look at the rabid aquatic creature. When he had brought the fish close enough to his face, the fish jerked its body in such a way that when it released its hold on the meat, its body would be flung toward Alexander. Luckily, the captain had the sense not to bring his face too close to the fish on the meat, and it fell impotently to the ground, where it violently flopped around. Sneering in disgust, Alexander used the broadsword to flip the fish back into the water.

"Well, that explains it," Alexander said.

"I do not believe the royal relic of a foregone age should be used for the lowly task of fishing," Lord Luxeniah said, himself sneering, but for a different reason.

After a moment of silence, Alexander turned to Stephan. "All right, Lieutenant, what is the solution?"

Stephan started to run a few scenarios through his mind, but then he decided to verbalize them since he understood all too well the captain's preference in knowing the foundation of his conclusions.

"The most obvious and efficient solution," Stephan began, "is to use a boat to cross the river, but it is not an option because the deni-zens of this area were not willing to provide us with one. We could attempt to make the craft, but without the requisite tools, it would be impossible. A boat would also be difficult, if not impossible, to carry through the dense forest from river to river. Traveling by boat down any one river would take us too far south and would also present its own unique problem since the threat of capsizing would a fatal one. The danger lurking in the water also prevents us from simply wading across it. Besides the current, the fish would surely kill us. I suggest we backtrack to Riverton, procure an ax, return, and chop down some tree in order to construct a simple bridge."

In response to Stephan's analysis, the captain looked away, clearly troubled. "That would take too long, Lieutenant," he said, as if the current predicament were Stephan's fault.

"There is no other solution, sir," Stephan said, remaining composed. He thought for a moment and then an idea came to him. "I suggest we walk farther downstream. The river might be thinner or there might be a rock we could use to cross."

Alexander smirked, appearing dissatisfied, but instead of responding, turned to Lord Luxeniah. "What are your thoughts, sire?"

The lord seemed pleased by the deference. "I think it is an excellent idea."

With that, they started down the river's bank, to follow Stephan's alternate plan to look for an easier way to cross the perilous river.

Further upstream, Fit Wit and Man Maul stood on the higher branch of a tree. The branch hung over the river, and the base of the tree was on the bank opposite the party of treelings. They had been watching and listening since the treelings had approached the river's edge. Underneath them, the dam they had helped build sat there. They feared it would not be used by its intended users because those they intended to help were walking away from it, unaware of its presence. When they looked at each other, they both saw a confused expression on the other's face. Man Maul turned back toward the treelings and opened his mouth. Fit Wit knew the meaning of this, and reacting quickly, covered his friend's mouth with his paw.

"Remember what the Guardian Elk said," Fit Wit hissed. "We can help them, but they cannot know of our presence! Your singing worked in the cave because we were hidden."

"Oh...right," Man Maul said sheepishly, looking down in embarrassment. It was then that he noticed, on the lower branches, a flock of blue jays perched, grooming themselves. Man Maul acted at once, jumping down to the branch below and continuing down from branch to branch until he reached the lowest one, which was populated by the birds. When he landed among them, they looked at him with disinterested glances before resuming their grooming exercises.

"Man! What are you doing?" Fit Wit whispered to his friend as loudly as he could without disturbing the elegant creatures in their moment of delicate caring for their soft, feathery pelts.

Man Maul merely gave Fit Wit a devilish smile and turned back to the birds who were still pecking at their feathers. He found the one who appeared to have the largest wingspan, stood behind the creature, and brought his arm back and up just before bringing his arm back down and slapping the bird at the base of its plumage. The bird squawked in a panic, and with the rest of the blue jays, it took off flying away from the branches in a cloud of flapping wings and fluttering feathers.

Horrified, Fit Wit jumped down to the branch on which Man Maul stood, prepared to give a more thorough chastisement. He feared the treelings might see them since they had been visible only moments before, and their attention would surely now be directed toward them. But as Fit Wit was pulling back his paw to smack Man Maul, he saw that the cloud of flapping blue wings was shrouding them from the sight of the treeling. He instead grabbed a tuff of the fur on Man Maul's arm and then ran back toward the trunk of the tree and the seclusion of the leaves.

As they peered through the foliage, they witnessed the treeling with the long, yellow hair look back at the sudden sound of the birds' flight. The treeling then noticed the dam-bridge farther up the river, somewhat in the distance and through willow branches hanging over the river. Once she got the attention of the other treelings, they walked toward Fit Wit and Man Maul. The squirrels had to stifle their squeaks of delight as they watched the lumbering creatures, who looked strangely small from their high vantage point, walk over to the dam-bridge. After some discussion, the slender treeling placed one foot and some of his weight on the structure as if to get a sense of its strength. Then the treelings crossed the river, each of them slow and careful, being fully aware of the mortal danger posed by the river's deadly inhabitants. When they all reached the opposite bank, the treeling dressed in the green and blue robe said something; he seemed to be marveling at the dam-bridge's fortuitous placement. When they found the next bridge, placed so that it would easily, but not too conveniently, be seen when one finished crossing the first, there was another expression of surprise, this time by the treeling with the large sword, over the sight of the next bridge and the clear path through what was once dense foliage. Fit Wit and Man Maul followed quietly behind, joyfully witnessing the fruition of their labors with the beavers in building the dam-bridges.

Traveling through the Riverwood forests was much easier and swifter now that there was a clear path for Stephan and his group to follow since the beavers who made the bridges across the many rivers also cleared trees from some of the denser parts of the forest between each of the dams. In time, the emissary came across a tall hill that Lord Luxeniah climbed to get a better view of the remainder of their journey to the Kingdom of Durathia. As he took in the never-ending forest, the lord found that if they would follow the river closest to them all the way south, they would eventually come to a break in the woods and then could head east, arriving in Durathia in much less time.

Lord Luxeniah decided to follow this new path, and on the second day of traveling along this river south, they came to the less dense portion of the forest and headed east until nightfall. It was then that they made their camp next to another unusually tall hill. They still had many days of travel before them on their way to the Tomb of Durath, in the place the poem had said it would be, where the White Sword of Durath rested. After making camp, Stephan made a fire around which they sat, resting from the day's travels. Fit Wit and Man Maul sat in a bush, enjoying the fire's heat while being concealed from view.

Later that night, after the fire had gone out and they were all fast asleep, dark figures surrounded the camp. When the figures completely encircled the camp, they moved inward and one of them brushed up against the bush Fit Wit and Man Maul slept in, waking the squirrels. Seeing the figures and that they were about to attack, Man Maul changed his voice and let out the loud screeching of a vampire bat. Stephan awoke. He got up and went to stir the remaining red coals from the fire when he stopped. Something was out of place. From the corner of his eye, he saw the many dark shapes closing in on the camp.

"Attention camp!" Stephan yelled the standard alarm. The others awoke. "Attention camp!" he repeated before crying, "Intruders!"

Alexander retrieved his broad sword in an instant. He was able to unsheathe it and wield the weapon in time to block a downward stroke by one of the shadowy figures. It was almost pitch-black in the campsite, but there was enough light from the coals and the moon to reveal the features of the attacker before him. He had long, matted, and unkempt hair and missing teeth. He was clothed in many different, unmatching articles of clothing.

Lord Luxeniah produced his own sword and fought several of the attackers at once with quick and precise blows. In a second, as he was retrieving his crossbow, Stephan witnessed the rapid movements and remembered the lord's fight with the Coltrous infiltrator near the Earthen archway when they had first come to Xaliud. In the moment, he noticed that the lord's movements did not seem to be as fast as before as he could actually see each of the strikes and parries. Before, near the Earthen archway, the two fighters could only be seen when there was a pause in the fighting. He worried that the nobleman was slower due to fatigue, but he also considered the possibility that his ability to see movement at that speed had improved. He also wondered if the attackers were Coltrous or were perhaps a rogue band of Riverton bandits.

In the second second, Stephan sensed the fighting Alexander was engaged in to his right and the fighting of Jessica on his left. With each flank covered, Stephan retrieved his laser rifle and slipped away into the woods to get some distance. He made for the hill overlooking the campsite. He loaded the crossbow and set up the rifle. He looked through the scope and knew that the use of the weapon on Cult Island, as well as the period of unuse since he had briefly used it on a patch of crystals near the Earthen archway, would mean that the rifle's power would be almost completely depleted. He had no time to check. Stephan cocked the weapon, engaging the power source. He heard the long unheard, but familiar buzz, and found a target—an attacker who was still secluded in the woods, who appeared to be waiting for an opportune moment to attack. It seemed as though he was going to attack Jessica since she was the closest and most vulnerable. Stephan wanted to use his rifle to shoot a laser beam through the waiting threatening figure, but the moment he took his shot, he knew the other attackers would become aware of his location and he would draw out much of their aggression toward him. Since he was still unprepared for any kind of close combat and since his rifle's power source would quickly become depleted, he would have to make his shots count. He would have to be patient and refrain from firing until the last possible moment. In the excruciating time while he waited, he witnessed the struggling of his companions below; Lord Luxeniah struggling to fight as many of the intruders as possible in a way that would protect Alexander and Jessica; Alexander struggling to fight on the same ground as even one of the attackers and succeeding in holding his own; and Jessica's success in dodging and parrying each attack directed toward her but not in any offensive strike.

When the fighting was reaching a fervor and as the waiting attackers were about to strike, Stephan took aim at the secluded figure
closest to Jessica and fired. The blazing hot beam cut through the
bandit, dropping him immediately to the ground. Fortunately, due
to the foreign nature of the attack, it being nothing like what the
other attackers had ever seen, the other attackers seemed to be confused by it, giving Stephan time to fire two more beams before they
could respond. When they did react, however, all of those who were
waiting to strike turned their attention to the hill, on top of which
Stephan stood. Stephan fired on another two attackers. When he
tried again, though, a weak and low rumbling came from the rifle
instead of the high-pitched shriek usually accompanying each blast.
He assumed the laser rifle's power source was too low to fire another
shot. The sight of so many of their comrades falling from the attacks
from a single position caused the bandits swarming the hill to hesi-
tate without stopping completely. As the bandits approached the
hill, they slowly encircled it. Before it was completely surrounded,
Stephan reacted swiftly and in a moment of inspired clarity. With
enough power for the rifle's light to still shine, he left his laser rifle,
with its scope's light still on, in a manner to give the impression that
he was still in the same place he was in when he had fired before.
With his crossbow in hand, he slipped quietly into the woods. He
then took up a position where he would have a safe shot at the hill's
apex where the light from his laser rifle would give him the vision
needed for some clear shots.

Three of the attackers reached the top of the hill and approached
the rifle. One of them picked it up and was slack jawed as he looked
over the strange weapon. Stephan waited until one of them was in
front of another and fired the royal crossbow. The arrow traveled fast,
so much so that it went clean through the first attacker's torso and

into the second's neck. Both fell as the other looked for the source of this new attack. As Stephan reloaded his weapon, he looked to his left at the other members of the emissary and was relieved to find them about to dispatch the last of the group they had been fighting. He was about to call out to them to inform them of the attackers who were on the hill when Alexander suddenly grabbed his own side and fell to the ground. In the darkness, Stephan thought he saw a marauder slice the captain there.

Alarmed, Stephan hurried and finished loading an arrow from his quiver and pointed his crossbow in the general direction the others were fighting in. When he did so, however, he found the place still and motionless. The sounds that usually accompanied a battle were silenced and replaced by the panicked cries of Jessica. By now, Stephan's sight had readjusted from the light his eyes had been exposed to from the laser rifle. He could now see that Alexander was lying flat on his back with Jessica kneeling over him, pressing down on his wound. Blood covered Jessica's hands as she pushed down on the wound. Stephan was about to run over to them to assist in any way he could, even though he knew he could do nothing, when some movement near the hill caught his attention. The remaining enemies were forming a line and loading their bows. Stephan could clearly see that they were preparing to release a volley of arrows at Jessica, Alexander, and Lord Luxeniah.

Jessica was frantically pressing down on Alexander's wound. She did not notice the forming line of bandit archers taking aim at them.

All she could focus on was Alexander. He was losing blood fast, so she needed to stop the bleeding. She searched the area around her for something she could use, but found nothing. Time then seemed to slow down in the moment of desperation. She wanted the wound to become cold so that the blood flow would almost stop. Normally, she would have had equipment that could produce temperatures well below zero degrees by displacing heat. She wished with all her being that the effect could somehow be produced now.

Movement in the distance in her general line of sight snapped her from her moment of reverie, and she saw the formation of a line of bandit archers, their bows with arrows set in them. In an instant, they had them drawn back, aimed directly at Stephan and the others. Lord Luxeniah stood and moved to be in front of Jessica and Alexander, with his sword drawn, as if ready to deflect as many of the arrows as he could and absorb any he could not. Jessica knew that though he had great speed in combat, he would not be able to stop all of the incoming projectiles. In a moment of despair, despair from Alexander's condition and despair from the danger from the line of bandits about to rain down death upon them, Jessica stretched out the hand not pressing down on Alexander's wound, and in a moment of sudden insight, which seemed to come from a place other than her mind, she closed her eyes and saw the bandits attack and the arrows flying toward them. In her mind's eye, she extended her arm and the air surrounding the arrows became completely void of all heat so that a wall of ice formed, trapping the arrows. Jessica opened her eyes and saw, to her surprise and astonishment, that the image formed in her mind had manifested before them. The attackers stood motionless, staring at the wall of ice that had formed before them—between them and those they were attacking. There was a moment of tense silence. Just as the bandits were about to act, the wall of ice rose off the ground, moved as if thrown, and landed directly onto the line of attackers with a sickening thud. The wall was about as long as the line of bandit archers, and it was clear that none of them remained alive.

Unsure of what had caused the sudden elemental manifestation, and even less sure of what had caused its movement, Jessica looked to her right over at Stephan. She saw that he had his arm extended, in a manner similar to hers, toward where the wall then lay flat on the ground. He was shaking a little, resting on one knee. He fell back into a sitting position, still shaking. Jessica looked down at Alexander below her and panicked when she remembered his critical condition. When she lifted the hand that had been covering Alexander's bloody side, though, there was no wound. Other than the blood on the captain's torn uniform, there was no sign of the gash. Jessica looked over to Lord Luxeniah, who appeared to offer no more answers than she had as to what had just happened.

After the shock of what had just happened passed, Stephan looked at his surroundings, particularly at the bodies of their attackers strewn about what used to be their campsite.

"They were bandits," Lord Luxeniah said, seeming to sense, in some way, Stephan's curiosity. "They most likely came here from in the Vile Gorge."

Stephan recognized the words describing the mysterious place to which Lord Luxeniah was referring, but he could not recall where he had heard it. After some thought, he found the memory of the lord mentioning it while conversing with Fortus, the blacksmith of Elk Lake Village. All Stephan knew about the gorge was its location, being east of the Kingdom of Geradia.

"How do you know that these Xalians came from this Vile Gorge?" Jessica asked. "They were not the Coltrous?"

"Look…." The lord used his sword to lift the cloak of a nearby dead bandit. "This chaotic arrangement of clothing is a dead give-away. They do not wear the feral, primal animal skins of the Coltrous. Furthermore, there is no way in the heavens the Coltrous could be this far east, outside the barren, common lands. The Durathians will not battle the ferocity of those of the Vile Gorge, but they are keen on keeping their forests clear of the Coltrous. They will not even travel through the Gorge; such is the fear of all regarding them."

Stephan did not doubt the truthfulness of what the nobleman said about the inhabitants of the Vile Gorge. His and his companions' little but dangerous skirmish with them and the sheer fortune that had given them their victory was enough to convince him.

Lord Luxeniah continued. "We should not be so far south; that much is my own fault as I had chosen the fastest possible route without regard to the possibility of their presence."

The lord and the others moved the bodies of the bandits out of the campsite. Afterward, those of the emissary got as much sleep as they could before setting off once again for the east. Fit Wit and Man Maul returned to the bush they were previously sleeping in to resume their rest, knowing they could easily catch up with the treelings in a couple of hours; they were content in a reassurance that they had done their duty for the night in lending aid to the treelings.

Chapter 25

The Mound Entrance

In the days of the easterly travel of Lord Luxeniah and his guard, there was a shared unease that there might be another attack, perhaps by those who had known the bandits they had defeated by the hill. To cope with this gnawing fear and prepare for the possibility, they trained more than they had before. Stephan and Jessica tried many times to recreate their respective feats. Their efforts produced nothing in the way of what power was manifested during the night the bandits attacked. There was a long period of impotence on both their parts, but also hope within both of their minds that if they continued to try, the power would return. After much effort with no manifestation, Jessica was able once again to freeze the moisture in the air around her. In that same instant, Stephan was able to manifest his power by suspending the chunk of solid ice in the air. From this experience, it became apparent that their powers were meant to be used in concert with one another. It also became clear that they would have to wait humbly and patiently for some opportunity to manifest the power; the manifestation would not come to them according to their whims or will. When it did come, however, they were then in full control of the power for however long it was within them.

On another occasion when the power came to them outside of their individual powers of will, Stephan could feel the internal structure inside the block of ice and succeeded in splitting it in two. Then he tried to split it into four pieces and then eight. Eventually, he was able to split the ice into thin sheets. They had been wondering how they could use this power as a weapon to fight the Coltrous, so when Stephan discovered he could split the ice into thin sheets, it dawned on him to try to sharpen them into projectiles. With these small blades, he was able to launch them through the air at various targets. This was much less draining for him than trying to throw chunks of ice with his mind, and much less draining for Jessica because it required her to drain less air of heat. The piercing sharpness of the ice blades also made them more deadly weapons.

When Stephan first attempted to hit targets, mostly tree trunks, the ice blades would merely shatter with no power of penetration. Then Stephan experimented with compacting the ice with the force of his power to make it denser. In this effort, the projectiles eventually became much more effective and durable as weapons, not shattering upon impact but penetrating the tree's bark and remaining as if it were an arrow sticking into the trunk. As their abilities rapidly increased and when the power was within them, Jessica was able to freeze more and more air to produce larger and larger blocks of ice.

Their progress east was slowed as the practice of honing these powers was draining on Stephan and Jessica, so much so that they required rest after each time the power was within them. The lord ordered them to practice and explained that although the slowing would be regrettable, the potential of their newfound powers made the delays acceptable.

As Stephan and Jessica trained, Lord Luxeniah taught Alexander the ways and techniques of the ancient Xalian sword-fighting masters. As a result of his training, the speed by which he was able to move while wielding his broadsword quickened. Over time, his strikes and parries began to be so quickly executed that they could hardly be seen. Though far from the lord's own level of skill, the gulf between their levels of skill lessened day by day.

While their travels were often interrupted by frequent periods of training and rest, Lord Luxeniah and his Earthen guard did, at last, arrive at the entrance of the Tomb of Durath, as was spoken of in the second half of the poem recited to them by the Supreme Vizier when they had visited him in the Chromas capital city. Since learning of it, Stephan had tried to imagine what the Tomb's entrance would look like. He imagined it to be opulent and ornate, adorned with statues of legendary heroes, columns, and artwork, in similar fashion to the stairway-monument leading to the Earthen Archway. What he saw now had none of that. It was a simple mound with a hole for its entrance that led to a stairway leading downward below the ground. Stephan did notice that there were flat areas on the mount, out of place. They seemed to be meant for the entrance's ornamentation.

Stephan made sure to stifle any unconscious expression of disappointment. He reminded himself that in spite of all that had happened and the length of time they had been on Xaliud, the Carn Doctrine had to be adhered to strictly. As part of this effort and to lessen his actual disappointment, he thought of the possibility that the mound had once been the sight of a glorious display but had either eroded over time or the individual articles that had once made up the monument were relocated or perhaps stolen.

Considering the entrance's relatively close proximity to the gorge, this explanation did not seem altogether implausible to Stephan. It was certainly more of a possibility than the first explanation since there would most likely be some remains of the statues or articles of decor for the monument, even considering whatever erosion would have taken place over a thousand years. The possibility of neglect by the Durathians in maintaining the appearance of the tomb's entrance crossed Stephan's mind, but he put effort into suppressing any expression of it.

The Geradian nobleman and his guard stood in front of the mound. The lord was about to speak when unexpected distant sounds interrupted the moment. The sounds were instantly recognizable as the rumblings of many boots striking the ground and the snapping of twigs and branches. Alarmed, all looked to Lord Luxeniah with inquiring and alarmed expressions. There was a mutual thought as to the possibility of more bandits from the Vile Gorge having followed them.

"No," Lord Luxeniah said, clearly understanding the concern of his Earthen guard, "they are not bandits." He paused to listen to the distant noise. After a moment, his eyes widened. "It is Ferekin! He has replenished his numbers and found us! I do not know how, but he is alive and he has found us!"

The lord's focus shifted to Stephan and Jessica. He spoke hurriedly. "I need to take Captain Bennet into the tomb to retrieve the sword. Hold them off for as long as you can! If you become overwhelmed, retreat into the tomb and come to us."

As Lord Luxeniah spoke, both Stephan and Jessica heard the words the lord was speaking, but with the words came mental images of the way through the tomb, for the stairway leading downward led into a vast labyrinth where one could easily lose himself and never be seen again. Along with the lord's thoughts came the impression that the Tomb of Durath was but one of many similar sepulchers located throughout the maze of catacombs, so knowing the precise location of this tomb was imperative to finding it in any reasonable amount of time.

When it was clear that the two Earthens understood, Lord Luxeniah and Alexander ran to the tomb's entrance, grabbed the torch on the wall just inside the mound's opening, lit the torch, and disappeared down the stairway. The light from the torch lingered after the Xalian and the captain vanished into the labyrinth and eventually faded. The darkness within the entrance returned.

Stephan and Jessica both stood facing the direction of the sounds, now louder than when they had heard them before. Stephan prepared himself by loading his crossbow. Jessica drew her curved sword. As they waited, and as the distant sounds grew, Stephan had an idea. "We could wait out of the way of the path here and flank them."

"No," Jessica said. "We're not going to be able to take them all even in the best scenario. We just need to delay them long enough to give Alexander and Lord Luxeniah time."

Stephan nodded in agreement, knowing she was right. Stephan ran over to the mound and climbed to its top, gaining a greater view. Although his sight was obstructed by the forest trees, he could see slivers through the foliage of the Coltrous armor type he had seen at the base of the Chromas mountain range. The tan and brown colors of the fur most Coltrous fighters wore contrasted distinctly with the green of the forest's foliage. The movement also gave a clear indication of how far away the Coltrous were and how much time they had to prepare. Stephan then had an idea and descended off the mound to rejoin Jessica. They stood and waited.

As they stood there, ready to contend with their pursuers, Stephan said to Jessica, "I know how we can defeat them…all of them."

On a cliff on Bloodfall Mountain, Saul gripped a rock and, after testing its stability, pulled himself onto the ledge above him. When he was completely on the ledge, he stood and looked up. He was nearing the mountain's top peak and could see then that it was within sight. He climbed the few remaining short cliffs. As he climbed, thoughts of the Alpha Z officers and the Geradian lord occupied his mind. He felt the familiar pang of guilt and shame for not accompanying them and doubted whether he would ever catch up to rejoin the emissary. His training on Bloodfall Mountain had taken longer than anticipated. He had planned on leaving much earlier, but he could not bring himself to cut his training short.

Saul reached a particularly large ledge, which stretched to both his left around the mountain bend and to his right, becoming a cliff. He was about to climb farther up to reach the mountain's highest point when, from around the bend to his left, he heard the deep snarling of what sounded like some gigantic beast in the middle of awakening. Something inside Saul moved him along the cliff's base toward the sound. He made sure to move silently, all the while listening intently to more and more of the beast's utterances. As he listened, he also heard something heavy being dragged on the ground. At first, there was a slight echo to the sounds, and Saul thought that the beast must have been moving inside of a large but shallow cave. He imagined it as more of a deep indentation in the mountain's rock face.

Saul reached the point of the bend where he would be seen by the beast if he went any farther and stopped. He felt fortunate to be downwind until he breathed in the rancid and rank odor the wind brought. He thought the smell must be coming from the beast itself until he heard the distant noise of the chomping of flesh.

Saul could not help but inch his way around the bend. When he did, he saw another rock wall, opposite of the opening to the cave. He stopped sharply when the carcass of a half-eaten green dragon was flung from the cave to the rock wall, striking it with a thunderous thud, and falling to the ledge ground. The ground shook when it landed. Much of the meat of the dragon's corpse had been completely sheared from the now visible bone. From the size of the creature, which was merely a meal for the beast, Saul gathered a sense of how large it must have been. He could not help but wonder whether it was the fabled lone survivor of Chromas lore who had been the first to survive the mountain's wrath and become transformed by it into this beastly form. He felt inside himself some insane yearning to continue his way around the bend in order to fight and defeat the beast. What was stranger than this death wish was the lack of any fear or caution from his mind to avoid the monster he was sure was a behemoth the size of a fairly large edifice.

Just as Saul was on the precipice of falling into the desire to engage, Lord Luxeniah came to his mind, supplanting the urge. *Saul! We need your help!* The thoughts were quick and surrounded by images and impressions of distress. In his mind's eye, Saul saw dark corridors and rushed movements. Even if the thoughts were expressed as words, Saul would have been able to sense the distress in the expression.

Saul! The thoughts continued to enter his mind. *I do not know if my mind can reach you, but we are in dire need of your assistance! It is my hope that you have left the Chromas capital city and are close to catching up to us.* The mind of the lord then grew distant. Saul stood still for a moment, not quite sure what to make of the thoughts and impressions. He considered the possibility that this was another moment when his mind had a weak grasp on reality. *Was this another false vision?* He decided immediately that this was unlikely. When he had seen the silhouette of the man in the sky, he was under a great deal of distress and torment, but at this moment, he was not. If anything, he was in a state of mind opposite to what could be described as distress, being excited, but not frenzied, even eager to fight the bestial being who was now only a few yards away from where he then stood.

Saul again heard the behemoth chomping on the dragon meat, apparently not finished with his moment of feeding. The desire to fight it remained, but instead of following it, he turned and walked in the opposite direction toward the southern facing cliff. He walked faster, not taking care to quiet his steps as he had done before. The behemoth around the corner stopped feeding, its attention caught by the quiet but distinct noises, arose, and exited its cave. It then made its way around the bend to find the small thing making the noise, walking away from the bend.

Saul was now running toward the southward-facing cliff, his gaze fixated on the direction from which the distressed thoughts of Lord Luxeniah had originated. It was roughly in the direction of the mountains Lord Luxeniah had shown him before his leaving the Chromas capital city.

As he neared the cliff's edge, Saul had the distinct notion that the way to reach the others in time to lend any meaningful aid lay in this direction. It was a notion similar to what he had experienced while training among the Chromas just before manifesting fire for the first time. What was different was the knowledge that this notion was preceding a different power.

Just as the pursuing behemoth was about to grip him with its mammoth-clawed hands, Saul reached the edge of the cliff and leapt off the mountain. As he fell, he felt the flames of fire surround him while the air below him grew thinner and his body lighter, until, he was soaring through the air toward the Tomb of Durath. After a moment of wind rushing over his body, Saul heard in the distance behind him the bestial cry ring out.

Chapter 26

The Durathian Labyrinth

Alexander and Lord Luxeniah sat in a catacomb away from the main hallway they had traversed until concealing themselves in their current hiding place. For the past long moments, Alexander had been peering from time to time into the hallway to keep watch for any pursuers. Lord Luxeniah sat, his fore and middle fingers on his forehead. He had been in this manner since he sat down, earlier muttering something about his thoughts reaching Saul. Alexander hoped he was not attempting alone what had taken the combined talents of the lord and four Chromas monks back at the temple. He doubted whether the lord could extend the reach of his mind to whatever corner of these lands Saul was in. He also doubted whether Saul could be of any use.

More time passed in the dark crypt. Its musty odor gave Alexander a sick feeling in the pit of his stomach that he might never leave the labyrinth. After a few more moments of silence, Lord Luxeniah opened his eyes and looked up at Alexander. The doubts within Alexander grew. The nobleman motioned silently toward the hallway, and they continued their descent deeper into the labyrinth toward the tomb of Durath.

Near the tomb's entrance, Stephan and Jessica stood, waiting for Ferekin and his band of Coltrous fighters. The sounds of their marching had been steadily growing louder and louder. Now they could clearly hear the horrible snapping of branches and crushing of leaves. Before long, they could see through the leaves the skin armor of the fighters and, in time, Ferekin's royal, garish armor, distinct in both color and shape from that of his underlings. When Ferekin and his men finally reached the clearing, they surrounded the Earthens, forming a circle. Stephan took note of the pattern and the irregularities of it. When the circle was complete, there was a few, long moments of silence while Ferekin stood watching them. Finally, the silence was broken by the Coltrouos royal leader.

"Well, it looks as though we have caught Luxeniah's pet Earthens," Ferekin said, appearing amused and confident to find Jessica and Stephan alone to stand against him. "Where is the Geradian liar now? Tell us and some good may come of it in your favor."

Jessica remembered what Stephan had said earlier about following his lead when Ferekin would arrive; she hesitated, looking to him. She found him silent, giving no order for action. He remained this way until his arms suddenly shot up, dropping the crossbow. Jessica mimicked him and raised her arms in a like manner, dropping her curved sword to the ground.

Ferekin took off his helmet and held it at this side. His face contorted in bewilderment as he said, "What is this?" His tone had stately authority in it.

Stephan put effort in preparing his voice so that it would not reveal the true place his efforts were being directed. "You must not be familiar with Earthen customs or body language."

Ferekin looked a little perturbed by this as his eyes narrowed. "I am familiar with all Earthen customs and manners that matter. This bizarre display, though, is nothing my scouts have ever reported to have seen."

Good, Stephan thought. *His attention and the attention of his men are fixed on us. I just hope it stays that way.* Stephan could feel his brow twitch slightly as his exertion grew. He glanced over at Jessica and could see a similar, almost imperceptible sign of exertion. *Keep it together,* he thought, partly regarding her, but mostly to himself. He looked back at Ferekin.

"This," he said, adjusting his voice to give the correct impression, "is how our kind show subservience. It is a sign of surrender." Stephan put on an air of weakness to further the impression, making the expression as convincing as possible.

Ferekin seemed pleased. *Excellent,* he thought. *Only a little longer.* The strain was beginning to take a toll. Stephan reminded himself that he must conserve some of his strength for later.

Ferekin continued. "You both surrendered without hesitation, surprising for being officers of Alpha Z," his tone then took on an exaggerated, mocking quality, "the most illustrious and skilled of Earth's fighting forces."

"Our skills," Stephan could no longer hide his effort and his voice showed it, "and our illustriousness…required training… which gave us the experience to know…when we are outmatched."

Ferekin's countenance grew dim with suspicion. "You are hiding something. Tell me now!"

Stephan felt the weight of the massive boulder of ice Jessica had been forming and he had been supporting with his power since he and Jessica had lifted their arms. The point was approaching when he would have to release the tension if he was to have enough strength to fight. He felt the boulder's interior structure and started to exert the force there in a pattern sure to create sheets of ice. It was fortunate that the resulting cracking of the ice was barely audible and Ferekin did not seem to notice it.

"What do you mean?" Stephan's voice was far from anything that could pass for unstrained.

"You are both shaking; your body and voice. And not in the way of fear, but…are you ill? What Earthen plague have you…?"

Stephan's use of power to break the interior of the ice boulder into sheets was now reaching its surface, and the resulting noises could now be clearly heard. In an alarming action, Stephan saw Ferekin look up. Stephan finished the breaking of the boulder into sheets and compressed the sheet's edges, forming them into pointed and sharpened blades in one final sounding crack. What now hung in the air was a cloud of ice blades. In his mind's eye, Stephan imagined the cloud taking on a new form and the blades obeying, each moving into its new place and forming a circular shape.

"Men! Ready the att—" but before Ferekin could finish the command, Stephan closed his eyes and brought down his arms. As he did so, every other blade of the circle shot into a Coltrous fighter. When Ferekin finished the command and the rest of the fighters began to close in, Stephan let loose a blade here and a blade there; only enough to keep them at bay and to prevent the whole of Ferekin's men from rushing in. He knew he did not have enough of his icy projectiles to defeat all of them and that Jessica more than likely would not be able to form the necessary amount of ice.

Jessica quickly picked up her curved sword and Stephan his crossbow. The ring of Coltrous fighters was now getting dangerously close and the two Alpha Z officers were finding themselves closer and closer to being up against the mound's side. Stephan motioned around the bend of the mound to the tomb's entrance and they both ran toward it. Before they could enter the labyrinth to escape to safety, they found the way blocked by Coltrous fighters. Instead, they climbed the mound itself, which provided some temporary protection.

On top of the mound, Stephan fended off a few climbing attackers with the last of the ice blades and Jessica produced smaller boulders of ice. As Stephan broke them into sheets, Jessica parried the attacks of their assailants with her curved blade. When Stephan finished compressing the edges and ends of the ice sheets into blade edges and points, he wielded them to fend off more of the onslaught of fighters.

When there was a break in the combat, Stephan looked over at Jessica and saw signs of her growing fatigue: her baited breath and the slowing of her parries. He felt his own weariness while noticing his own signs of it as the wielding of the ice blades was becoming more and more of a struggle. As the circle of Coltrous fighters continued to close in, the fighters were becoming less intimidated by the death of a nearby comrade. Stephan was losing hope that they could defeat all of the Coltrous fighters. It was becoming more and more difficult to suspend the ice blades in the air, and the forming of the ice boulders was clearly taking a great toll on Jessica. Just then, a thought came to Stephan's mind.

"Jessica!" Stephan shouted over the shouts and taunting of the Coltrous fighters. "I need you to make a longer brick of ice!"

"I don't know if I can!"

"This will be the last one, I promise!"

With a great show of effort, which pained Stephan to watch, Jessica slowly created the long ice block. When she finished, Stephan could see her shaking as she struggled to stand and fight. While using the last of the ice projectile blades to delay the Coltrous fighters, Stephan broke up the ice lengthwise into two thinner blocks and then those into four, long ice sheets. He used the usual method for compacting the ice, but instead of making small projectiles, he made four long ice blades. Along with wielding Jessica's blade with his power, which she had dropped in her exhaustion, he fought off the line of fighters with the ice blades as well as he could, considering he had very little sword training, being more skilled as a marksman. In consideration of this, Stephan made a split-second decision to avoid engaging in intricate swordplay. He used three of the blades to keep the circle of fighters at bay with crude but powerful and intimidating swings while he used the remaining blades to strike from behind and above. The strategy was working surprisingly well, but what was also unexpected was how draining it was for Stephan to wield the blades with his mind. In this moment, he felt for Jessica, who was on the ground, still struggling to get up. He knew that her role had been a more taxing one than his, and some part of him hoped she would stay down, out of harm's way.

As the full depletion of his strength approached, Stephan looked around for an opening in the enclosing circle to escape through, but he found, to his horror, that they were completely surrounded, isolated from any way out. He used the last of his strength to break the long blades into shorter, projectile-shaped blades and flung them at the thinnest and weakest part of the enclosing circle of Coltrous fighters in a desperate attempt to create an opening through which he and Jessica could escape. When the small cloud of ice blades hit their targets, an opening was created, only to close immediately with more fighters. Stephan fell to his knees. Jessica's blade seemed to fight by its own strength as he waited for the inevitable end: death or capture. Just as the circle of frenzied, bloodlust-consumed Coltrous fighters was about to envelop them, both a distinct and familiar sound of intense flame pierced the sounds of their assailants surrounding them. The sound grew before erupting in an explosion in the ranks of the Coltrous. The bodies of many of the fighters were flung like rag dolls into the air in every imaginable direction.

Stephan looked up, expecting to see a Chromas dragon rider swooping in to save them as they had done before at the base of the Chromas mountain range. At first, though, there was no rider to be seen through the rising plumes of smoke obscuring their vision. But then Stephan saw a small ball of fire in the distance growing larger as it neared. Stephan put his arm around Jessica, pulling her to him to protect her as the ball of fire seemed to be directed at them. It landed, however, among the Coltrous, and the explosion threw more of the fighters into the air. Another ball was headed for the top of the mound where Stephan and Jessica lay, unable to move, and although the Coltrous were directing their attention away from them, they had no place to flee. However, instead of increasing in speed as it neared, it slowed. When it was just above them, the flame dispersed and Saul landed next to them.

"Stay down!" Saul yelled just before he knelt and a ring of fire formed around the mound. With great and deadly force, the ring extended, bursting outward and engulfing the remaining Coltrous fighters in flame.

Stephan and Jessica struggled to stand. "Saul?" Stephan said between exasperated gulps of air. "How…?" But instead of inquiring about the dramatic change he had just witnessed in Saul, Stephan remembered their mission and looked around at the bodies strewn around the mound.

"We have to find Ferekin's body! We will not repeat the same mistake as before!"

Ferekin must have been buried, Saul thought, immediately feeling foolish. He understood Stephan's hastiness. He and Jessica joined Stephan and searched the bodies.

Stephan thought the search was proceeding quickly because the Coltrous fighters were all dressed in the furs and skins of beasts. Finding Ferekin's body would be a simple task since the Coltrous leader was dressed in armor, and although it would be charred, it would still be unmistakable from the other bodies.

After many moments of checking and rechecking their slain foes, neither Stephan, Saul, nor Jessica found Ferekin's body. Stephan was about to search the area again when, while near the labyrinth's entrance, curious shapes caught his attention from the corner of his eye. He walked over to the mound's opening, and when he got a closer look, he could see that they were footprints. He placed his own foot onto the charred marking, comparing its size to that of his own foot. The print was dramatically larger. Alarmed, Stephan called to the others.

"He's in the tomb!" Jessica and Saul came immediately to the labyrinth's entrance, and upon seeing the footprint, they understood and followed Stephan when he hastily entered. The stairway leading downward from the entrance became pitch-dark almost at once. Stephan held up his laser rifle and activated its light source. Light filled the cavernous, stone stairway, allowing them to see the way downward. As he held the rifle, Stephan contemplated the possibility that it might be more than merely a large flashlight so there might be enough power for one more shot, and if there was a need for that shot, he would have to use it wisely.

The stairway continued downward farther than one could see. On its left, catacombs branched outward, level with the stairway. On the right was a dark abyss, the bottom of which could not be seen, even when Stephan shined light into it.

Stephan tried to think back to when Lord Luxeniah had thought to him the way through the labyrinth to the Tomb of Durath. When the way came to him, Stephan motioned toward Jessica and Saul to follow. They continued down the main stairway until they reached the appropriate catacomb and entered it. Each of the catacombs was either a dead end, the way to small isolated labyrinths within the larger labyrinth, or a hall leading to the rest of the underground maze. With most of them appearing to be very similar in appearance, getting hopelessly lost was a serious danger.

In spite of this, they hurried on their way toward the tomb, worried they would arrive too late, only to find the White Sword of Durath in the hands of a Coltrous Warlord.

Chapter 27

The Tomb

The echoes of rushed footsteps were all that could be heard in the long hallways of the labyrinth as Alexander and Lord Luxeniah hastily made their way through never-ending catacombs. They made their way down stairway after stairway until at last they came to the entrance of the tomb of the one who was called Durath, the fabled archhero of the First Great Conflict.

Upon seeing the tomb's entrance, Alexander noticed right away that it was decorated with many triangular shapes. He wondered for a moment whether the shapes were symbolic of the fabled union of the three northern kingdoms, but he let the thought pass almost as soon as it had entered his mind.

Lord Luxeniah silently and reverently entered the tomb, his torch still lit from when they had entered the labyrinth, and revealed the tomb's interior. In the center was a stone sarcophagus. The walls were covered in an array of artifacts and carvings, each relating in some way to some event of the First Great Conflict. In the back of the tomb was a small catacomb, the entrance of which was flush with the left wall. Alexander expected the Sword of Xaliud to be in the stone sarcophagus and that the lord would move toward it to open it. He was surprised when the Geradian instead moved toward the small catacomb, but Alexander followed. When they reached the catacomb's center, Lord Luxeniah held his torch up close to the left wall, revealing a large, opulent, crystal, shaped in a perfect diamond. From its shape, and the craftsmanship that had clearly gone into its forming, it was apparent that the diamond meant to serve as an ornamental piece. Alexander could tell that it was the clear, most common kind of crystal found all over the parts of Xaliud where they had traveled, but many times larger and much more opaque. Alexander thought he could see something trapped within the confines of the crystal. He wondered how it was made. Alexander looked back at the stone casket. He wanted to open it and retrieve the White Sword he had heard spoken of in so many corners of the realm of Xaliud.

"Here it lies!" Lord Luxeniah said in reverent whisper.

Alexander looked at the nobleman and responded in the same manner. "Here lies what?"

"This is the white claw of the gold lion!"

Alexander returned his attention to the crystal and stepped forward to get a closer look. "It doesn't look like a claw to me," Alexander said, referring to the gigantic crystal's diamond shape. "It looks more like a…." He broke off when he remembered the poem that the blacksmith had spoken of back in the Village of Elk Lake. He also remembered the blacksmith's ability to imbue weapons with the dust of Mylenian crystal and how he could disintegrate a crystal into a fine powder with his mind. Alexander pushed these thoughts away, trying to understand why they filled his mind. What was the connection between them? The crystal, Fortus the blacksmith, Mylenian crystal as a material for crafting…. Alexander's thoughts stopped. He then knew what the lord was referring to when he spoke of the white claw of the gold lion.

Alexander turned sharply to Lord Luxeniah. "The sword is in the crystal!"

The lord gave a slight smile and nodded softly. Alexander turned back to the crystal; his elation from the realization was now being replaced with the dread of another. "How are we going to get it out?"

"*We* will not." The lord faced Alexander. He pointed at him. "*You* will." And without another word, the lord walked toward the tomb's larger room and placed the torch on the wall where the small catacomb met the rest of the tomb.

"Me?" Alexander scoffed. "How could I possibly...without training...?"

"Give thought to it and...." The lord stopped when he heard something from outside the tomb. They listened as the sounds grew louder until they became more audible. It was the unmistakable clanking of heavy metal boots striking the floor. Accompanying this sound was the light clinking of chainmail. Lord Luxeniah knew immediately who it was and where he was heading.

"Give haste and free the sword!" the nobleman commanded Alexander, and he drew his own sword, turning to face the tomb's entrance, standing between it and Alexander.

Alexander turned to the crystal. *How am I going to get the sword out?* he thought frantically. He had no idea. He had no tools, and he knew of none that could penetrate the crystal. He assumed there was nothing that could. He remembered how Stephan had once attempted to cut a crystal shard with his laser rifle with no effect. A sick feeling grew inside him. The only other person he knew of who could do what the lord was demanding was on the other side of the Realm of Peace. *Why hadn't they brought him Fortus?* Alexander thought, almost bitterly. He thought about the blacksmith, about their intimate conversation on the craft of turning the crystal to dust. *It is something the crystal wills,* he had said. *I merely look for the chance and I am grateful.* Alexander thought about what Fortus had said. *What did he mean by that?* Alexander was growing frustrated and was about to give up all hope when those thoughts, before rotating in his mind independent of each other, aligned in his mind. *He had spoken about the crystals as if he had known them.* Alexander thought back to the countless interviews, personal conversations, and other interactions he had had in the past with those from whom he had wanted something and had to convince to give it to him. Even at a young age, it had been a game to him to imagine the person was something to dismantle with the prize in its center waiting for him to free it. At times, in his mind, it was a treasure chest to open, or a Chinese puzzle to dismantle, but one way or another, he always got what was waiting for him. The prize was always his before he even started the task of dismantling.

From these thoughts and memories, Alexander came to the sudden realization that he could imagine this crystal as being one of those he had always been able to pick apart. The notion still seemed bizarre to him, even considering what he and the others had been through up until now in the Xalian realm. The picking apart of a person was an effort dealing with emotions and influence, whereas this was physical dismantling and freeing.

The sounds of Ferekin's powerful, rumbling steps and clinking armor grew louder, dividing Alexander's attention between the task of freeing the sword and Lord Luxeniah's solitary stance against this formidable foe. *Do not waver in your task!* The lord's thoughts filled his mind. *All that matters, all that can defeat Ferekin now is the sword. Even if you hear me dying, do not attempt to aid me. Ferekin's armor is of ancient Geradian craft, legendary in its fortitude. Without the power of the sword, both of us will die!*

Alexander understood and focused on the crystal, blocking all else from his mind. He resolved then to heed the nobleman's words. He avoided the doubts he had thought only moments before and willed his mind's eye to the sword to feel out the crystal's weaknesses, imagining it as a person. *The blacksmith said it had a will.*

Lord Luxeniah stood in front of the tomb's entrance waiting, stealing himself for what lay ahead. He considered searching the tomb for armor suitable for his stature, but he decided against it. He would be much better off relying on his speed because Ferekin would be slowed by his heavy plate armor. The footsteps were now loud, and the lord thought he could feel the ground shaking a little with each thunderous step. The Coltrous royalty stepped into the tomb's entrance and into view. He seemed much larger now when compared to their last encounter where Lord Luxeniah had only seen him from a distance. Seeing him this closely, he realized that Ferekin was gargantuan, towering over the Geradian.

Ferekin held his already drawn sword, letting the point of it rest on the tomb's floor. "Lord Luxeniah, at last we meet properly, under much more appropriate circumstances."

"Yes," the lord answered. "I could scarcely hear you in the desert wind last time we conversed. You seem well to me; however, I am at a disadvantage for I do not know how you found us."

Ferekin bellowed a booming, unsettling laugh. Lord Luxeniah worried about Alexander's focus. He continued, "Just like a Geradian, stalling for time to avoid battle!"

The royal Coltrous raised his sword; it was now level with the lord's chest. The lord gripped his sword tightly as Ferekin spoke again. "The great and wise Lord Luxeniah, so insightful, yet alone in his anticipation of the impending Second Great Conflict." Ferekin stepped forward; Luxeniah stepped backward. "How could one so wise be so foolish as to allow himself to be trapped in a tomb, relying on the strength of pathetically weak Earthens as his guard?"

The towering behemoth before the lord stopped and help up his sword as if admiring it. "We have been looking on you for some time, Lord Luxeniah. You and your vain notions of defeating us. Gathering the Earthens and snatching them from the grasp of Yenien was a most skillful move on your part; I give you that much. However, your efforts have been in vain." He looked up from the sword to the lord. "The white sword will not be released, and the four will die tonight!" When he had finished saying these words, he lunged forward. He lifted up and then slashed his broadsword downward toward Lord Luxeniah. The lord parried the attack, barely avoiding the blow as the sword crashed into the tomb's floor. It crushed a few of its tiles, sending pieces of them up into the air.

In a single moment in the midst of the fight, the lord could sense Alexander's focus about to slip and thought to him, *Do not even think of stopping! I would kill you myself!*

Ferekin pulled his sword from the rubble and slashed sideways at the lord, who blocked the blow with his own blade. The force of the attack sent the lord sliding backwards, his boots grinding the dust on the floor while still maintaining balance. There they stood, the blades locked, pressing against each other, Lord Luxeniah shaking to hold his own.

Outside the tomb, Fit Wit and Man Maul hid near the tomb's entrance, cowering at the terrifying power of the two titan treelings locked in mortal combat. They had followed Lord Luxeniah and Alexander down the many catacombs and stairways to the tomb and hid outside when they heard Ferekin coming.

"There's no way we can help!" Man Maul pleaded to Fit Wit.

Fit Wit hesitated to answer. As he watched the titans fight, his hind legs were bent and his fur stood up as if to say he wanted to jump in and help. His posture then eased a little. "Right," he finally answered. "We best double back; the others may need us. They should have arrived by now." Fit Wit thought it was odd the other treelings were not there yet. The strange larger treeling had arrived, so why had they not? The two squirrels ran down the catacomb, in the direction the others would most likely head.

Further up the labyrinth, Stephan, Jessica, and Saul were now rushing toward the tomb. Stephan had a sickening premonition that Lord Luxeniah and Alexander, as powerful and as skilled as they both were with the sword, would be in desperate need of their help. *If Ferekin's armor, and Ferekin himself, had withstood the full force of Saul's attack, there's no telling what it would take to penetrate it and defeat him,* Stephan thought. He hoped their combined strength would be enough.

They had made considerable progress through the catacombs and winding stairways, but Stephan was becoming less and less sure of the way. The lord had thought to him the path he would be taking throughout the labyrinth in haste, and furthermore, the nobleman had no personal knowledge of the labyrinth itself, but he had been communicating the way he learned from the poem Fortus had described. It was a shaky description at best. What added to the confusion was the likeness the catacombs and hallways shared with each other.

Stephan stopped at a point where several catacombs converged and where there were many different ways they could go; there were several ways down several sets of stairs; there was another hallway, or they could continue down the catacomb they had been walking through. Stephan had no idea which to take, and the others were surely relying on him. He was about to explain to the others the dire predicament he had put them all in when the sound of a rock rolling down one of the stairways caught his attention. The noise was familiar and strangely resembled the sound he had heard of a rock falling from a fissure when they had been in the blue caves. It would be foolhardy to trust such a whim, but he knew they were close to the tomb and that they could always double-back to choose another direction.

Stephan motioned to Saul and Jessica regarding the stairway and they took it down. In a crevice above the stairs, Fit Wit and Man

Maul hid, slinking into a hole so they would not be seen. To the delight of the squirrels, and according to their hopes, the three treelings descended the stairway and headed in the direction of the tomb.

When they had reached the bottom of the stairs, Stephan could hear the sharp clanging of swords echoing throughout the halls of the labyrinth. Stephan motioned to Saul and Jessica eagerly, and although they hurried to reach the tomb, they were careful to step more and more lightly the closer they got. The sounds of fighting grew louder as they neared the tomb. When they were nearing its entrance, they softened their steps to quietly creep up to it. At this point, there was no denying that the two who were fighting, from whom the noises originated, were Ferekin and Lord Luxeniah.

Saul, who had hurried past Stephan, being closest to the tomb's entrance, peered around the corner. He found the two Xalians in heated combat, fighting vigorously. Saul could tell from the way Lord Luxeniah fought that the lord was quickly becoming exhausted. He looked battered, and he was bleeding from many minor wounds. He also noticed Alexander in a small catacomb staring at something on the wall and wincing in confusion. Saul was about to rush into the fray when Lord Luxeniah, while parrying Ferekin's massive sword during a particularly powerful slash, was caught off balance. Ferekin kicked and toppled him to the ground. Ferekin lifted his sword for the killing blow. The lord did not look as though he had the strength to block, parry, or even move out of the way. Saul saw his opportunity and ran into the tomb, took a shield from the way, and yelled as he ran toward the Coltrous warlord, "You Coltrous bastard!" Ferekin turned toward the sudden noise just in time to see Saul throw the shield and feel the edge of a shield striking his throat. Ferekin dropped his sword and staggered backward, clutching his throat. He struggled to breathe and reeled from the blow. Stephan and Jessica then rushed in and moved the battered and bleeding lord out of the way of the fighting, which was about to ensue.

When Ferekin recovered, he retrieved his sword, lifted it in the air, and slashed it down at Saul, who moved quickly and dodged the attack. He then jumped up toward Ferekin, his leg in perfect position to strike Ferekin's head, but the Coltrous warlord reacted quicker than Saul and punched him. Saul flew across the room, bouncing off the wall and landing on the tomb's floor.

In the corner of the tomb, the power was still upon Jessica, and she was doing all she could to heal Lord Luxeniah of his injuries. She felt the familiar sensing of the potential, the opportunity for power beyond her own that she could see in her mind's eye, and drew upon it. But instead of the cold that had accompanied the healing of Alexander's wound sustained during the bandit attack, a light illuminated from Jessica's hands as she laid them on Lord Luxeniah's body, and she started to heal him.

Stephan was dividing his attention between Saul battling Ferekin and Jessica healing the lord's wounds and fatigue. He knew that, once again, this was another instance where he could not help Jessica and turned his attention to the fight. He clutched his laser rifle. In terms of physical strength, Saul and Ferekin were two gods fighting in a higher realm, their attacks like the forces of nature Stephan could not even hope to affect. He cocked the rifle. It gave an unusually high-pitched humming. He knew he was pushing it past its normal limits.

Saul stood and faced Ferekin. Ferekin gripped his sword with both hands, readying himself. Saul took up a defensive stance just as

Ferekin launched forward with a torrent of slashes and thrusts. Saul struggled to dodge them, sliding, ducking and jumping to avoid the blade's deadly edge. Ferekin was becoming more and more enraged with each failed attempt to land a blow. After much of this, he saw an opportunity. He withdrew his sword while placing a kick squarely onto Saul's chest. Saul flew back a few feet and landed on the floor in a way so that field of vision was directed toward the others huddling in the corner. He saw Stephan finish charging his rifle. He understood what Stephan had in mind, so he stood and jumped. While his back was toward Ferekin, he pushed off the wall just right of the entrance, sending himself into a backflip over Ferekin. Ferekin looked up, watching the display. Stephan saw Ferekin's distraction and his chance. He aimed his laser rifle at his now-exposed neck and pulled the trigger. The searing, red-hot beam struck Ferekin directly on the exposed flesh of the neck with no perceivable effect. Stephan dropped the now smoking and intensely hot rifle onto the ground. He knew it was now internally destroyed and useless.

Stephan stood, staring, not believing what he had just witnessed. He had read in the Grand Library in the Kingdom of Geradia of the legendary invulnerability of some ancient armor. He now realized it was the armor Ferekin now wore, but he had not anticipated that characteristic extending to his skin as well. Stephan felt a sudden sinking feeling of hopelessness that he was now utterly worthless in this fight.

Ferekin let out his disturbing, mocking laugh, which echoed distinctly in the halls. Saul, now behind Ferekin, facing his back, jumped and tore the warlord's helmet off his head on the way up, interrupting him. Ferekin turned around, and Saul fell striking him on the forehead with his own helmet. Ferekin staggered, holding his head and howling in pain.

"You may be invulnerable," Saul yelled, "but we're going to beat you to a bloody pulp!"

Ferekin took up his sword, gripping it tightly with both hands, and raised it high. Shouting in rage, he brought it down toward Saul, but instead of dodging or parrying the attack, Saul clapped the blade, halting it with little space between the edge of the blade and his face. A small bit of hope returned to Stephan as he saw another vulnerability on the part of Ferekin, and took one of his last arrows from his quiver. In an exaggerated movement, he threw the arrow at the Coltrous warlord. The arrow flew through the air at a speed you would expect from one who was proficient in throwing. As it bounced off his face, Ferekin gave an incredulous look and his mouth formed a tense line as if it were about to break again into laughter when the falling arrow stopped in the middle of the air. Stephan extended his arms and the arrow flew with great speed toward Ferekin's exposed neck. Without time to react, it struck its target. The arrow, whose point was not buried in the neck, but had only barely penetrated the skin, stayed for a brief second before falling to the tomb's floor. The small cut the arrow made did not even produce a drop of blood.

That confirms my suspicions, Stephan thought to himself. *His skin in impenetrable to any piercing force!* The earlier feeling of worthlessness returned more intensely than before. He turned to Jessica, who was healing Lord Luxeniah. He wanted to ask her to lend her power, but it was clear that she was too involved, and the whole of her abilities were directed to the nobleman's wounds. Stephan turned back to Saul and Ferekin, who were still locked; Saul shook to maintain his hold on Ferekin's blade, and the warlord exerted overwhelming force to push the blade through Saul's clapped hands. Stephan could see Saul's body quivering more and more. Even with Saul's remarkable surge of strength and power, he would eventually give way to Ferekin's colossal strength. *Is there any hope?*

In the tomb's rear catacomb, Alexander struggled to remain focused on the task of freeing the sword from its diamond-shaped crystal prison. Although he could feel the crystal's integrity almost completely compromised, a part of his mind was aware of the fighting in the tomb's main room. Though he strove to stay focused, a thought to help the others crept through.

There is no aid you can lend without the sword, Captain! The lord's thoughts were in his mind once again. *Do not fail us! Your failure would be the death of us all!*

Alexander clutched his mind and forced it into complete focus. He was close; a few more moments and the sword would be freed.

In the main room of the tomb, Stephan could do nothing but look on impotently to observe Saul shake more and more, his strength waning and growing fainter. Then, Saul's body ceased to quake. Ferekin had stopped pressing. Saul kept his hold, unsure of what could be a farce. In an instant, Ferekin lifted his sword, lifting Saul off the ground with it. Saul let go reflexively, and as he fell, Ferekin kicked Saul, sending him across the room and knocking him against the wall. He fell to the ground. Ferekin let out another maniacal, cruel laugh.

The Coltrous warlord looked over at Jessica, who was still trying to heal the lord. Stephan knew it was slow going as Jessica was using the very last of her strength. Ferekin looked alarmed and walked toward Jessica in quick, broad steps. Not knowing what to do, but having to do something, Stephan picked up the lord's royal sword and clutched the handle tightly. He stood in front of Jessica. Ferekin did not stop his progress. While walking, he effortlessly lifted Stephan, by gripping his engineer's uniform, and flung him into the adjacent corner.

Stephan looked back in horror as Ferekin, now standing in front of Jessica, grabbed her and threw her like a rag doll onto the ground. Lord Luxeniah cried out as he tried to stand in agonizing futility. His internal wounds were not yet fully healed, and the movement was causing the many small tears inside his body to reopen. Miserably, he slumped back into a lying position on the ground, almost passing out from the pain.

Ferekin then placed his foot on Jessica's chest, and when he shifted a portion of his weight onto her, she let out a piercing and desperate cry. Ferekin laughed maniacally. "This is one of the four? This is all the Realm of Peace has to offer? This is truly pathetic!" Ferekin continued to press his weight onto her, and she continued to wail in pain.

Stephan, holding his throbbing arm, turned to the corner of the tomb opposite Ferekin. "Saul!" he yelled. "You've got to help her!"

Saul was motionless, witnessing what the warlord was doing to Jessica, wide-eyed and paralyzed. Stephan kept urging him, "Saul, you're the only one strong enough!" Saul remained still. "Saul! Saul!"

Finally, Saul moved. He turned towards Stephan. Stephan fell silent and took a step back. Saul raised his hand, felt the power within him, and produced a heavily concentrated ball of fire. Stephan could tell it was more a concentrated ball of heat. The flame burned more intensely, and its color was brighter than it was before. Saul took a step toward Stephan. His face was becoming contorted in rage. Stephan took a step back, shaking as he did.

Ferekin, who was watching Saul, said, "Well, well, there might be hope for you yet!"

Saul brought the inflamed hand back into throwing position, but as he was about to throw the fireball at Stephan, he suddenly turned toward Ferekin. He threw the ball of fire at him. Without time to react, the Coltrous took the full force of the fireball's explosive impact, which knocked him backward and removed his boot off of Jessica. Wild-eyed and crazed, Saul leapt forward with a frenzied speed toward Ferekin, grabbed him by his breastplate, and with a strength unknown even to himself, launched Ferekin across the room and against the opposite wall. With a crash, he fell to the floor, and many artifacts landed on it, as well as pieces of the wall itself falling on top of him. Without a break in the assault, Saul launched himself toward Ferekin, grabbed him by the top of his breastplate, and struck his face again and again with his fist. Ferekin took a few more blows as he stood, but when he did, he grabbed Saul, continuing to take the painful strikes to his face, and threw him, with much force, toward the opposite wall. As Saul approached it, however, he turned his body and landed on the wall on his feet before immediately launching himself back at the warlord. As Saul was approaching him, Ferekin was crouching to retrieve his sword. As he stood, Saul tried to deliver a powerful punch on his exposed face. Ferekin caught Saul's fist and held it inside his own massive grip. Ferekin attempted to counter with his own punch, which Saul caught in turn. The two stood there, struggling, shaking, once more locked in a standstill, neither able to gain an advantage over the other.

In the tomb's alcove, Alexander stood, vigilantly focusing the whole of his attention on the crystalline encasement of the White Sword of Durath. He was about there. Until then, the massive, diamond-shaped crystal had shown no visible sign of deterioration. In spite of this, Alexander could sense the crystal's interior structure faulting, growing weaker and weaker. The structure of it on its smallest level breaking in a cascading reaction until, at last, the crystal broke apart in large chunks, falling into a pile and leaving the sword suspended for a brief instant. It stood on the tip of its blade, buried in the pile of crystal shards. In that brief moment, Alexander's mind beheld all of the sword's features. The sword's pommel was made of crystal shards of pure white crystal. The grip was of fine leather bounded by golden rings. The cross guard was crafted in the shape of two pairs of snakes, each pair extending outward from a golden chappe, their bodies intertwined, and the head of each snake biting a small, blue orb. A blue, diamond-shaped crystal sat fastened in the chappe. The blade was pure white, made of a different kind of crystal they had not seen in any other part of Xaliud. The fuller came to a shallow point, itself having the shape of a diamond.

The White Sword of Durath fell into Alexander's hands as if it had wanted to. The sword was somewhat longer than the Geradian broadsword he had wielded since they had departed from the kingdom in what seemed like ages ago. The white sword, heavier too than the Geradian royal sword, seemed to have an energy. Alexander could feel it in his hands and then throughout his entire being. He felt as though he were becoming one with the sword. As Alexander held the blade, he was locked in a reverie about the sword and its potential; their potential together, until sounds from the main room commanded his attention. He looked, finding Saul and the Coltrous warlord locked in a struggle of strength and will. Alexander gripped the white sword tightly and ran toward them. Ferekin, upon seeing the oncoming threat, expended most of the rest of his strength in an attempt to free his hands by throwing Saul. To counter, Saul expended the rest of his strength in a desperate attempt to hold Ferekin there. The struggle became so great that fire burst from Saul, surrounding him. In spite of the Herculean effort, Ferekin's strength overcame Saul's, and he threw him onto the tomb's floor. Ferekin, with unholy speed, crouched, retrieved his sword from the floor, and turned to meet Alexander's blade with his own. Ferekin tried to parry the thrust of the white blade, but Alexander ran the white sword easily through Ferekin's blade—through his chest plate and his chest.

There was a moment of tense silence as all who were present stared in silent disbelief, unable to accept in mind the reality of what they were seeing. After the moment passed, Alexander withdrew the sword, its white blade now the dark red of royal Coltrous blood. Ferekin gasped for air before collapsing to the tomb's floor to lay there in his gore, coughing up blood as he did.

Alexander hurried to clean the White Sword's blade, restoring it to pure whiteness as he watched Ferekin's breath leave his body. He laid there, still and motionless. Jessica moved slowly and with great pain over to Lord Luxeniah to resume healing him. When that task was completed, she healed herself, Stephan, and Saul. In profound silence, for none knew what to say, or had the will to speak, they left the body of the royal Coltrous in the tomb. There was a mutual thought they all shared that the presence of the body, out in the open within the tomb, would serve as a record of what had happened there.

By torchlight, the lord, the officers of Alpha Z, and the private returned, through the labyrinth, to the surface. They had no tools to bury the bodies of Ferekin's fighters, so they used stones to cover them. There was another unspoken, mutual thought that the fighters were merely following orders and, therefore, had died honorably in battle; whether they were being controlled by Ferekin or some unseen power like the privates on Cult Island, they knew it did not matter.

When the rows of rock mounds were laid, they walked into the forest just south of the tomb's entrance and up a hill all the way to its summit. From there, they had a view of the rest of the way to the Kingdom of Durath and sat to rest. Stephan noticed the fair weather and the birds flying past them. As they sat safely and carelessly, they all felt an assurance that all would be well in the end, that although the way would be difficult and perilous, they, and the Northern Kingdoms of Xaliud, would prevail against the enemies of peace and freedom.